SNIPER!

Linda J. White

Linda J White

Cover design: June Padgett, Bright Eye Designs

First Printing July, 2017
SNIPER! -Paper-9 c1.pdf
Printed in the United States of America

Scripture quotations are from the ESV® Bible (The Holy Bible, English Standard Version®), copyright © 2001 by Crossway, a publishing ministry of Good News Publishers. Used by permission. All rights reserved.

White, Linda J., 1949-
Sniper! / Linda J. White

ISBN 978-0-9912212-4-0 paperback
ISBN 978-0-9912212-5-7 ebook

For Faith, lover of language, who,
like me, awaits that Glorious Day

Sniper!
Character List
In Order of Appearance

Kit McGovern, Katherine Anne; FBI agent, Norfolk; honey blond hair; 5'6"

David O'Connor, Kit's boyfriend; a former detective; works at the Norfolk Police Academy; brown hair, brown eyes; fit

Gail Massey, Assistant U.S. Attorney

Amos Cantrell, Leader of the Covenant Sworn Army; gray haired, old

Pete Sterne, an agent; is at the courthouse when Gail is shot

Steve Gould, Kit's boss; square-jawed, no nonsense

Charles Cunningham, Gail's boss, U.S. Attorney; tall, gray-haired

Brian Massey, Gail's husband

Lincoln Sheffield, former U. of Alabama. football star; an agent with ambition; Black, about 6' and 220 lbs; a sharp dresser

Jason Swagger, Norfolk, VA police chief

Jesse Crawford, Mayor of Norfolk

Joe Langstrom, Assistant to the mayor of Norfolk; short, curly hair

Emilio Valdez, Firearms Instructor; friend of David

Alex Valdez, Emilio's son

Charles Lipscomb, Insurance Salesman; victim #2; late middle-age

Shirley Bailey, African-American; 32; mother of a toddler, Laticia; CNA

Cissy Singleton, a teacher; David's neighbor; single woman; diabetes, chin-length dark hair, blue eyes

Annie, Cissy's service dog; a yellow Labrador retriever

Mrs. Lipscomb, heavyset wife of Charles; big cat, yappy dog

Raymond Bailey, Shirley's brother

Gary L. Walters, a gun enthusiast who goes missing

Mrs. Walters, Gary's wife; 50s; gray, wispy hair

Chase Carter, young, first-office agent; blond hair, fresh-faced; eager

Brick Bresner, ATF special agent; short, square, tough; USMC wrestler

Tom Packer, Detective, Norfolk PD; short, gray hair; wolf-like

Ralph Ellis, Chesapeake homeowner and bus driver; 65; victim #4

Mitchell Silverman, car salesman; Victim #5

Joe & Judy Swigert, car buyers; witnesses to shooting #5

Fred Nelson, Big Bob's Cars to Go sales manager

Candace Stewart, FBI, profiler with CIRG; 55; blond, attractive, gray eyes; wise

Capt. Mark Mahoney, VA state police; governor's security team

Frank Mancini, Governor of Virginia

Kathy Emory, VA Beach; Victim #6; waiting for the bus.

Dr. Sullivan, Medical Examiner

Julia Rankin, Student at ODU; 23; victim #7; lives in Orion Towers

Patrice Sweeney, 7-Eleven cashier; sniper shot #8 missed her

Samuel L. Jones, Head of the Norfolk FBI office; Fifty; 6'4", hair edged in gray

Susan Bondurant, Clerk at the Sunrise Inns and Suites

Clifford Tryon, former military; gang ties; sniper training

Tomas Mathus, Teen; Victim #9; he survives;

Tyson Mathus, his brother; age 8

Juanita Mathus, their mother; Latina

Karin Crawford, the mayor's wife; lawyer and stay-at-home mom

Travis Crawford, the mayor's brother; lives in WV; did jail time; ties to Tryon

Buzz Reynolds, Editor at the Norfolk Times; Piper's boss

Mary Knowles, Associate Publisher at the Norfolk Times

Darryl Minor, David's boss at the Academy

Jack Black, an alias

Henry Hardison, Norfolk resident; 42; 5'7"; wiry; former Navy

Mabel Grady, his landlord

Joseph D. Prather, Director of the FBI; 50s piercing gray eyes

Charles Bettcoe, another alias

Jared Thomas, Night Editor at the paper

Cara Burns, Piper's babysitter

Renee Boudreau, Kit's mother

PROLOGUE

THE HAWK'S HAND SHOOK A little as he took the rifle Alex handed him. He felt the coolness of the metal, the weight of the barrel, the perfect balance. He lifted it up and looked through the scope, sighting on the schoolchildren playing a hundred yards away. Perfect.

"It's like the M16s," Alex said, "but it's so adjustable. You can up-size the caliber, change the stock." He hesitated. "Is this for you?"

The Hawk looked at him. *What business is it of his?* Still, he answered. "Yeah."

"Deer?"

He lowered the gun. "Varmints."

Alex nodded. "You just can't do better than an AR15."

The Hawk nodded. "It'll do." He decided to push the kid. "Throw in some ammo."

Alex hesitated.

"Two boxes."

The young man rummaged in his car, found some .223 bullets and handed them over.

The Hawk pulled a wad of cash from his pocket and peeled off three hundred-dollar bills.

"It's $500!" Alex said.

The Hawk shrugged. "I'll give you the rest after I've shot it." He smiled a crooked smile. "Or did you expect me to try it on those kids over there?"

Alex's eyes widened. He opened his mouth to protest, then closed it again. "Two weeks, man. I want the money in two weeks." His face looked red.

"Sure." The Hawk grinned as he watched Alex drive off. Stupid kid. Where'd he get the gun, anyway? Stole it most likely, to pay for weed. The kid reeked of it.

He caressed the smooth, clean metal of his purchase. "I think I'll call you 'Payback.'"

CHAPTER 1

FBI SPECIAL AGENT KIT MCGOVERN jabbed the apartment elevator "door close" button a half-dozen times. "Come on, come on." Shifting her briefcase to her right hand, she checked her watch. "I'm still okay," she said, consoling herself. By the time the door opened at the basement garage level, she was tapping her foot again. Being late to court on the final day of a major case was not something she would tolerate.

Stepping off the elevator, she moved toward her assigned parking place. When she looked up, she saw a familiar figure leaning against her car. She smiled and quickened her pace. "David!"

"This is for you," he said, handing her a latte as she drew near, "a pre-celebration of the end of your case."

"Thank you."

"And here's something for later." He put a folded piece of paper in her jacket pocket. He placed his hands on her shoulders and leveled his brown eyes at her. "I'm so proud of you." He kissed her. "See you tonight."

She touched his cheek. "Thanks. We should be finished by five."

"See you at my house."

Later, at the courthouse, she pulled the paper from her pocket. In David's characteristic block print letters he'd written, "'No weapon that is fashioned against you shall succeed, and you shall refute every tongue that rises against you in judgment.' Praying this for you today."

✝ ✝ ✝

Nearly nine long hours later, after a grueling day in court, Kit and Assistant U.S. Attorney Gail Massey exited the courtroom at the Norfolk Federal Courthouse. Their case had concluded, but the solemn faces of the members of the jury signaled trouble ahead. Maybe the jurors liked the white-haired, bearded, grandfatherly Amos Cantrell, leader of the Covenant Sworn Army. Maybe they hated the government. Maybe they resented a female prosecutor and female FBI agent ganging up on the old man. Maybe they couldn't tell the difference between legitimate protest and criminal conspiracy.

The two women walked side by side, stride for stride, eyes straight ahead, willfully ignoring the lawyers and spectators in the courthouse hallway, the click of their heels on the smooth, white marble floor and the creak of the leather of their briefcases punctuating their march. "Do you think we got him?" Kit asked. Months of investigation and preparation had gone into this trial. Now it was up to the jury.

The older woman, her hair and makeup still perfect after a full day in court, cast an encouraging glance in Kit's direction. "Your work was impeccable."

Kit took that as a yes, maybe. She pushed open the door, squinting as the bright September sun assaulted her eyes. She and Gail stepped out toward the gaggle of reporters waiting on the sidewalk, six steps below. "Ms. Massey!" one shouted. "Do you expect a guilty verdict?"

Before Gail could open her mouth, before a solitary word could escape her lips, a single gunshot split the air. The prosecutor uttered one shocked gasp, dropped her briefcase, and fell to the ground, blood spreading over her white silk blouse like a target.

Kit's adrenaline surged. She grabbed her gun, crouched beside the prosecutor, and searched for the threat. She saw reporters scattering like geese, and two pedestrians, their faces filled with shock, staring at Gail. She saw a white box truck, several cabs, and a minivan. She saw a mother covering a baby with her own body and a light plane overhead. She saw an empty field and buildings across the way. But no gun, and no gunman.

Holstering her weapon as two U.S. Marshals rushed up, she ordered them to call 911. "Gail, Gail! Help is coming. Breathe, Gail, breathe." The sun beat down on her back. Sweat formed on her neck. Kit opened Gail's blouse, searching for the wound. She jerked off her jacket and pressed it down with the heel of her hand where she had seen blood pulsing, pulsing, like a dam had broken. She pressed hard to keep life from ebbing out of Gail Massey's body like a tide pulled by the moon, hoping against hope that God would save this woman who loved him and loved justice and loved her family.

"Gail, I've got you. Stay calm," Kit encouraged, her own heart pounding. Sirens wailed from blocks away.

Kit fought for Gail's life. She pressed and prayed and pressed some more. Still, Gail's face turned pale, her eyes glassy. As the emergency vehicles approached, the prosecutor mouthed one word. "What is it?" Kit asked, not catching it. "Gail, what …?"

EMTs appeared and Kit stood up, making room for them. Her head spun. She inspected her own hands, red and sticky with blood. Later, in the silence of the night, or in a grocery store line, or while staring at food in a skillet, she would remember the sound of the EMTs snapping on gloves, ripping open gauze packets, reciting Gail's vital signs.

Someone touched her elbow. "Kit! Are you all right?"

Another agent, Pete Sterne, had been in the building on another case. Now he stood on the steps next to her, scanning her face, his jaw taut. "What did you see?"

"It happened so fast." The EMTs lifted Gail onto a stretcher. She looked at Pete. "I need to go with her. She was trying to talk."

He frowned.

"I need to go with her," Kit repeated.

He nodded. "Go. I'll handle things here."

✞ ✞ ✞

David O'Connor fingered the little white box in his pants pocket. Tonight was the night. He was pushing ahead, taking a risk, because it was time. Time to call the question.

As he finished getting dressed, he went over his plan again in his mind. This morning he had staged flowers at the end of his dock. On the way home, he'd pick up steaks and salad. He'd make an excuse, once Kit got to his house, to walk out to watch the sunset. Just as the sun kissed the waters of the Lafayette River, he'd drop to one knee, produce the ring, and pop the question.

He didn't understand Kit's reluctance to talk about marriage. And he had no idea what he'd do if she said no. Straightening his tie, he realized he was as nervous as a 16-year-old boy.

"Hey, did you hear?" One of his co-workers at the Norfolk Police Academy walked up. "Shooting at the courthouse. FBI agent, I heard."

Fear shot down David's spine.

"She's dead."

✞ ✞ ✞

The jostling of the ambulance threading its way through the streets of downtown Norfolk turned Kit's stomach. She sat next to Gail Massey, fighting nausea, her mind already compiling a list of possible suspects and paths of investigation, her heart still in a state of shock. Outside the back window of the ambulance she could see traffic and pedestrians, stores and shops. In her mind's eye she could see the members of the militia group, each one of them. She tried picturing them killing Gail, sighting the target, squeezing the trigger. Who did and who did not have that kind of heart? Her stomach rolled.

The murder of a federal prosecutor would be an FBI case. Clearly, she would be the best person to investigate it. After all, she'd worked closely with Gail for eight months! She knew her family, what she liked to eat for lunch, whom she admired, and what she did to relax. Her boss, Steve Gould, might object, saying it was too personal, but Kit would counter those objections because she had to have this case, she had to pursue justice for Gail.

Lost in thought, Kit never felt the vibration of her personal phone. Over and over it signaled her, but she was oblivious, focused on Gail, who was hooked up now to fluids and swathed in bandages. "Gail," she said, hoping the prosecutor would speak again. "Gail!"

✞ ✞ ✞

Norfolk traffic varied from horrible to infuriating. The police academy was maybe ten miles from the federal courthouse. Today it was the worst ten miles of David's life. An accident in the Downtown Tunnel had produced gridlock. Sweating in his old Jeep, his heart drumming with anxiety, David tried first one side street, then another. They all were blocked. Finally, he pulled the Jeep up onto a grassy median strip, jerked off his suit coat and tie, threw them in the back seat, and ran the remaining two miles.

The old four-story courthouse was blocked off as he knew it would be. Sweaty and red-faced, his leg aching, he flashed his Norfolk PD badge and pushed his way through the crowd of spectators and reporters until he got to the steps. There he saw blood. Whose blood? Her blood? In the blazing sun, his head began to spin. He searched for a familiar face, an agent he knew or a U.S. Marshal. He found no one. "Who was it?" he asked a uniformed officer.

"Woman. Not sure who," the uni said, shrugging. "One shot." He shook his head. "Somebody wanted her dead."

"They take her to Sentara?"

"Where else?"

A mile. It was only a mile to the Sentara Norfolk Trauma Center. David began running again, working his way through the streets, trying to stay clear-headed, trying not to panic, trying to pray. "Oh, God, please, not her, not her ..." His words beat in time with the drumming of his heart.

☫ ☫ ☫

Kit stood next to the wall in the trauma room, watching the activity as a medical team tried to lure life back to Gail's still body. The efforts failed. A doctor pronounced the time of death.

Ask not for whom the bell tolls ...

There would be no other doctors called for Gail, no more nurses, or IVs. No dinners with her family, no Christmas, no grandchildren, not one more birthday.

Kit raised her eyes to the ceiling. A verse jumped into her head: *For me to live is Christ, and to die is gain.*

Really, Paul?

Kit stared down at her own hands, now clean, thanks to the kindness of an emergency department nurse who had given her some wipes. She had tried so hard to stop Gail's bleeding. So hard. Why, God?

Footsteps. She looked up.

"Kit. You okay?" Her boss, Steve Gould.

"Yes. I'm just …" What was she? Shocked? Stunned? Sad? All of the above.

Another man followed Steve. Charles Cunningham. Gail's boss. The U.S. Attorney. The tall, slim man had the look of a greyhound. He nodded to Kit, and glanced at the sheet hiding Gail's body. He cursed and shrugged and said, "She was so good." Then he pressed the hand sanitizer dispenser and began rubbing his hands. "What happened?" he asked Kit.

There wasn't much to tell. The steps. The sun. The shot. And Gail was down.

"Militia group," he responded.

"They certainly had motive and means."

"And we gave them the opportunity. Why'd you go out that door?"

"Press conference," Kit said. "Gail wanted to update the press following closing arguments."

Cunningham nodded. He looked over at Steve. "She working this?"

"I …"

"Yes. Please. I know this group. I want the case."

Steve eyed her, as if measuring her grit. "I'm not …"

A nurse entered the room, followed by a man dressed in a golf shirt and shorts. Gail's husband. He turned. "Wait there, kids."

Kids? Gail's kids were here?

Cunningham and Steve fell back, yielding to the power of the moment. Kit watched as Brian Massey moved toward the bed wanting to see but not wanting to see. The nurse gently pulled back the sheet, revealing Gail's face, and Brian collapsed. "Oh, no, oh, God, no!" he cried and fell to his knees, his hands folded, his face buried. The nurse rubbed his shoulder. His sobs filled the room. The two other men quietly left.

Kit moved forward. "I'm so sorry, Brian," she said, touching his arm. "I'll do everything…"

"Oh, God, no!"

"Dad?" Two teenagers, a boy and a girl, pushed into the room. The girl was holding her hands to her face. "Oh, Dad."

Kit's stomach lurched. Gail's kids. They shouldn't see her like this.

More people came. A doctor. A chaplain. A neighbor.

Kit needed air. She walked out into the main trauma area. She looked toward the entrance. There she saw a familiar figure, the sleeves of his white dress shirt rolled up, arms braced on a desk, trying to talk his way past an admissions clerk. David. David! Her throat tightened.

At that moment, he looked up. Their eyes met. And even from that distance, she could see his body sag with relief.

CHAPTER 2

KIT ENTERED HER APARTMENT AND flipped on the lights, with David right behind her. "What I'm thinking is that it could have been Jace. He's the enforcer of the group and it seems logical to me that he would do it. On the other hand, Crease is on meth half the time. He can be volatile. Or Trent."

"Kit," David said.

"I wonder if we missed something in the investigation, some warning, some indication they would risk going this far …"

"Kit."

"Jonas, too, he beat his wife. I know that. And then there's Amos's son …"

"Kit, Kit …"

She turned toward him and looked at him, saw his face furrowed with concern, saw his eyes, those golden-brown eyes, full of compassion, saw the softness in his jaw and the slight parting of his lips and the texture of his skin and the throbbing of the artery in his neck. And the love. Most of all, love. The kind of love that completely disarmed her, unraveling her defenses and defeating the armor that she so carefully and intentionally built around her heart every day. She gasped as she felt her interior walls collapsing and she sobbed, "Oh, David!" and buried her face in her hands.

He caught her and she collapsed into his arms, and he held her and let her cry. He spoke soft words, soothing words, and stroked her head. He held her as his shirt became sodden with her tears and her breath came in desperate gasps. "It was terrible," he said, softly. "She was your friend."

She nodded, her face rubbing against his shirt. "I couldn't save her! I tried, but …"

"You couldn't. The blood just kept coming."

"Yes, it was awful," she sobbed. "And I prayed, but God…"

"He was there," he said softly, and he kissed the top of her head. "Trust me. He was there."

✟ ✟ ✟

It wasn't just the water that went down the drain as Kit showered. Her energy dissipated as well. But after drying off with one of her ragged towels, she selected a practical outfit —a navy golf shirt and khaki tactical pants—and went out to the L-shaped living room/dining area in her new apartment.

David had helped her find this place after pointing out that her old building, a three-story walk-up, lacked security and a safe parking area. Elizabeth Towers offered "upscale urban living" in a "vibrant community" in the "heart of downtown Norfolk." Having seen Norfolk's heart first hand, Kit remained skeptical. But she did like the security, the underground parking, the fitness facility, the indoor pool, and the easy access to coffee bars and eateries. And it wasn't far from her office.

David was setting out dinner in the dining area. With placemats, even. "What's this?" Kit asked.

"Salad with some of that stuff you like—quinoa—and a little apple and sweet potato I found in the fridge. And soup. Chicken soup."

He was such a good cook. Years of living alone, he said. But that hadn't helped her. "Thank you! But I only have a minute."

He glanced at his watch. "You're going in to work?"

"Yes. I have to get started, check to make sure the evidence team has what we'll need, look over my files, be interviewed. I am a witness, after all." She pulled out a chair and sat down. The clock on the wall across from her read 7:32. He brought her water from the kitchen and joined her at the table. "Grace?" she asked him.

And so he prayed … a long, heartfelt, prayer of thanksgiving for the food, for Kit's protection, for ongoing wisdom and mercy, for comfort for Gail's family. Kit got lost in his words, lost in the sheer blessing of hearing his heart, lost in the feeling that in his prayer she was climbing Jacob's Ladder.

Why couldn't she pray that way?

"Amen."

As she opened her eyes, she realized that the shirt he had on, the one she'd wet with her tears, was a white dress shirt. And he was wearing suit pants. Hadn't he worked today? His normal job uniform was blue cargo pants and a golf shirt. That's what he'd been wearing that morning, in the parking garage. "Why are you all dressed up?" she asked.

He shrugged. "Just am." Stabbing his salad, he said, "Where will you start?"

"The militia group. The case we just finished. And the reporters. I want to see their pictures, video, security camera footage … everything from around the courthouse." Just talking about it was starting to re-energize her.

"Somebody document the cars in the vicinity?"

"I hope so. I don't know. I was with Gail." Kit bit into a piece of tart apple, images swimming in her head. The sound of the shot. The shock of Gail falling. The blood. "She was trying to say something."

"What?"

"I don't know—it was just one word. Like 'Gordon.'"

"That mean anything to you?"

"Nothing. I'm going to check to see if she was investigating anyone by that name."

He shifted his jaw. "Will they give you the case?"

"It's federal. And I want it."

David exhaled softly. He studied her, his brows slightly furrowed.

"What? I'm the best one to pursue it. I know the militia group." The soup felt warm going down.

"You knew Gail. Well. You were friends."

Kit paused, her throat clenching as her friend's face appeared in her mind's eye. She reached for her water, hoping he wouldn't notice.

But he did. "Don't you think you need a little time to absorb what's happened?" he said softly.

She doggedly pursued her salad—the green lettuce caressed by the light vinaigrette, the tiny grains of quinoa, the sweet potato and the apple—each bite was a pleasure and yet … Kit looked up at David. Their eyes met. "I need to do this."

They finished their meal in silence, rose, and began cleaning up, the clatter of dishes punctuating Kit's talk of potential suspects. When they were finished, Kit strapped on her gun and grabbed her go-to blazer, the navy blue one she wore to work more often than not. No one ever accused her of being a fashionista. She was sliding it on when he spoke again.

"You could consult on the case."

"No. I want to be the case agent."

"Why you, Kit?" he said, throwing up his hands. "There are three hundred other agents in that building that could handle this case. Why you?"

"Because I want it done right. She was my friend. She deserves justice."

"And you're the only one capable of pursuing it. The only one."

"Her children have no mother."

"Even justice won't solve that."

"It's all I can do." Kit's face was hot. She shrugged her blazer into place.

"What about you?" David said.

"What?"

"If someone from that group did take her out, don't you think you could be next on their list?"

She waved her hand dismissively. At the same time, a cold chill ran through her.

He shook his head and turned away, his hands on his hips, his head lowered. Even from behind she could see he was angry. Standing there, staring at his back, Kit remembered when they met on Chincoteague Island. From across a parking lot, when he pulled his shirt off, she could see the scar on his shoulder, the remnant of an old bullet wound, her first clue to his troubled past.

Her heart softened. She moved toward him and touched him.

He turned around and took her in his arms. His chest heaved with emotion. "They told me an agent got shot," he said. "I thought it might be you." He closed his eyes momentarily as if that scene was playing across his mind. She thought she felt a tremor run through him. "I couldn't stand the thought of losing you, Kit. I really don't want to lose you."

She pulled his head down and kissed him. "I have to do this. I just have to. Trust me. I'll be fine."

✝ ✝ ✝

They caught a cab back to the courthouse. Kit retrieved her Bureau car and drove David to his Jeep. The streets of Norfolk remained filled with people headed to and from the clubs and restaurants of downtown. Kit's mind raced, pinging from the evidence she'd want collected to suspects she'd want to interview. She fielded phone calls from her boss, the senior U.S. Marshal at the courthouse, and the head of the Evidence Response Team. While talking to the medical examiner who would do an autopsy on Gail, David interrupted.

"Make sure he gets the angles."

She looked over at him.

"You want the trajectory angles," David explained, "so you can estimate about where the shot came from. Street. Building. Roof. Whatever."

Kit repeated the request to the ME. She clicked the phone off. The light turned green and she pressed the accelerator. "It's so handy having a boyfriend who knows homicide investigation." She smiled at David but he didn't react.

"Up here, on the left," he said, motioning.

Kit saw his car, up on a median strip, and pulled up behind it.

"Take care of yourself, Kit. I love you."

"I love you, too. Go home. I'll call you later."

✝ ✝ ✝

David walked up to his car as Kit drove off, spinning some gravel as her Bucar popped off of the median strip and she accelerated into traffic. The lighting was dim on the median and only after he was next to his Jeep did he see that someone had bashed out the back driver's side window. The contents of his glove box lay scattered in the front, his iPhone charger was missing, and his suit coat and tie were gone. He uttered a word of frustration, considered calling the cops, and rejected that idea. The car was old. He'd given up all but the liability insurance. He'd pay for the window himself. And the suit coat? Just another casualty of a bad night.

David started the car and eased off of the median just as a kid in a Mercedes with a throbbing sound system jerked into the lane in front of him. BDUDE23, his license read, and for a split second, David considered writing it down, then rejected that idea. Still, he was irritated, and instead of turning toward his home, which is what he had planned to do, David took a right and drove to the courthouse. "You can't give it up, can you?" he muttered to himself. Questions regarding Gail's death taunted him, daring him to chase them, and all it took was a moment of weakness triggered by the annoying boom-boom-boom of a seventeen-year-old's stereo to distract his head long enough for his impulsiveness to take over.

The streets around the Federal Courthouse were empty, the evidence team gone, when he arrived. He drove slowly down Granby Street, imagining the possibilities. He spotted a few fragments of yellow crime-scene tape stuck to the bushes out in front of the courthouse. Then he pulled his car up on the sidewalk. Gail was as tall as Kit, he figured, about five foot six inches. If she had been shot from a car, the bullets would have been angled slightly up; if shot from the building down the street and on the other side, the angle would be downward. So much could be told from trajectory angles.

That would be the start, anyway. If it were his case he would want to know the ballistics—what type of bullet, did it remain in the body, and what about the lands and grooves, the "signature" of the individual gun barrel that the bullet traveled through before it pierced the body of Gail Massey.

There was so much to discover in a homicide investigation. And so he drove home, thoughts bouncing around in his head.

Home was a two-bedroom gray and white cottage on Knitting Mill Creek off the Lafayette River. "Creek" was a misnomer: the water in front of his house was as broad as most rivers, and deep enough for a four-foot-draft sailboat. His dock stretched out seventy feet into the creek and was sturdy enough for any boat he'd want. For now, though, he was happy with his kayak.

He'd just been in the house for a few months and didn't really know his neighbors, except for the Grays, an older couple who lived right next to him, and Cissy Singleton, a teacher who lived across the street and had a dog. Because their street was a dead end, the neighborhood was quiet, which is just the way David liked it.

He took a shower, pulled on shorts and a T-shirt, and walked out onto his dock. At nearly midnight, the creek was quiet, the soft blue glow of a television in a house across the way the only evidence that anyone was up but him. The lights of the city created a constant glow, obscuring the stars. The air felt soft and warm, thick with humidity, and the bugs buzzed in the marshy edges of the creek.

The flowers were still there, in their glass vase. David sat down next to them, his feet dangling over the end of the dock. Gail's death would send echoes down the hallways of Kit's mind for a long, long time. She just didn't know it yet. He wished he could protect her, wished he could have talked her into leaving the investigation for someone else, wished he could shelter her from the evil that seeped through civilization like a poisonous gas.

Like him, she was a warrior. She could not walk away from the challenge evil presented. She had grit and tenacity. He loved that about her. And yet …

After years of being alone, he had someone to lose.

David plucked a flower from the bouquet and tossed it into the creek. He repeated that action, tossing another, and then another, until a stream of flowers was floating in the current like ducks, bobbing their way to the Lafayette River, nodding and bowing with the little waves, disappearing into the night, like one prayer after the other.

CHAPTER 3

AN ENDLESS LINE OF BRAKE lights stymied Kit's progress toward the FBI field office, some eight miles from the city's center. She hoped the jam was left over from roadblocks local police had erected after the shooting. Her hope was more wish than conviction. Restlessly shifting in her seat, she tried to use the time to good advantage, plotting out responses to Gail's shooting, making notes to herself on the notepad she'd placed in the passenger seat. In all likelihood, finding the killer would be a joint task force effort. Since 9/11, so many of the Bureau's resources had gone into anti-terrorism efforts—both foreign and domestic—that few offices had the luxury of dedicated violent crime squads any more. The investigation would involve state and local police and possibly other federal agencies. She'd have to work hard to keep her authority over the mostly male crew. That was nothing new.

Kit finally reached the field office and parked her car. Inside the building, she waved to her boss, Steve Gould, who was at his desk with his phone cradled on his shoulder. Steve looked up and acknowledged her presence.

"Where are we?" he said a few moments later, appearing at her desk.

"You probably know that better than I do."

He nodded. Steve was a no-nonsense kind of guy, an attribute Kit had come to respect in the year and a half she'd worked for him. "The Evidence Response Team is sifting through the evidence. The ME is preparing to do the autopsy in the morning. Right now, it looks like a hit, plain and simple." Steve hesitated. "You okay?"

She nodded.

"You need to talk to an Employee Assistance Coordinator."

"A counselor?" Kit frowned. "I'm fine." She shifted in her chair. "I talked to the ME on the way over, and," she looked down at her notepad, "Mason Kellogg, the U.S. Marshal in charge." She tapped her pen on her lips, thinking about all that had transpired in the trial before the shooting. "Will the judge declare a mistrial?"

"I'm sure he will."

Kit sighed. "All that work."

"Look, I've got messages out to Norfolk PD, the U.S. Marshals Service, ATF, and a bunch of agents. We'll meet at 7:30 a.m. Why don't I take your statement and then you go home and get some rest? And you need to see a counselor. It's the rule."

"Do we still have a cot back in that room?" Kit asked. Every once in a while, an agent felt the need to spend the night.

"Sure, but ..."

Kit stood up. "Let's go do that statement."

They went into an interview room and Steve began the recording. He methodically asked her questions, and as she walked through the events of the day in response, Kit could hear the pounding of her own heart in her ears, feel the tension crawl up her back like a snake, sense the shock and the outrage wind around her neck until it was wrapped up tight. When she described the spreading blotch of blood on Gail's blouse, nausea gripped her. She leaned forward slightly and covered her emotions with a closing assertion: "I want justice, Steve, for Gail and every other prosecutor out there."

He clicked off the recording. "I know, Kit. But you have a tendency to overrun your headlights."

☩ ☩ ☩

Kit found the cot, slept for a few restless hours, and rose at six in the morning to prepare for the preliminary task force meeting. She was hungry, but she didn't want to leave the building. When Steve showed up at six-thirty, he had coffee, yogurt, and a bagel for her. "I figured you wouldn't go home," he said.

"Thanks. I am starving."

He handed her a slip of paper. "You have an appointment with the counselor at 10 a.m. You go or I'll put you on admin leave."

She grinned at him. "You drive a hard bargain."

At 7:25, Kit walked into the conference room. Steve, at the head of the table, nodded to her, but then his eyes shifted.

Kit turned around. Lincoln Sheffield was right behind her. He was new to the field office, and from what she'd heard, he was ambitious and smart and difficult. Full of himself. Over six feet tall and a good two-hundred and thirty pounds, he towered above Kit and had the kind of confidence-bordering-on-arrogance that being a highly sought-after University of Alabama football player creates in a man. Word was he was in Norfolk to get his ticket punched on his way to a higher position in Washington. Most people who'd worked with him hoped that happened sooner rather than later.

Dread washed over Kit. Why was he here? To join the investigation? She glanced at Steve and saw he was staring at her with that don't-argue-with-me look in his eye.

"All right, let's begin," Steve said five minutes later. A dozen agents and other law enforcement officers took seats around the giant walnut conference table. "Kit, fill us in."

Kit perched on the edge of her leather seat, her notes in front of her, very aware that this was her time to set the tone of her leadership role. Professional. Unemotional. Logical. Strong. Even while her insides felt like quicksand.

The fluorescent ceiling fixtures emitted a stark and sterile bluish light. Kit felt like she was in a paper gown in a doctor's examining room. Every eye was focused on her, every ear tuned in on her words, every brain scanning for some weakness, some vulnerability. Welcome to law enforcement.

She began with the shooting itself. Then she backtracked to the trial and profiled the militia group. She finished with a description of Gail, including just enough personal information to trigger the determination to find her killer in the heart of each and every law enforcement officer there.

When she finished, she looked up. Steve Gould's microscopic nod signaled his approval.

Pete Sterne was next. He outlined what he'd done after Kit left with Gail in the ambulance. The evidence he'd collected included security and press camera footage. He'd ordered interviews with each reporter and called out the Evidence Response Team, which conducted a grid search and photographed the steps for blood spatter analysis.

Kit took notes. "No shell casing?"

"No. And no bullet, yet. The medical examiner is doing an autopsy this morning."

"We'll want the angle of trajectory of the bullet."

Pete frowned and tilted his head. "I assume he knows his job."

Just checking, Kit thought.

Pete continued. "I asked Norfolk PD to block off egress immediately after the shooting. We were not successful in accomplishing that."

A Norfolk police captain sputtered. "We had all but 168 covered. Well, and 264 east."

Only the two most logical ways of escape, Kit thought, her blood pressure rising. But it was too early to get into a spitting match with the locals.

After everyone had spoken, Steve described the memorandum of understanding between agencies that he'd drafted. Investigators would form a joint task force, with the FBI as lead agency, and Norfolk PD and the U.S. Marshals Service contributing staff. "Special Agent Kit McGovern will take the lead role, along with..."

Kit's brain stopped. Along with?

"... along with Special Agent Lincoln Sheffield."

Oh, no. Oh, no!

"We'll meet again at seven tonight. After that, it'll be 0800 and 1600 routinely."

She confronted her boss when she got him alone after the meeting. "Really, Steve? You had to give me Lincoln?"

"Orders from above," Steve admitted. "Somebody's pushing him. And this is a high-profile case. Or it will be." He sighed. "Let him handle the press. He's supposed to be good at that."

✞ ✞ ✞

As she suspected, working with Lincoln was like harnessing ocean waves. He pounded Kit with one assertive statement after another, one plan after another, one reminder of his competence after another.

At least when the preliminary autopsy report was delivered at 8:23 a.m. it landed on her desk, not Lincoln's. She stared at it, the clinical, cold analysis of a body that had so recently been a warm, intelligent, loving, and beloved human being. Weight of liver, condition of spleen, size of heart.

Kit shook off her emotions and scanned down to the relevant portion. The ME had retrieved a bullet lodged in Gail's spine. Before it caught there, it had cut a devastating path through her torso. If the ME had retrieved the bullet, though, why hadn't he called her to come pick it up?

The answer walked in the door. "Oh, I see you got a copy of the autopsy. Cool," Lincoln said.

Kit looked up. "You got one?"

"I went down there. Watched him finish up. Got that bullet fragment going up to Quantico. It's all good." Lincoln grinned.

"Did you overnight it?" she asked.

"No way. I got a first-office agent running it up there. Top priority." He smiled again. "I got friends at the lab."

Great, Kit thought.

"Hey, can you get me that list of militia members? ASAP?"

"Yes." She looked at her list. "What about security camera footage?"

"Pete's looking at it. Two of the cameras were out."

Her cell phone rang and that was Lincoln's cue to exit. Thankfully, he took it.

Kit looked at the number on her phone. David. She clicked it on.

"Guy got shot over in Portsmouth," he said. "Just before eight this morning."

"That's news?" Portsmouth had some rough places but even she had to admit she sounded testy. Maybe no sleep didn't help her mood. Lincoln certainly didn't. "Why does that surprise you?"

"Just seems odd. He was just walking into a grocery store."

She didn't respond.

David continued. "Did you get the autopsy report? On Gail?"

"Yes."

"And?"

She told him.

"Did it describe the entry and exit wounds?"

"No exit wound. The ME found a bullet in her spine."

"Caliber?"

"Not sure yet. It's going to the lab."

"Angle of penetration?"

Kit leafed through the report. "Says here that the bullet entered her chest, penetrating the sternum, aorta, and left lung, lodging in 'L4.'"

"Lumbar vertebrae number 4. So the angle would be down."

"She was on the step."

"Right, so she was probably shot from above, from someone in a building."

"We've got agents and police officers canvassing the area now, and we're checking surveillance video."

"Handgun or rifle?"

"We don't know yet."

David hesitated. "If the bullet was from a rifle, I'll bet she was shot from a distance."

"Why?"

"Because the bullet stayed in her body."

Kit had a lot to learn about homicide investigation. "Thanks, David."

"You going to check this other shooting?"

"What? In Portsmouth? No. I've got my hands full. We're getting ready to go roust some militia members. Oh, and don't worry. I'll be with a big, handsome, hunky guy. I'll tell you about it later."

☩ ☩ ☩

Jace Anderson worked as a mechanic in nearby Chesapeake. He'd been putting a Ford pickup back together after tearing down the engine with two other guys at the time of Gail's murder, so Kit had to scratch him off her list. Jonas was at the hospital with his wife, attending the birth of their fourth child. As for Amos's son, Jed, he had been in the courtroom for the trial, and had not yet shown up for work, according to his boss at a construction site. Kit kept him as a possible.

Lincoln had insisted on driving, and that was fine with Kit. Her lack of sleep was catching up to her, although her "counseling appointment" had nearly made her doze off. What a joke. Meanwhile, she couldn't help but notice that the black SUV the Bureau had assigned to Lincoln was a whole lot nicer than the ratty Ford she'd been stuck with lately.

"Where you from?" he asked her.

"D.C. area. My dad's a lawyer there."

"Oh, yeah? I love that area. Where'd you live? In the city?"

"No, Falls Church. Just over the river."

"I've got my eye on the perfect place—a condo in Northwest D.C. The M Street area, you know? Clubs. Bars. Women. Restaurants. Everything you'd want."

"Are you planning to move there?"

"Someday. Someday. When I get my dream job." He drummed his fingers on the steering wheel, waiting for the light to turn green.

"What is your dream job?" Kit braced herself for the answer, calculating her response.

Lincoln smiled. "I am going to be the first African-American director of the FBI. I got my five-year plan and my ten-year plan. I'm working my plans and someday, I'm going to be sitting in that high-back leather chair, looking across that oak desk at congressmen coming to ask me favors." He glanced over to see her reaction.

Kit kept her expression neutral. She didn't want to throw cold water on their relationship right away but she sure didn't want to encourage him either. David's face flashed into her mind and suddenly the desire to be with him gnawed at her heart. She closed her eyes momentarily.

"What about you, Kit? What's a chick like you doing carrying a gun and chasin' thugs?"

Kit bristled. "First of all, I'm not a 'chick.'"

Lincoln laughed. "Whoa, whoa, sorry!" He raised his hands up off the wheel. "I forget you people are sensitive about that."

You people?

Traffic was stopped up ahead. Kit wondered if he noticed. Her grip on the door handle tightened.

"But seriously, why an agent?" he asked again, braking hard.

"Why shouldn't I be an agent? Because I'm a woman? What is this, 1950?" Kit shifted in her seat and tried to swallow her annoyance. Was she going to have to fight him all throughout this investigation? She decided to try to change the tone. "It's about justice, Lincoln. I have a passion for justice. I'm sure you can understand that. But I didn't want to be tied to an office all day long. So I became a cop, then applied to the Bureau."

He nodded. "I'm down with that."

"I think women bring something to the Bureau that wasn't there before," she said.

"Me too. Skirts!"

Her anger flared. Just then her cell phone vibrated. David again. She answered it. "Hey."

"How'd your rousting go?"

"So far, everyone has an alibi."

"Hmmm," David said. "I went to see a guy I know in Portsmouth."

The other shooting. Why should she care? "Yes?"

"Guy was walking into a grocery store on his way to work. A businessman, dressed in a suit. Witnesses heard a single loud bang, and he fell over. Bled out on the parking lot. Small entry wound. Large exit wound. Looks like a .223."

"But nobody saw anything?"

"Nothing."

Kit frowned, pushing away the thought creeping into her mind. "We're almost to the office. Can I call you later?" She hung up and turned toward Lincoln, whose raised eyebrows indicated his silent question. "Friend of mine. He's a cop, teaches at the Norfolk Police Academy. There was a shooting in Portsmouth this morning. A man walking into a grocery store."

"Folks get shot all the time."

"He said the wound looks like it came from a rifle. The victim was a businessman, no police record, no known enemies, intact marriage."

Lincoln turned into the FBI office parking lot, using his key card to open the security gate. "'Pop' and he's gone. Some folks can't catch a break." He pulled into a parking space. "Right now, I got a press conference to prepare for."

Lincoln had arranged for a press conference in front of the courthouse at five. Kit thought that having it at the same place as Gail's murder was foolish, but it was a done deal before she had any input. Frankly, she was happy to have Lincoln take the lead with the press.

A reporter, Piper Calhoun, called her. "Hey, Kit. Agent McGovern. What's going on? Can you clue me in?"

Kit took a deep breath. Piper had actually helped her resolve a human trafficking case a while back. Still, Kit didn't want to talk to her. "We're having a press conference at five at the courthouse."

"Yeah, yeah, I know. But I thought you could give me a preview. Why Gail Massey? Was it retribution from that militia group? And I'm curious about the shooting in Portsmouth. Any connections?"

"We'll release what information we can in the news briefing, Piper. I really can't add ..."

"People are scared. They need to know what's going on."

"There's no reason for everyone to panic."

"You bet there's a reason: People don't want to die." Piper said. She hesitated. "You ought to know that, being right next to that prosecutor that got killed. It could've been you!"

An unwanted tremor ran through Kit. "Just come to the news conference. I think a lot of your questions will be answered."

As Kit clicked off her phone, Lincoln appeared. She looked up at him. "We're just making a short statement at the news conference, right? No questions."

"Sure. Yeah. Hey, I just talked to the SAC."

Kit frowned. The Special Agent in Charge? What gave Lincoln instant access to the FBI's top guy in Norfolk?

"The mayor's office called him. Joe Langstrom's going to

join the task force."

The mayor's aide? Joining the task force? "Why?" Kit asked.

"The mayor wants to make sure we've got everything we need to succeed. Joe gives us direct access."

"It's a bad idea."

"Why?"

"To have a politico involved? They talk, Lincoln. That's what they do. They have no idea how to keep their mouths shut. And we don't want information getting out until we're ready to release it." Didn't Lincoln know that?

"You worry too much, Kit." Lincoln grinned. "Me? I'll be playing golf with the mayor by spring." He winked at her. "It's part of my plan."

Later, she saw Steve in the hallway. "I object to Joe Langstrom joining the task force," she said.

Steve pulled her off to the side. "Can't help it."

"It's wrong."

"I know." He exhaled and looked up at the ceiling. "I can't do anything about it. The mayor and the SAC are tight."

She fumed. "Lincoln doesn't know squat about investigations. He's a grandstander, Steve, nothing but an egotistical ..."

Steve held up his hand for her to stop. "Can't help it. It's gonna happen. Make the best of it."

Kit watched him walk away, anger burning hot in the back of her neck.

CHAPTER 4

DAVID PULLED HIS GUN BAG out of his locker and slid his newly cleaned Glock into it. He liked his job teaching Norfolk police recruits, shepherding them through the twenty-week training academy. Most of them were kids in their early twenties and their exuberance and energy brightened his life. They looked up to him, most of them anyway, and thought of him as the wise old man. They loved his stories about his days as a Navy military police officer and then a beat cop and then finally a homicide detective. About being shot twice. About the murders he investigated and the death scene puzzles he'd put together. He saved the hard story, the one about killing the kid in the alley, the one that almost made him walk away from policing altogether, for their last week.

For David, mentoring these young men and women was the closest thing to being on a team that he'd had since high school. He found himself constantly using football metaphors with them, and so in turn, they called him "Coach." His current class graduated in a week. Today was their final qualification test on the shooting range.

Emilio Valdez, firearms training instructor and all-around good guy, approached him. "So I take it that wasn't your girl that got shot."

A flood of emotion ran through David. "No, thank God. But it was her friend, the prosecutor she'd been working with, and it happened right in front of her." And could have been her, he thought. By the grace of God, it wasn't.

Emilio looked around. "Can I talk to you a minute?"

"Sure." Something in Emilio's eyes told David it was personal. "Let's go for a walk."

They left the building, walking down a path that led through the woods to the small pond. The air was warm and the sun bright overhead. The oppressive humidity of summer had lifted and leaves were beginning to change. David turned to his friend. "So what's going on?"

Emilio took a deep breath. "I just found out my son's washing out of the Navy."

David had met Alex one night at Emilio's house. "What happened?"

"Drugs. One month away from the end of a four-year enlistment. I can't believe he couldn't wait one more month to smoke pot."

"The Navy's famous for its zero tolerance policy."

"And my son's famous for screwing up."

"So what's he going to do? What's his plan?" David asked.

"I don't know. My wife and I are arguing about whether to let him come live at home." Emilio kicked a stone. "She thinks we should. I don't."

"She's his stepmother, right?"

"Yes."

"What's your concern?"

"I don't want drugs in the house. I don't want to enable his irresponsibility. And …"

"And?"

"And I'm angry with him!"

David mulled that over for a minute. "What alternative does he have? Are there friends he could stay with?"

Emilio frowned. "I wish there was." A jogger ran toward them. The two men stopped talking until he was well past. "I don't know where else he could go. He's lost touch with his high-school friends."

"Grandparents?"

"They're all in Texas. And they don't know anything about his problems." Emilio looked at him. "He grew up with his mother, and I don't think she ever disciplined him. She always gave him whatever he wanted. Now," he gestured with his hands, "we get this."

They walked in silence for a few minutes. "You're good

with these kids," Emilio said, breaking the silence. "Would you talk to him for me? He won't listen to anything I say."

David hesitated. He barely knew the young man. But then, Emilio was a friend. "Sure. If I can help, I will."

They reached the end of the path and turned back. David's cell phone rang. "Hey, Emilio. I've got to take this."

"Go ahead. I'm going back. Thanks, David."

The call was from David's friend in Portsmouth. The bullet that took down the man walking into the grocery store in Portsmouth was a .223 Remington, a common rifle bullet used by hunters and the military. It was on its way to ATF for analysis. They'd enter it in NIBIN, the National Integrated Ballistic Information Network, and compare it to other bullets used in crimes.

Kit should have it run against the fragment retrieved from Gail Massey's body. Why? Most homicides were committed with handguns. A rifle killing was unusual. Even in Norfolk.

Did she know that, David wondered?

✞ ✞ ✞

Approximately twenty-four hours after Gail Massey fell mortally wounded, Kit stood on the same courthouse steps facing the same descending sun and the same gaggle of reporters as she had the day before, standing beside Gail. This time, the person next to her was Lincoln Sheffield. Next to him was the Norfolk Police Chief, Jason Swagger.

Kit squinted into the sun, her heart drumming, her thoughts swirling around Gail's murder. It had happened so fast. Once again, she scanned for places a shooter could have hidden. In the buildings across the way, in the next street over—there were hundreds of possibilities. What about the surveillance cameras? Had they caught anything? FBI techs were going over the footage now.

The sun felt hot on her face, just as it had the day before. Kit shivered.

Lincoln stepped up to the cluster of microphones."Good afternoon, ladies and gentlemen," Lincoln began. "Yesterday afternoon, just before five o'clock, Assistant U.S. Attorney Gail Massey …"

His words droned in Kit's ears and she found herself fighting a creeping vine of tension. It was crawling up her back, over her shoulders, up her neck. Why Gail?

Her attention snapped back. A short, curly haired man had worked his way through the police officers gathered behind the mics and had wedged himself into the small space next to Lincoln. Joe Langstrom, the mayor's assistant. Great, Kit thought. He's interjecting himself already. If this becomes political …

"Any questions?"

Questions? Her attention snapped back to Lincoln, who had obviously forgotten the agreed-to format. Or was ignoring it.

"Why was Gail Massey targeted?"

"What exactly are you doing to identify the sniper?"

"Do you have any evidence to link this morning's shooting in Portsmouth with the murder of Gail Massey?"

"What is the ballistics evidence telling you?"

The questions from reporters popped like automatic weapons fire, one after another, and Lincoln tried to field them. But when he got flustered and started to reveal the caliber of the bullet, Kit intervened. Stepping up to the microphone, ignoring the surprise on Lincoln's face, she asserted, "That's all for today. We'll put out a schedule of regular press briefings. But no more questions today."

"How about the shooting in Portsmouth …"

Kit held up her hand. "No more …"

"What about public safety? Should the people …"

"I can speak to that." Joe Langstrom pushed in.

Kit wanted to slug him.

"The mayor wants to assure the people of Norfolk and the greater Hampton Roads area that they are perfectly safe, and should keep to their daily routines without fear. Go home, enjoy your weekend …"

Blah, blah, blah. Kit steamed. She gave him three sentences, then leaned in front of him and said, "That'll be all." The reporters resisted at first, then perceived she was serious. They shifted and began to move away. That's when she saw David, standing in back of them, grinning at her.

☥ ☥ ☥

The Hawk slouched in his seat at McDonald's, watching the wall-mounted TV as the news conference ended. *Idiots! You don't see the connection?*

Irritated, he stood and walked toward the front. If law enforcement didn't link the shootings, if they didn't give him credit, would they count?

"Three chocolate-chip cookies and coffee," he said to the young blonde woman behind the counter. She was taller than him and slender.

"What size, sir?"

The way she asked irritated him. "Large, sweetheart. Always." When he pulled his change out of his pocket, he intentionally included the two bullets that were also in there. He saw her eyes widen. He smiled as he handed her the proper change and slid the bullets back in his pocket.

He picked up his coffee and cookies and left.

✟ ✟ ✟

"You are beautiful, you know that?" David said, as Kit slid into the front seat of his car.

"What?"

"You handled that so well."

Kit, adrenaline still surging, tried to decide if he was kidding or sincere. She looked over at him and saw the approval in his eyes. He was serious. She relaxed into the seat. "I am so tired."

"Sure! That was gutsy—standing right there, where Gail got shot, just one day later. Right there, bold as anything. You're amazing. And you must be exhausted. That's why I'm driving."

"Thank you." Her voice sounded weak even to her. No need for masks with David. He pulled away from the courthouse and headed toward her apartment.

"You want to go home, right?"

"Yes, please." She leaned her head back, then glanced at her watch. "I have to be back at seven."

"What?"

"We're meeting. The task force."

He shook his head. She settled back, then raised her head again. "I'm sorry, David."

"About what?"

"I snapped at you earlier. About the Portsmouth shooting."

He shrugged.

She cleared her throat. "I think I just blew the whole teamwork thing."

"How?"

"By shoving those men out of the way."

He smiled. "They were talking too much."

"That's what I thought!"

"And that political guy, what's up with him?"

"Ridiculous." Kit propped her chin in her hand. Then she remembered something. "Hey, I tried calling you earlier."

"Oh, yeah? My phone never rang."

She picked his phone up from the console. "It's silenced. You need to remember to un-mute this when you get out of class."

"Sorry."

She rolled her eyes. It wasn't the first time she'd had to remind him. "And keep it charged, David. What if I needed you?"

"What if you did? Now, let's see, that would mean you're not as feisty and independent as you pretend to be. And that you find me useful. Not only useful, but attractive. Irresistible, in fact. And that would mean, well, you can't live without me!" He grinned at her.

"Not a chance, cowboy."

"But close, right? Very close."

She laughed. Only David could make her laugh in the middle of a big case. Kit watched as he entered the security code into the box at her apartment garage. The gate arm rose, and they entered the dark garage.

"So what do I do?" she asked him.

"About your case? Leading the team? Do exactly what you're doing. Choose your battles. But don't let 'em push you around." He pulled into a guest parking space. He turned off the car and put his hand on her knee. "And always remind your team why they're working so hard."

✝ ✝ ✝

Kit walked down the hallway of the FBI Norfolk headquarters building to the conference room where the joint task force would meet in just fifteen minutes.

Her ears were ringing with the conversation she'd had with David over a delivered pizza. He offered her more information about the Portsmouth shooting. Kit's brain was locked in on the militia group. The Portsmouth shooting was a distraction. She tried to push his message away. Still, his logic had stuck with her. As she strode down the hall, she went over it again in her head.

There were about one hundred homicides in the whole Hampton Roads area in the past year. Sixty-eight percent were committed with firearms. Statistically, fewer than twenty percent of those would be rifle-related. Some of those would have been hunting accidents. A handful maybe.

So eight or ten homicides by rifle would be committed in the entire Hampton Roads area in a whole year. To have two in two days in adjoining jurisdictions in broad daylight in public places was notable.

Should they try to see if there was a link between the Portsmouth businessman and Gail? Was he related to her? Had she had dealings with him? Did they go to the same church? Shop at the same stores? Use the same tax guy?

Kit moved into the conference room where the other members of the task force investigating Gail's murder were already gathered. Representatives from the U.S. Marshals Service, the Norfolk Police Department, and ATF stood around the room talking. Lincoln stood with a small cluster of men, back in the corner, laughing.

Everyone looked up as she came in. "Gentlemen, let's begin," she said.

Lincoln led off with a review of the TV news at five and six. "We were the third story in at six o'clock, beat out by a multi-car accident on I-64 and a sewage spill. At least they reported what we told them at the press conference. So far so good."

Using the press to generate leads remained a mainstay of law enforcement, though Kit was leery—once the press got its teeth around a hot story things could quickly get out of control. If the public got riled up, pressure could force premature arrests. It became harder for law enforcement heads to remain coolly methodical.

Kit was hoping one of the other investigators would have turned over a rock and found one of the militia members unaccounted for during the time Gail was shot. After Lincoln finished, she turned to them. One after another, each reported the same thing she and Lincoln had found—every one of the militia members had a solid alibi.

Kit's thinking was already going to the next degree of separation. Could one of them, maybe even Amos himself, have hired a contract killer?

In fact, before she could bring it up, Lincoln started down that road. "What I'm seeing is they don't want to get their own hands dirty, so they hired somebody to do the job for them. Anybody got a lead on a hit man? Where would they go? Who knows the bad boys in Hampton Roads?"

"All those guns they have, they've got to be connected with all kinds of shooters," an NPD task force member said.

"I'm saying we need to push these guys. Go after them again. Press 'em. Find out who their friends are, their family members, offer a reward."

But as she listened to Lincoln, David's logic began playing in her head.

Finally, she spoke up. "This morning, as you know, at about 7:58, a man walking into a grocery store in Portsmouth was shot. It was a single rifle shot, a .223 bullet. I believe we need to see if there's a connection."

"Hold on, hold on," Lincoln said, leaning forward, his dark blue suit straining to contain him. "Let's not get off track. It could be coincidence. I say keep to the militia group."

That's when Kit repeated the statistics David had given her. Honestly, the odds of two rifle murders in two days in broad daylight were slim. She saw the other men in the room frown as they considered her argument. Lincoln was not backing down. But then she saw his eyes shift as the door to the conference room opened. She turned. Steve Gould stood at the door. Seeing the look on his face, her heart began beating hard.

"Kit, gentlemen: There's been a shooting in Virginia Beach," he said. "A woman filling up at a gas station. Witnesses heard a single loud bang. A Marine who was also there told police he's positive it was a rifle." The skin on Steve's face looked tight. He leveled his eyes at the group. "I think we have an active serial sniper."

CHAPTER 5

SHIRLEY BAILEY, THIRTY-TWO, HAD been in the process of putting gas in her 2010 Nissan at 6:55 p.m. Thursday when the shot rang out and she fell to the ground, blood gushing from a wound in her head. The mother of a two-year-old girl never regained consciousness. She died forty minutes later.

News of the third shooting initiated a tornado of activity in the FBI. The Critical Incident Response Group from Quantico mobilized. Their Rapid Deployment and Logistics Unit began working with Steve, arranging for space for a task force that would increase in size—critical now that a third local jurisdiction was involved. Profilers and support staff were on their way to Norfolk. And the SAC had assigned an evidence response team to the task force full time.

"We're getting agents from Richmond and Washington field offices," Steve told Kit, "as well as from Quantico. And Homeland Security is getting involved."

"Because it could be a foreign terrorist group."

"Exactly, although no one has claimed responsibility."

Within hours, CIRG and Steve had worked together to arrange to lease an empty warehouse just down the road from the FBI office. It had good security and no windows, which meant the prying eyes of reporters would be stymied. Workers began delivering tables, computers, phones, and chairs, a couple of refrigerators, and a dozen cots. An IT team began setting up the computer stations and the phone system and arranging for a tip line. Someone else began working on designing security badges with embedded access codes for members of the team.

The investigations, of course, could not wait for the entire support structure to be in place.

Three victims, three very different lives: a prosecutor, an insurance salesman, a certified nursing assistant. Two married, one single. Two women, one man. One in Norfolk, one in Portsmouth, one in Virginia Beach. They didn't work together, worship together, or play together as far as she could tell. Their one connection? They were dead, shot on the street by what was probably a rifle using a .223 bullet.

"Why," asked Kit, leaning over the shoulder of an intelligence analyst reviewing video, "is that camera so foggy?" The security camera footage from a parking garage downtown looked grayed out. Indecipherable images moved jerkily on the screen. Kit guessed they were cars, but identifying them was impossible.

"The security guy didn't know," the analyst reported.

Kit stood up. "You've got three shooting scenes now. Make a list of commonalities with what you've got. Any car, any person, any motorcycle you see that may match with the others. And keep me apprised."

"Yes, ma'am."

Kit stood behind the video tech, thinking, one arm across her midsection, her other hand pressed against her mouth. She reviewed in her mind the police reports of the three shootings. She knew what she had to do: go interview the families.

She checked her watch: nine o'clock. First thing tomorrow.

† † †

Steve had insisted she go home. She had to walk a line with him—he had the power to take her off the task force, and that was the one thing she didn't want to happen.

Her dad had called right after she arrived at her apartment. News of the shootings was beginning to spread.

"I figured you'd be right in the middle of it!" he said after she told him about the task force. She didn't tell him she'd been right next to the first victim, her friend, Gail.

Why hadn't she shared that, she wondered later?

Around 11 p.m., Kit forced herself to go to bed, but she couldn't shake images of the shooting. The crack of the rifle.

The shock of seeing Gail fall. The blood. Every time she closed her eyes, she relived that moment.

She didn't want to go to sleep. She couldn't go to sleep! She had to work this case.

Steve might be able to make her go home. He couldn't control how early she got back to the office.

Kit checked the time: 11:18. She'd give it four hours.

✞ ✞ ✞

On Friday morning, Cissy Singleton opened her eyes. Fear vibrated in her chest like a trembling piano wire. Was it her blood sugar?

She looked down toward the foot of the bed. Annie, her yellow Labrador retriever, opened one eye, yawned and stretched. No, Cissy knew Annie would be going crazy if her blood sugar had dropped. The trained service dog could smell it.

Then she remembered. The sniper. Three people shot dead. According to the news last night, the shootings appeared to be random. She shivered involuntarily.

Annie jumped off the bed, anticipating that she would get up. Cissy complied, shuffling out of her bedroom and toward the back door. "Go on! Go poop," she said to Annie, motioning toward the back yard.

The coffee brewing in the kitchen filled the house with its fragrance. She was glad she had remembered to set up the timer on the automatic pot the night before. She glanced out of her front window. The lights were on in her neighbor's garage across the street. David O'Connor would be working out, she knew. He did every morning.

He was such a nice guy. Just yesterday, he'd taken Annie with him on a run. She was thankful for that—Annie just didn't get enough exercise, hanging out with her all day at school. The dog had come back with her tongue hanging out and had slept all evening, allowing her to grade papers.

Annie was invaluable to her, sensing her low or high blood sugar episodes before they became dangerous. Before Annie, Cissy never knew when she might pass out, or become disoriented, or start shaking. Even with an insulin pump she had problems. The dog proved to be a godsend, giving her much better control over her diabetes. And Cissy did walk her. Still, Annie obviously loved running with David.

She looked again across the street and crossed her arms in front of her as if comforting herself, quieting the fear within. David was a cop. Maybe she should talk to him, ask him how soon he thought this sniper would be caught. Were they even close to identifying him?

She shivered again. The kids at school were scared. So were the teachers and the administrators. Everyone was already on edge. How much more of this could they take?

Annie barked at the back door. Cissy let her in, poured a cup of black coffee, and returned to the bedroom. Shower, get dressed, then eat. And try to survive another day.

✞ ✞ ✞

The alarm had gone off at five-thirty Friday morning, waking David from a restless sleep. He pushed his feet over the edge of the bed, sat up, and stretched. Coffee first. Then the book study he was doing. Then his workout. Pushups. Situps. Leg lifts. Weights.

Would he have time for a run?

He had just finished with the weights when his cell phone signaled the delivery of a text message. He glanced at it. From his boss: *Need to support Sniper TF. Can you take students to Granby scene by 0800?*

Absolutely! David's heart jumped. He texted back a quick *yes* and headed for the shower.

An hour later, David stood at the front of the lurching school bus, facing back toward twenty-two police cadets. They were a week from graduation; he'd been their mentor for nearly five months. "What we're doing first," he said, speaking loudly to overcome the roar of the bus engine, "is a basic grid search in the empty field directly across from the courthouse steps. Form a line. Stay within arm's reach of each other. Walk slowly together across the field, eyes planted on the ground. You find something, you call Casey. He's the designated evidence collector. We're looking for anything: a scrap of paper, a button, the imprint of a shoe, a thread caught on something, a cigarette butt. A shell casing wins the big prize."

"What's that, coach?" a kid asked.

David grinned. "Dinner with me."

"And Agent McGovern? Because otherwise ..."

Everyone laughed. David narrowed his eyes, feigning anger.

A big, hulking cadet in the front of the bus raised his hand. "Sir, won't having all of us out there together put us directly in the line of fire, as it were?"

"Thank you for volunteering to be closest to the road," David said. "I'll be right behind you."

When the laughter subsided, David grew serious. "Kevin is right. Every one of you will be vulnerable out there. But then, every member of the public is as well. If you're not willing to put your body on the line to protect them, then don't become a police officer. Drop out now. Don't accept the badge." The bus lurched to a stop and David grabbed the upright bar to keep from falling. He bent down to look out of the window and pointed. "That's the field. When we finish with that, we'll break up into groups and canvass the streets."

"Sir, hasn't the Norfolk PD done this already?" a woman asked.

"Yes, and the FBI ERT did it, too. So, yeah, we are recovering some ground, but then again, if you find something, we'll have bragging rights."

"You mean you'll have bragging rights, with Agent McGovern," said a wise guy.

David grinned. "That's right. After we finish here, we've got two other assignments. So let's do this thing."

Ten minutes later, a line of blue-uniformed police cadets slowly walked across the open field across from the federal courthouse, all eyes focused on the ground. David, the sun warm on his back, walked behind them, watching them and thinking about Gail's murder. Where did the shot come from? He looked across the field and down the street, cataloguing each building, each window on each floor and imagining a shooter inside.

They finished the field, and David split them up into five teams of four each, and gave them streets to cover, telling them to do an exhaustive search for evidence and identify and map every security camera they could find. They would meet back at the bus in half an hour to go to the Portsmouth site.

While they wandered off, he went back to the courthouse steps. He wanted to stand where Gail had stood and envision the scene.

And so he did, climbing the six steps up to where the bloodstains had been, looking out over the city and imagining the reporters down below. He tried to estimate the angle from which the bullet had been fired, counting for gravity's pull as it traveled through the air. And as he stood there thinking, emotion filled him. It easily could have been Kit.

☩ ☩ ☩

Kit heard a noise and then Lincoln's voice.

"Hey, girl!"

Girl?

"What's up?"

Kit unfolded her arms and slowly turned around. "Lincoln," she said acknowledging his presence. Behind him trailed Joe Langstrom, the mayor's aide.

"I've been showing him the ropes," Lincoln said.

"It's fascinating, just fascinating what you all do," the political guy responded.

Kit allowed him a nod. Couldn't Lincoln see the danger in that?

"So, what's up?" Lincoln asked.

"I'm going out to talk to the families after the meeting," Kit said, and was instantly sorry she'd shown her hand.

"Great!" Lincoln rubbed his hands together. "Where to first?"

An hour later, they were in Lincoln's Bureau car. Kit supposed she should be thankful she was able to shake off the political guy. The mayor needed him, he said, for a briefing. But the idea of spending half the day with Lincoln made "thankful" out of reach as far as Kit was concerned. What an ego.

As they drove through Norfolk, she heard all about his high school football career, his college football career, his predictions for the NBA, and his exploits at the FBI Academy.

Finally, they arrived at their first destination—Gail's house.

"This guy still a suspect?" Lincoln asked.

"We have to consider family members could be involved. I don't think that's the case here."

The Massey's two-story brick traditional colonial stood in the pricey Ghent area of Norfolk. It was a large house with a walled courtyard in back and a Palladian window above the front door. Hardwood floors and large, comfortable rooms filled the inside, along with a gourmet kitchen. Kit had been there many times during the course of the militia group investigation. She couldn't imagine the place without Gail. The home had lost its heart.

As she stood on the porch waiting for Brian to respond to the doorbell, Lincoln chattering away next to her, Kit could only hope that he knew when to shut up. He'd had very little field experience, from what she understood.

Brian ushered them into the formal living room, painted a dark green to match a color in the flowered drapes. The artwork on the walls—paintings of gardens and formal family portraits—just screamed "Gail."

Kit could hear noise coming from the back. The kids, she presumed, were in the family room. She sat down on the couch as did Lincoln. Brian sat perched in a wooden armchair with an embroidered seat. "What can I do for you?" he asked.

"Brian, first of all, how are you?" Kit asked. She dared not look at Lincoln, seated to her right. He was quiet, for once.

Gail's husband shook his head. "In shock, I think. I mean," his eyes teared up, "I can't believe she's not coming home, can't believe I'm not going to see her again." He looked up at Kit. "I keep calling her phone, just to hear her voice on her outgoing message."

Kit reached out and touched his hand briefly. "I'm so sorry, Brian. She was a wonderful woman."

"This, this person who killed her. Who is he?"

"We don't know yet. That's one reason we're here. To ask you for help."

"What? How?"

"Did Gail ever share concerns with you? Did she tell you about threats or weird phone calls or anything like that?"

Brian shook his head. "Nothing lately. I mean, she was all

wrapped up in that militia case. I assume one of those guys …"

Lincoln said, interrupting, "We got nothing on them."

"But I thought …"

"Nothing," Lincoln repeated.

Kit shot him a look, warning him with her eyes to be quiet. "Brian, do you remember her talking about any concerns for her safety?"

He shook his head.

"Did she have any visitors you didn't know?"

"No." The grieving husband looked up. His eyes were red from crying.

"How about debts," Lincoln asked, chiming in. "You owe anybody money? Or vice versa?"

"Just the mortgage. And some credit card bills." Brian rubbed his hands on his thighs. "I just don't know what to do!"

"You'll figure it out in time," Kit assured him. She only hoped that was true. "What arrangements have you made?"

Brian rubbed his forehead as if trying to remember. "Funeral is next week. I had to wait until her parents could get here. And the burial is at Oak Grove." He looked at Kit. "We hadn't planned on this."

"No one plans to die prematurely," Kit said. "You'll work through it, Brian, with the help of your friends and family."

As Lincoln drove away from Brian's house, Kit called back to the office. "Check his financials," she told someone. "Debts, large withdrawals, that sort of thing."

"You think he did it?" Lincoln asked when she clicked her phone off.

"No, but we have to check everyone. I doubt he had anything to do with it. He's not a serial sniper anyway."

"They had it all. And now he's got nothing."

"He still has the kids," Kit said, "and a future. He'll have to adjust, but life will go on." After all, she thought to herself, my dad and brother and I survived. You can live without a mother. You just have to be tough.

Lincoln grinned. "I like being single, but I'd miss my momma, that's for sure," he said. "I'd miss her corn pudding, and her chicken and dumplings, and the best country fried steak in the world." He glanced at Kit. "Most of all, I'd miss that big smile on her face when I come home. She is my biggest fan."

"I'll bet."

"Every time I show up, she throws a party. Like I'm the prodigal son." He smiled.

"Are you?" Kit's phone vibrated. She glanced at it. David. He'd have to wait.

Lincoln pulled over and parked. "Not hardly."

Their second stop was a smaller suburban house just off I-460 in Portsmouth, home of the late Charles Lipscomb, shot walking into a grocery store. The blue-gray rambler had a small fenced backyard with a yappy dog. A battered sedan sat in the driveway.

"Charles was just getting back on his feet after that storm knocked his business down," his heavyset wife explained to the agents. "He was working so hard." Her pink pullover shirt barely covered her blue stretch pants. She stroked a large white cat lying on her lap.

"Did he receive any threats? Was he worried about anything?"

She shook her head. "Charles was a good man. A good man. He kept his customers happy."

"How long were you married?" Lincoln asked.

"Thirty-four years. Charles was my high school sweetheart. We'd planned to grow old together." She started to cry. "Every day on the way to work, he'd stop at that store and get two doughnuts. Two! I told him his doughnut habit was going to kill him. But I never thought it would be by getting shot. How can a man just walking into a store be murdered? In cold blood! Who would do something like that?" She dabbed her eyes.

Yes, Kit thought. A man walking into a store, a prosecutor standing on the steps—who would kill them, and why? ISIS? A domestic terrorist? A crazy person with a grudge? What kind of person was she looking for?

Another half hour of talking to Mrs. Lipscomb didn't lead to anything—no rationale for the shooting, no links to the other victims. "We got nothing there," Lincoln said as they drove away.

"At least," said Kit, glancing at her cell phone, "we've got no more bodies."

"So far."

Shirley Bailey's house in Virginia Beach sat on a street filled with identical three-bedroom ramblers built in the 1960s. Her brother, a man in his late 30s, let them in. Over the green velvet couch in the living room was a collection of professional portraits of one person: Shirley Bailey's two-year-old daughter, Laticia.

. The house was filled with family members: Shirley's mother, her two brothers and three sisters, and a multitude of kids. Lincoln looked at Kit as if to say, "I got this."

"Hey, man, can we talk?" he said, spotting what looked like the oldest of the brothers.

His name was Raymond Bailey and he led them back to a bedroom and shut the door. "Mr. Bailey, we are sorry for your loss," Kit said.

Raymond nodded. "She was my little sister, you know? The baby of the family." He looked straight at Lincoln.

"We are going to catch who killed her, yes sir, we are," Lincoln responded. "But we need some help." He nodded toward a picture of Laticia on the nightstand. "Who's the baby daddy?"

"Jayvon Coombs." Raymond shook his head. "Great guy. Good job. Wanted to marry my sister." He looked at Lincoln, his eyes white against his dark face. "Works down in one of the hotels, as a manager." He raised his eyes and gestured with his hands. "He helped her buy this house. Didn't want her and the baby living in no apartment."

Kit felt a pain in her back. Tension. She moved to try to stretch it away. "So what was wrong with marrying the guy?"

"We never could figure her out on that."

"Did you ever see evidence of abuse? Bruises? Fear on her part? Did you notice her being under stress when he was around? Afraid to make decisions? Overly deferential?"

Raymond just kept shaking his head. "I'm telling you they were happy together. He'd come to all our family gatherings. Brought food. Played horseshoes. They'd joke around together and play with the baby. He wanted to marry her. Make it right. But I guess … I guess she just wanted her space."

Kit felt her personal cell phone in her blazer pocket vibrate. She glanced at it. David again. They were supposed to go to Chincoteague for a long weekend beginning tomorrow. The water would still be warm enough for him to surf, and she had been looking forward to some beach time. With the sniper case, though, there was no way she could go. He knew that, right?

"Any other men catting around?" Lincoln asked, going for the jealousy angle.

Kit's attention returned.

"No, man. I'm telling you, they were happy. Just not married."

"Where'd she work?" Lincoln asked.

"Old folks' home." Raymond went on to describe an assisted living facility nearby.

"Who kept the baby?" Kit asked.

"Our momma, his momma. Jayvon's that is. The daddy."

They were finished here. Kit could feel it.

But Lincoln kept going. Asking about work associates, asking about the other family members, asking about Shirley's hobbies and where she shopped and what she did for fun and who she dated in the past.

And in the end, he came out the same place Kit did—a dead end. She glanced at her watch: noon. She was anxious to get back to the office.

They were getting in the car when Steve called her: The task force would meet at four o'clock. But a woman had reported that her husband, who was a gun collector, had been missing. Could Kit stop by and interview her?

"We've got one more stop," Kit told Lincoln.

Gary L. Walters had been missing from his Norfolk home for two days. The house, a ramshackle one-story bungalow in a lousy neighborhood, looked like an armory as Kit and Lincoln walked through the front door. There were guns on the wall, guns in a gun safe, guns on shelves where books should be.

A Norfolk PD officer had responded to the missing persons report, but Steve thought the Bureau should check it as well, because of the guns.

Mrs. Walters, a woman in her fifties with gray, wispy hair and a sturdy frame, gestured vaguely around her. "This is what I live with. It's crazy. The man can't stop buying guns."

"When is the last time you saw him, Mrs. Walters?" Kit asked.

"He stormed out of here night before last. Didn't even watch the rest of the game."

"Had you argued?"

"Just over the TV. I wanted to talk to him and he had that stupid football game on."

Lincoln looked over at Kit. "Chicago-Green Bay. Good game."

"Where'd he go?" Kit asked.

"If I knew that, I wouldn't have reported him missing, now, would I have?" Mrs. Walters picked up a pack of cigarettes, tapped one out, and lit it. "Some bar, I'm guessing. Some place with a TV." She exhaled a stream of smoke.

"Friends? Family?"

"They haven't seen him." The woman tapped her ash off into a soda can. "He'd better show up before tomorrow," she said, gesturing with the hand holding the cigarette. "He knows that's my mother's birthday. She's eighty. And everybody's going to my sister's house."

Kit looked around. "Any of his guns missing?"

"Who knows? He's got more guns than he does hair." The end of her cigarette glowed red.

"Would you mind if we take a look around?"

"Suit yourself." Mrs. Walters gestured toward the rest of the house and plopped down into an overstuffed armchair.

The house had two bedrooms cluttered with clothes and knick-knacks and old magazines. And guns, of course. Kit checked the closets and under the beds, behind the doors and even in the bathroom. "I'm not seeing any obvious empty spaces, are you?"

"Nope. But who knows? This guy is like Rambo." Lincoln's eyes ranged over the room they were in.

Mrs. Walters appeared behind them. "Have you ever had a break-in?" Kit asked her.

"Everybody around here knows what they'd get back at

'em. And everybody knows I'm just as mean as my old man."

They walked out into the kitchen and continued the search. A door led to the back yard, and Lincoln started to open it.

"I wouldn't ..." Mrs. Walters began.

As soon as the door moved, ferocious barking erupted. "Whoa, whoa, whoa," Lincoln said, as the nose of a brown dog pressed through the door's crack. Kit put her hand on her gun, her heart pounding.

"Get out, Sugar!" Mrs. Walters yelled, and she smacked the dog's nose repeatedly. "Get out!" Finally the dog retreated and Lincoln shut the door. They could still hear it growling.

"You need to keep that dog up!" Lincoln said.

"He is up! You're the one's not up," Mrs. Walters said.

"How many people has he bitten?"

The woman narrowed her eyes. "Three. Every one of 'em deserved it."

Kit's cell phone rang. "Excuse me," Kit said, and she answered it, walking toward the front of the house, aware that the two were still arguing. "Yes. Where? When? Cause? Okay, thanks." Clicking off the phone, she returned to where Lincoln, hands on his hips, gun exposed, was still lecturing Sugar's owner. "Mrs. Walters," Kit said, "they've found your husband."

"Where is that no-good man! I'm tellin' you, he has it coming to him this time."

"I'm sorry, ma'am. But they found him dead in some woods about a mile from here."

"Dead? Dead? Well, if that don't beat all."

CHAPTER 6

"SO, NO EVIDENCE OF A gunshot wound?" Lincoln asked as they drove back to the office.

"None. The ME will give us the results of the autopsy, but so far, it looks like Gary Walters died of natural causes."

Kit stared out of the window. Three people shot by someone, some anonymous someone, out there on the streets of Norfolk. Or Portsmouth. Or Virginia Beach. The thought of finding him seemed overwhelming. She turned toward Lincoln. "Steve says he's moved us to the new office."

"He got that up and running quick."

Quick*ly*, Kit thought, but she kept her mouth shut. Fifteen minutes later, she was guiding him to the warehouse-type building just down the street from the main office. Already reporters were hanging around the temporary chain link fence erected around the parking lot. They were hungry for news.

"Look at the vultures," Lincoln chuckled. "Waiting for me to throw 'em some meat." He eased past them, showed his badge to the guard, and pulled into a parking space. "I like that we're meeting at four. That'll give me time to get out and say something that'll make the five o'clock news."

They entered the building. Kit felt relief along with fatigue. There'd been no more shootings. No more victims. No more trauma. After all, three was enough.

Or was it that the sniper just took days off?

As Lincoln disappeared in the cavernous building, Kit noted the time: 1:43. A couple of hours to get a lot done. She'd gotten the ball rolling with some messages while she was out. She hoped they'd been able to accomplish what she'd asked. Using her badge to enter the locked door, she marveled at Steve's efficiency and CIRG's. They were well on their way to having a complete, IT-enabled office in place.

"Agent McGovern." Chase Carter, fresh-faced, blond-haired, and smelling of aftershave greeted her. "I got those pictures you wanted." He was young, a first-office agent, eager to help.

"Great!" Kit walked into the hastily assembled conference room. Chase had posted large eleven by sixteen-inch pictures of each of the sniper's victims on one wall. Kit looked at each one, summarizing in her head what they knew so far.

The first was Gail's official portrait, she in her black suit, smiling, flag in the background. Kit felt a twinge in her gut. Charles Lipscomb was next: a late-middle-aged portly insurance agent, killed in a grocery store parking lot in Portsmouth. Shirley Bailey, a mother and a certified nursing assistant at an assisted living facility, was filling up her car on her way to work in Virginia Beach when a single shot felled her.

Always remind your team why they're working so hard. That's what David had said. "Good job. Thank you, Chase. That was very fast."

Next to the photos, Chase had hung a map of the sprawling Hampton Roads area: Newport News, Hampton, Norfolk, Virginia Beach, Chesapeake, and Portsmouth. Each locale sat perched over a body of water. Together, the rivers, bay, and ocean formed the busiest deep-water port in the Eastern United States. Connected by a crosshatch of roads, bridges, and tunnels, honeycombed by lakes and marshes, the jurisdictions also formed an investigative—and transportation—nightmare.

Still, with Hampton Roads' traffic snarls a common occurrence, how'd the sniper get away each time? Kit stood staring at the map, arms crossed in front of her. Over 1.7 million people lived in the area—she'd looked it up. A massive naval presence and a huge international port with its foreign ships and crews would make identifying a serial sniper like finding a single, marked piece of confetti in a Madison Avenue parade. Ridiculously hard.

Kit shook her head, and grabbed three red pushpins from a box on the table nearby. She pressed the pins into the locations of the three shootings, beginning with the Granby Street courthouse. Three dots. Three deaths. One shooter? Who was he?

At three fifty-five, members of the task force started straggling in: The group now included representatives from Norfolk, Virginia Beach, and Portsmouth police, as well as the Virginia State Police, two ATF agents, some U.S. Marshals, Homeland Security, and others from the FBI.

Lincoln Sheffield made a grand entrance at one minute after the hour. He glanced at the victim wall. "That's a little creepy," he joked. Then he dropped copies of that day's newspapers in front of the investigators seated around the table. "The sniper is on a roll, and newspapers are happy, happy, happy," he said, before taking a place next to Kit.

She looked down at the paper he'd placed in front of her. Indeed, the ink was flowing. The front page included a major story suggesting that Hampton Roads was under attack, profiles of Charles Lipscomb and Shirley Bailey, and an info box outlining what each victim had been doing when he or she was shot. A skybox promised an interview inside the front section with a "security expert" outlining what investigators should be doing to arrest the sniper and just what citizens could do to protect themselves. Already, journalists were analyzing law enforcement's performance.

Kit lifted her eyes from the paper and opened the meeting. "We've had nothing since 6:55 p.m. yesterday, right?"

"All's quiet," Lincoln said. He and Kit were at the end of the rectangle of tables and chairs assembled to serve as a conference table. To their left, Chase was just taping the last of the victim profiles on the wall under their pictures.

Kit looked out over the group, determined to keep them on task. Just one woman besides herself sat at the table. She opened her mouth to begin when the mayor's aide, Joe Langstrom, walked into the room. Annoyed, Kit stood up straighter and stared at him, willing him to make eye contact. He didn't. She turned back to the others. "ATF? Could you tell us what you've got?"

ATF Special Agent Brick Bresner looked like his

nickname: short, square, tough. He was a weightlifter and former Marine Corps wrestler. "The lab's preliminary report on the second shooting verifies probable .223 bullet. When we get the autopsies the lab will do a trajectory analysis on all three. In addition, we have dogs on the way here."

"Good, thank you. Can we send agents to gun shops to check for .223 rifle sales?"

"We are doing that as well. Over thirty rifles can use that caliber bullet, so it's not easy to break that down. And with hunting season here ..."

"Gotcha."

"Dogs? Why dogs?" Lincoln asked.

"They're trained to sniff for explosives. We will use them at every shooting site to check for gunpowder residue, shell casings, et cetera."

Lincoln nodded.

"Thank you, Brick." Kit looked out over the assembled group. "Let me outline what resources we plan to have available for your use." She began going through the usual—the online database to correlate information gathered by the investigators, the access to the lab and to ballistics and other evidence testing, and then the profilers from the Behavioral Analysis Unit who would soon be on the scene.

Tom Packer, detective with the Norfolk Police Department, sat staring at his hands. He was rolling a small piece of paper between his fingers. He looked up at Kit. "How helpful have profilers been in other cases? The ones I've worked," he said, "they got everything wrong."

Kit reacted to his demeanor. Why the hostility? Packer had short gray hair and he reminded Kit of a wolf. She wasn't sure why. Kit made a mental note to ask David if he knew him. "My understanding," she responded, "is that the media-heads doing their own profiling are often wrong. The official profile are usually right, on many aspects, at least. Not all, but many."

Packer responded, "So, is Uncle Sam going to pony up to help local police departments with overtime and other expenses? Our pockets aren't deep."

"I'll ask about that."

A police officer from Portsmouth raised his hand, drawing

her attention away from Packer. "911 is already going crazy. People are calling in and reporting everything from firecrackers to suspicious cars, most of which turn out to belong to their neighbors. A real emergency couldn't get through if it tried."

"We'll activate the tip line," Kit checked her watch, "about five today. That should take some of the heat off."

"Who's doing the follow-ups on the leads we're getting?" the Portsmouth officer asked.

Lincoln interjected, "We'll have agents ..."

But Kit interrupted him. She knew these local cops were territorial, and justifiably so. None of them would want the FBI taking over their turf. "Actually, we'll all need to follow leads. You have a shooting in your jurisdiction, we're counting on you to pursue it in conjunction with your FBI team member. Basically the tip is yours." She was aware Lincoln was staring at her but she didn't care. "How are we doing with the security camera footage?"

Erin Lansdale, the only other woman assigned so far to the task force, spoke up. "We're going over that now. Well, the techs are. We do have one problem—a couple of cameras weren't functioning. We're not sure why."

"Just like computers, you can't count on those things," Lincoln said. He looked straight at Kit. "That all? 'Cause I got one question."

"Yes?"

"Who's in charge of coffee? Because so far, it ain't happening."

Before Kit could even think of how to respond to that, multiple radios and phones sounded in the room.

Another shooting. This time in Chesapeake.

✝ ✝ ✝

Ralph Ellis was raking leaves in his front yard in Chesapeake just before five in the afternoon. Neighbors heard what they thought was a truck backfire. By the time Ralph's wife came home from the store twenty minutes later and found him, Ralph had bled out.

Kit stood in front of the neat brick rambler, a warm September sun on her back, her heart in her throat, watching as the medical examiner made an initial assessment. Ralph Ellis lay on his stomach, his rake on the ground next to him, his feet in a pile of leaves.

"Gunshot wound to the back," he said, rising and facing Kit. "Looks like the other ones." He gestured to his assistants. "Wrap him up."

Out of the corner of her eye, she saw Lincoln taking notes. Beyond the mass of police cars and emergency vehicles, neighbors stood clustered in little groups. A jogger moving by, slowed, then stopped, staring at the scene. "Do you have any idea of the angle of penetration?" Kit asked the ME. Her eyes ranged across the street, looked for the sniper's perch.

"Not yet. I'll let you know once I get into him."

"Thank you," Kit said. She turned to Lincoln. "I'm going inside to talk to Mrs. Ellis."

"I see reporters down there," Lincoln said, gesturing. "I'll go speak to them."

Mrs. Ellis, of course, had no idea who would want to kill her sixty-five-year-old husband. He was a bus driver, that's all, just a bus driver. She'd wanted him to go to the store with her, but no, he was a yard guy, and having those leaves covering his lawn was bothering him. She sobbed. "He was set to retire at the end of the year. We were going to go to Florida."

"We will find the person who killed him, Mrs. Ellis. I promise you that." But as she was speaking, Kit felt her phone vibrate. "Excuse me." She pulled it off her belt. The call was from Steve. Just then, she heard an ambulance siren wailing. "McGovern," she said into the phone.

"Three blocks away, at a car dealership," Steve said breathlessly. "Guy was showing someone a car on the lot when he got shot."

"Tell CPD to block off major egresses," Kit said. "I'm on my way."

✝ ✝ ✝

Enough! Kit thought as she eased her car out of the traffic jam around the Ellis's house. Adrenaline sparked through her system. She flipped the air conditioner on high and aimed it at her face.

Lincoln drove ahead, screaming around the corner, flying

toward the car dealership.

Mitchell Silverman lay next to the right front tire of a fairly new "Moonlight White" Nissan Rogue. Medics surrounded him. A blood smear down the side of the car showed Kit exactly where he'd been standing. Her mind raced.

"I knew you were going to make me work all weekend," the ME grumbled as he emerged from a Chesapeake police car.

"This one's not yours yet, doc," she replied.

Kit moved to where she could see the victim, who lay on his side, blood pooling on the black asphalt. The EMTs already had an IV going. They placed him on a stretcher and two of them lifted him into the ambulance. "How is he doing?" Kit asked the driver.

"He may make it."

The manager of the dealership appeared at Kit's side. "Can we move all these vehicles?" he asked, gesturing toward the flashing lights on the law enforcement cars. "It's bad for business."

Kit turned and stared at him. "Sir, one of your salesmen just got shot. I hardly think the presence of cop cars should be your chief concern."

"Press followed us," Lincoln said, nodding toward a bunch of cars coming down the street.

The sales manager straightened his tie. "Some good may come of this after all."

Kit rolled her eyes. "Where are the customers who were looking at the car?"

"I've got them inside. Come with me."

Joe and Judy Swigert had been looking for a car big enough to handle their growing family. They sat in the manager's office, a thirty-something man and woman dressed in shorts, T-shirts, and flip-flops. The woman had been crying. A tow-headed three-year-old boy played with cars on the floor while his infant sister lay nestled in their mother's arms.

As the sales manager introduced her to them, Kit's mind flashed back to what they'd just been through. It could have been them. It could have been their baby or their son. Right now, they could be deep in shock.

Kit sat down in a black plastic chair. "How are you doing?" she asked softly.

The woman squeezed her daughter closer to her as tears streaked her cheeks.

The husband spoke first. "One minute the salesman was showing me this cool SUV, and the next thing I knew, *bang!* He was on the ground."

"Joe tried to stop the bleeding," Judy added. "There was so much."

Kit said, "He was still alive when the ambulance took him. I think there's a chance he'll make it." She rested her elbows on her knees, leaning forward. "Where were you positioned when it happened?"

"I was in the driver's seat," Joe said, "and the salesman was standing just in front of the open door."

That fit.

"Judy, where were you?"

"Heath had just run behind the car and I was chasing him. Otherwise …" she dissolved into tears, unable to finish.

Kit reached over and touched the woman's shoulder. "You're here. You and all your family. That's what counts."

☩ ☩ ☩

The tension back in the task force office was palpable. Kit had assigned two members from Chesapeake to oversee the evidence collection at the two most recent sites. Brick Bresner stood by ready to take the bullets to the ATF lab.

"How'd it go?" Steve asked as she walked back into the office.

Kit shook her head. "Still nothing definitive." Behind, news of the latest shootings blared from a television hung high on a wall. "Did they break in with that?"

"No, they've been live on the air since five o'clock. Nonstop coverage."

"How can they find that much to say?"

"What they don't know, they make up."

A perky blonde reporter standing outside the car dealership appeared on the screen. "I'm standing here at Big Bob's Cars-To-Go, site of the latest sniper shooting. With me is the sales manager, Fred Nelson. Fred, what was it like to have your own salesman targeted?"

"Of course, we were most concerned about our customers. In fact, it wouldn't surprise me if our salesman, Michael Silverman ..."

"Mitchell," Kit interjected. "He doesn't know his own salesman's name?"

"... took the bullet himself, saving the Swigerts from certain death." Fred hitched up his pants.

Kit turned to Steve. "This is nonsense."

"How is that victim? He survived, right?"

"Yes. I sent two uniformed officers to the hospital to follow through."

"And just like before, no one saw anything."

"That's right," Kit said. "But our shooter isn't a ghost. And we will get him." She looked around. "When will the CIRG profilers get here?"

"Early tomorrow morning."

She checked her watch. David had invited her to his house for dinner. No way she'd have time for that.

CHAPTER 7

THAT EVENING, DAVID STOOD AT the counter chopping onions and green peppers and humming along with The Civil Wars, hoping Kit would return his call, hoping she would say she was just a little late to dinner but she was on her way. He heard a soft knock at the door and his heart jumped. He threw the door open, expecting to see Kit.

Instead, his neighbor, Cissy Singleton, and her dog Annie stood on his front porch. The two were a study in contrasts: Cissy, her arms folded across her chest, her brow furrowed, and Annie standing calmly and confidently, her otter-like tail wagging slowly.

"Come in, come in!" he said, opening the door. "What's up?"

Cissy was short and slim, with straight, dark hair that cupped her chin. She wore jeans and a Virginia Tech sweatshirt, and on her wrist was a large, square watch. "What smells so good?" she asked.

"I'm just fixing dinner." David's phone buzzed. "Excuse me," he said. He looked down. *Tied up. Can't make it. Sorry!* Kit's text message sent disappointment rushing through him. He texted her back. *Love you. Be safe.* Returning his eyes to his visitor, David said, "Have you eaten?"

"No, but …"

"Come on, then." He turned down the stereo. "Is she off duty?" He gestured toward Annie.

"She can be," Cissy said, unsnapping the yellow Lab's leash and removing her vest.

"Hey, Annie!" David reached down and began playing with the dog, who exploded with joy. After a few moments, David said, "Okay, now, settle down," and he patted her ribs. He walked over to the sink and washed his hands. He heard another text message coming into his phone and glanced at it before resuming his chopping. "Have a seat." He gestured toward the small table. "What's going on?"

"I really didn't mean to invite myself to dinner."

"I'm glad for the company. My date cancelled." David grinned.

"I just wanted to talk to you about, about this thing going on."

"The sniper?"

"The whole school is terrified. The kids, the teachers—we're all scared. Every day we're getting new rules, new instructions on how to handle the kids, what to do if there's an alert. Shield the kids as they're getting on the bus, stay away from windows in the classroom, don't let the kids play outside, watch for slowly moving cars. We're all freaking out." She propped her chin on her hand, her brow furrowed. "I saw your lights on and I just wanted to ask you, when will this end? How worried should we be? How close is law enforcement to ending this craziness?"

David scooped up the onions and peppers he'd been chopping and added them to the skillet. Then he began slicing the flank steak in thin strips as he considered how to respond to her. Dumping the steak in with the vegetables, he inhaled deeply. "Ah, that smells good," he said, stalling.

"I'm really worried. This morning, I think I had a panic attack, or the beginnings of one, anyway."

"You got enough going on; you don't need this, right?" Between her diabetes, which was difficult to handle, and the ugly break-up she'd recently had, David knew Cissy had enough stress for several people.

"Yes."

"Well, look, there's about 1.7 million people in Hampton Roads, right? So the chances of any one of us becoming a victim are pretty small."

"These people that were shot, they were doing normal things. Pumping gas, walking into a store, standing on the steps of the courthouse. That's what's so freaky." Cissy folded her arms. "It scares me. I don't know what's safe."

"It's the randomness that ramps up the fear."

"Yes." She shivered.

David saw her eyes fall on his Bible and the notebook for the study he was working on in Hebrews. *We have this as a sure and steadfast anchor of the soul, a hope that enters into the inner place beyond the curtain.* Hebrews 6:19, the verse he'd texted to Kit that morning.

Should he reach out to Cissy? Share his faith? He deftly slid the steak stir fry mixture onto a platter. "You want to pull out some plates?" he said, nodding toward the cabinet.

"Sure." Cissy got up, removed two stoneware plates, found the silverware, and put them all on the table.

"Drinks? Water okay?"

"Sure."

They sat down. "Do you mind if I say grace?"

"No, sure, go ahead."

David prayed, for their meal and for their safety.

They began eating, and it gave David time to think. What could he say to her? He felt a flicker of anger toward a man he didn't even know, an old boyfriend who had recently moved out, leaving her lonely and abandoned, then a bigger flicker, more than a flicker, toward the sniper who was causing such fear around Hampton Roads.

"This is really good," she said, lifting a forkful of stir fry.

"Thank you." David finished chewing.

"So help me. How do I deal with these shootings?"

"Well, remember, there's been a huge law enforcement response. FBI, Norfolk PD, ATF, all the surrounding departments. Everybody's looking for this guy. And they will find him."

"But how long will it take? I mean, I've got a quarter tank of gas. I'm waiting for the next shooting to fill up, 'cause I figure the odds of two in a row are slim. So I'm calculating, how long can I delay getting gas? As soon as the next one happens, I'll be at the pump."

David nodded. "Lot of people are thinking that way."

"Today, I had to stop at the store. People were zig-zagging through the parking lot, terrified they'd be shot. And the kids

—oh my gosh, the kids. They're freaking out."

"What grade do you teach?"

"Third. And you would be amazed at how much they know. The other day, the teachers heard about that shooting at the gas station. The kids didn't know it yet, but they knew just from our demeanor something else had happened. From our body language, the expressions on our faces." Cissy put down her fork. "I caught a kid the other day drawing the sniper lying on a rooftop aiming at a school, blood dripping off a girl."

"What did you do?"

"Asked the school counselor to talk to him. She pulled in his parents. But what could they say to him? What he drew was something that could really happen, something he was afraid of, something I'm afraid of." She looked at David.

Her eyes were a beautiful, clear blue, the bluest eyes he'd ever seen.

"Aren't you afraid?" she asked him.

"I'm a cop. I just want to get this guy."

"But are you ever afraid?"

"No." Instantly David knew it was a lie. The thought of losing Kit scared him. The thought of never being with her, of never holding her, of never having her for his wife sent fear racing through him in waves.

How odd. After all these years of being alone.

He corrected himself. "A few things scare me, but not the sniper." He took a deep breath. "I have to trust God for the rest. He's a big God." David pushed it a little. "I know he loves me. I'm learning to trust him."

Cissy stared at her glass of water, not meeting his eyes. Finally, she looked up. "I don't ... I don't believe in God. Not like that. I'm spiritual and everything. But I think god is more ... part of nature. A force."

"Okay," David cleared his throat. Should he go further? Press her thinking? Not today, he decided. Take it slowly. "As a cop, I'd say be smart. Don't expose yourself unnecessarily. The chances are 1.7 million to one that it'll be you. Probably less than that, because you're inside most of the day."

"That makes sense."

"Quit watching the news."

She looked at him oddly.

"Don't even read the newspaper. These reporters are just amping up the fear factor. Sells papers, but it heightens anxiety."

"Thank you."

"We'll get through this. We will."

He wasn't sure he'd convinced her, but she smiled at him anyway.

Hours later, David lay in bed wide awake, wondering if he should have said more, thinking about how to help Cissy grab on to hope.

He'd had the same problem with Emilio. His son, Alex, who'd been discharged from the Navy, was now missing. David had tried to call him, but the kid wasn't answering his phone and wasn't returned the messages he left.

Now Emilio was panicking.

Dispatches crackled on the police radio on his bedside table. Normally, he kept it on a setting that alerted him only in an emergency; lately, though, he couldn't stop listening to it, couldn't stop waiting for the next call for the next shooting.

His years as a detective had deeply shaped his thinking. Figuring out the puzzle, fighting for justice for the victim had been his passion for a long, long time. And now, he had to admit, with Kit on the line, he felt restless that he wasn't in the game. He was a coach now, not a player, and it bothered him.

✟ ✟ ✟

Nights spent sleeping on a cot at the office meant bad mornings for Kit, punctuated by terrible coffee. Still, the expected arrival of the CIRG team from Quantico early Saturday morning necessitated the uncomfortable night, at least according to Kit. Among the agents CIRG was sending was a profiler named Candace Stewart. She was a specialist in both geographic and psychological profiling. Kit planned to work closely with her. But before Candace arrived, Kit wanted to be up on every detail of the cases, so she stayed late at the office, pouring over files and drinking cold, black coffee for which the term "burnt" was a compliment. David called to see if she wanted to go to church on Sunday, but there was no time for that. Not this week.

Profiling had evolved in the forty years the FBI had been using it. The original breakdown between "organized" and "disorganized" killers had become much more sophisticated. Techniques like geographic profiling and linguistic analysis had added nuance and accuracy. Still, the principles were the same: People's actions were prompted by something hidden in their psychological makeup. Discovering that "something" could help identify what the Bureau called the UNSUB, the unknown subject, and close a case.

At seven on Saturday morning, Kit stood in the task force conference room staring at the map on the wall. She heard a noise and turned to see Steve Gould standing at the door. With him was a fifty-ish woman with short, blonde, stylish hair. The jacket of her raspberry pink suit fell right at her waist. As she stepped in the room she adjusted her grip on a thick leather attaché case.

Attractive, professional, and smart: that was Kit's instant reaction.

"Kit!" Steve walked toward her. "This is Special Agent Candace Stewart. Profiler with CIRG." He turned toward the profiler. "Special Agent Kit McGovern. She'll bring you up to date."

Steve walked away. Candace set her briefcase down and walked over to the wall. "Nice summary," she said, gesturing toward the map and the photos. She turned toward Kit, her bright blue eyes like searchlights on Kit's face. "You were there, when the prosecutor was shot."

Kit nodded. "Yes. Gail and I were working on a case."

"It must have been a shock, being that close."

Kit pressed her lips together momentarily. "I'm hoping you can help us catch this guy. I think geographic profiling will help." She moved closer to the map. "You can see, we have multiple jurisdictions involved and quite a complex metropolitan area."

Candace waited a beat before responding. Kit had dodged the deeper issued Candace had addressed, but she had the sudden sense that *she* was being profiled. She tucked a stray strand of hair behind her ear and raised her chin.

Thankfully, Candace returned her focus to the wall. "Yes, all the tunnels and bridges, waterways and interstates make movement around the area quite complicated. Three sites wasn't really enough to hone in our UNSUB but now we have five." She walked to the pictures and seemed to study each victim's face, and then their profile. "So random." She turned to Kit. "I assume you've checked for a common denominator."

Kit nodded. "There are none. We, Lincoln Sheffield and I, interviewed the first three victims' family members and the wife of a man who was missing. Of course we haven't had time to extensively interview yesterday's survivors, but I'll have someone on that today. I don't see any commonalties between the victims so far. They're different socio-economic groups, different races, different ages, different everything. So what's the sniper doing? How is he choosing his victims? Why is he killing? That's what we need you to help us figure out."

"What about chatter?"

"Homeland Security isn't picking up on anything so far, from ISIS or any other terrorist group." Kit cocked her head. "They tell me it would be normal, if it was a foreign terrorist, for there to be something." Kit thought, What if it was ISIS? She refocused. "Would you like to see the case files?"

"Very much."

Kit had just shown Candace how to log into their database when Steve appeared, holding a sheaf of papers. "The latest from ATF." She took the papers and began leafing through them. "Two of the three bullets from the first shootings are confirmed as .223," Steve said. "That's why they did so much damage. They're small and fast. Three thousand feet per second."

"So basically, the sniper can fire from far away ..."

"And get out of the area before anyone can react."

Kit looked at him. "We had two witnesses report a car leaving the area at a high rate of speed where Shirley Bailey was shot."

Chase Carter had joined them. "We checked that out, Agent McGovern. Found the car on the gas station's security video and interviewed the driver. He was just scared. Said he heard the shot and floored it."

Kit nodded "Good work. On the other hand, the suspect could just drive slowly away while innocent bystanders beat feet out of there, drawing everyone's attention. I suspect we're going to get a lot more of that."

"Yes, ma'am."

Chase crossed his arms. "In the Bailey shooting, more than one security camera was inoperable."

"What?" Kit said. Was that the link between the shootings?

"I've been talking to the tech. He was trying to get pictures of that car speeding away. An agent went out to find more video from nearby security cameras. On two of them, the lens was obscured. Maybe just dirty. He couldn't tell. But still …"

"And whoever owned the cameras hadn't noticed?"

"I asked them to go back and find when they'd had the last clear footage from those cameras. It was two days before Bailey got shot." Chase shrugged. "I guess they look at that stuff all the time, and get complacent. They're used to nothing happening."

"So how'd you track down the car of the guy you interviewed then?"

"Cameras from further away. We had a bumper and a partial plate. We tracked it down that way."

"Good work." Kit tapped her pen on the table. "Chase, make sure we stick with the camera angle. That may be the link we've been looking for."

Steve nodded toward Candace. "Does she have what she needs?"

"I've gotten her started." Kit brushed her hair back. "I'll stick close to her today, unless something else breaks."

"Okay." Lincoln Sheffield cruised into the room with a stack of papers in his arms. "Now we are cooking." He plopped them down on the table. The front page banner headline blared, "Sniper terrorizes Hampton Roads."

Kit glanced at Steve. "Our purpose is to stop this guy, not get headlines."

"This'll help. We'll have more eyes looking for him," Lincoln claimed.

"Somehow I doubt that." She looked to Steve for support,

but her boss just shook his head and walked off. She crossed her arms and refocused on Lincoln. His wardrobe today, she noted, featured a black suit, pink shirt, and pink, black, and yellow patterned tie. So stylish.

He was such a peacock! Did he think the FBI gave extra points for fashion?

She pulled her eyes away from Lincoln as the other members of the task force began filing in. Some, she knew, had been up all night, managing the crime scenes. A surge of appreciation washed through her.

Kit checked her watch. Seven fifty-five. Just enough time to grab a cup of coffee.

Candace apparently had had the same thought.

"May I introduce you to the task force?" Kit asked.

"Sure!"

Moments later, Kit rapped her pen on the table, calling the task force to order. "First of all, let me introduce you to Candace Stewart. She is an agent, and a profiler with CIRG. Candace, would you please tell everyone how you will be contributing?"

Candace was so poised, Kit thought, as she faced the table of mostly male investigators and outlined her profiling methodologies. "I look forward to working with you," she said, ending her introduction.

"Okay," Kit said. She noticed a few of the investigators frowning. "Let's have an update on the two new shootings. Jim?" She called on a Chesapeake police detective who had taken over the review of the crime scene for the fourth shooting.

Jim Braden stood. He had a sheaf of papers in his hand. "Ralph Ellis, sixty-five. Bus driver. Gunned down while raking leaves in his own front yard. So far, nothing in his background to suggest he was specifically targeted. We're checking his financials and with his employer and coworkers this morning, but so far we have nothing. And there are no security cameras. It's normally a quiet neighborhood."

Lincoln snorted. "Reporters may get into his life before we do. His widow called me an hour ago saying the newsies were coming. I told her she could refuse to talk to them, but both she and her daughter want to."

"Okay, that's victim number four. How about number five?" Kit nodded toward another Chesapeake officer, Sean Boyd.

"Mitchell or Mitch Silverman," he began, "age forty-four, a salesman at Big Bob's Cars-to-Go. He was showing customers a car when the shot rang out. The customer said he didn't see anything, nor did anyone else at the dealership. We're again checking background and security camera footage and will update the task force later. The victim did survive. He's still at Sentara Hospital."

Kit nodded. While Boyd was talking, Joe Langstrom had entered the room and was standing with his back against the wall.

He raised his hand. Kit nodded to him. "I just want to say that Mayor Crawford is very concerned about the public's safety and would like to offer any assistance he can. That's why I'm here."

"Plus, he's the guy who got us the coffee pot," Lincoln quipped. "Good job, Joe."

Kit wrested the control back. "If there's nothing else, let's meet back here at four."

✞ ✞ ✞

"Kit, how familiar are you with geographic profiling?" Candace asked as they walked back from the conference room.

"I got about fifteen minutes on it at the Academy. That was eight years ago." Eight years and one marriage ago. Time flies. "But I learned enough about it to believe that it could help us."

"Let me show you something."

Candace led her over to the Hampton Roads map on the wall. "So we've had shootings here, here, here, here, here, and now here." She made little ink dots on the map. "You know the concept, right? That we carry with us a 'mental map' of our surroundings and the places we usually travel?"

"Right."

"Offenders usually have some kind of home base—their own residences, or a close friend's house, or work, or a recreation location like a bar. Most won't commit crimes in their own immediate area. It's too likely they'll be recognized. So there will be a 'buffer zone' around the home base. Then the crimes will form some sort of pattern."

"These shootings seem so random," Kit responded.

"They do at first. But geographic profiling can clarify the picture. One of the researchers who developed this methodology was a law enforcement officer in Canada. He found that by cataloguing the locations of the crimes, often a pattern emerges: They'll be along a well-traveled route, or in a similar neighborhood, and so on. The locations, then, form a core crime set which, when plugged into a logarithm can establish probable neighborhoods in which the UNSUB may live or work. Layer over that information about known felons and so on and it can narrow your list of suspects substantially."

Absorbed in the information, Kit hadn't noticed that Chase had joined them.

"So there's an actual mathematical formula that analyzes the data?" he asked.

"Right." Candace shuffled some papers.

Chase looked like he understood. "What kind of output do you get?"

"There are several. I tend to use a choropleth map, a sort of 3-D representation of likely geographical locations for the suspect."

"What if the guy isn't from around here?"

"It doesn't work on 'commuter' suspects," Candace replied, "unless, of course, he's become a temporary resident. And just looking at this map," she turned to Kit, "I'm thinking he knows this area. Hampton Roads isn't the easiest place to negotiate, travel-wise." Candace walked to the white board and began writing. "We could be looking at a suspect who is operating almost at random. He's cruising around looking for an opportunity."

"Except for Gail, right? That was planned," Kit suggested.

"Not necessarily. Think about it: He was looking to take a shot downtown. He saw the reporters. Now he has an audience. And he loves that."

"None of the other victims were high-profile."

"He's being careful. Everyone's on the lookout now. No one expected that first shot."

True, Kit thought. No one expected it. Least of all me.

"Then again," Candace said, "he could be just hunting his victims."

"If he obscured the cameras, that would indicate he planned the attacks, right?"

"Good point." Candace rubbed her fingers together as if she were trying to urge some thought into expression.

Kit noticed she wore just a little makeup: a light foundation with a hint of blush, and just a touch of lilac eye shadow. Kit touched her own cheek, aware she hadn't even thought of makeup. Or moisturizer. What would she look like at fifty-five?

"We normally need six sites but running the program, even with five, should help us," Candace said. "I'll need some information on the earlier crime scenes—descriptions of the neighborhoods and so on. If Chase could work with me on that, I'll begin the analysis."

"Chase?"

"Yes, ma'am. I'm on it."

CHAPTER 8

SOMETHING CANDACE HAD SAID WHEN they were going over the ballistic reports the day before had resonated with Kit. Then she'd gotten a text from David asking a question on the same subject. He'd walked the shooting sites with his kids, and Kit got the feeling ideas were popping into his head.

He'd wanted to have dinner with her last night, but she was all tied up with reports coming in from investigators, so she'd put him off, again, and then spent half the night regretting it.

Truth was, she couldn't eat much anyway.

Two blocks away from and diagonally opposite the courthouse steps where Gail had been killed was a six-story office building. Google showed it as having a parking garage on the roof. The reports weren't clear that it had been thoroughly checked—it was pretty far away. But then, if a bullet could travel 3,000 feet per second, a shooter didn't need to be close to kill someone with a rifle.

David had asked if that building had been checked thoroughly. She couldn't confirm that, so, climbing into her Bureau car, Kit drove back downtown. The building sat on Boush Street, across Brambleton Avenue.

At 6:30 a.m., traffic was light. Kit pulled over to the curb. The building housed a law firm and other offices, and sure enough, there was a ramp on the left side, the entrance to a parking garage.

Kit pulled in and drove up the incline. She emerged into the light and pulled onto the roof. There she saw an old, battered Jeep Cherokee. A familiar rush, like coming home after a long absence, ran through her.

David, standing next to his Jeep, turned around, a surprised look on his face.

"Why haven't you gotten that fixed?" she teased, pointing to his broken window

He grinned. "It's symbolic of my heart." He wrapped his arms around her. "I'm missing my girl."

The warmth of his body and the strength of his arms covered Kit like a balm. Tears sprang to her eyes. She hoped he didn't notice. "What are you doing here?"

He kissed her before he answered. "My kids checked these streets, but I noticed they didn't look at this building, except to say there was no footage from security cameras. I decided to find out why." David cupped his hand under her jaw, cradling her face. "How are you?"

He loved her. Kit could feel it. "I'm fine. Busy, that's all."

"And how is Lincoln?" He dropped his hand.

Kit rolled her eyes. "Please, let's not go there."

"So what made you come up here?"

"Your text."

"You're stalking me!"

"I didn't know you were coming here this morning. You just asked a question I didn't have the answer to. Plus, the profiler from CIRG arrived. We were going over the ballistics and it struck me again the angle of penetration of the bullet that hit Gail. When I checked our database, I couldn't find much on this building. So I came to see if this could have been the sniper's location."

"My thinking exactly," David said. "Look at this." He lead her over to the edge of the roof, and handed her a rifle scope. "Check that out."

She peered through the scope, adjusting the focus, and aiming it toward the courthouse steps. "You'd have to be a good shot," she said, looking to David for affirmation.

"Yes, but the angle is about right."

Kit glanced around. "What about security cameras?"

"That's what's interesting," David said. "Look at this."

She followed him to a camera set on a pole about ten feet off the garage floor. His car was parked right next to it, and to her surprise, he jumped up on the hood and reached toward the camera.

"There's something on the lens. Some kind of gunk." He looked down. "You got any swabs with you? Any evidence collection stuff?"

"Sure. One second." Kit jogged back to her car, grabbed an evidence kit, and came back. Retrieving swabs and a plastic bag, she handed them up to David.

He collected a sample of whatever was on the lens, then dropped the swabs in the bag, and handed it back to Kit. She sealed the bag, dated and initialed it. "I'll have this checked," she said.

"Let me know." David climbed down. "Didn't you say the footage was missing from some of the other scenes? I have a theory—the guy is obscuring the cameras, maybe the day before, maybe the night before."

"Wow."

David hesitated, as if he were mentally transitioning from work to personal. He took her in his arms again. She felt his smooth cheek against hers, and smelled his aftershave. "Finish this case up, will you?" he said, nuzzling her ear.

The sound of a car engine made them both turn around. "Oh, no," Kit said.

The black SUV was as Bureau as Italian leather shoes and square jaws. It might as well have had a seal on the side.

Lincoln and Joe Langstrom got out. Kit moved slightly away from David. "Well, you are up with the chickens," Lincoln said. "Is this the boyfriend?" He nodded toward David.

How did he know where she was? Or that she had a boyfriend? "David O'Connor," she said, "Special Agent Lincoln Sheffield and Joe Langstrom, the mayor's assistant."

David shook hands with them. "Lincoln Sheffield … wait, University of Alabama? Wide receiver?"

Lincoln beamed. "Roll Tide, man! You got it."

David grinned.

"You go down there? I'll get you tickets some time, man."

"Maybe after we catch this sniper?" Kit stared at them, her arms crossed.

David, she could tell, was trying to stifle a laugh. How

annoying!

Lincoln looked around the sparse parking garage. The sun had edged up over the horizon and was warming up the day. "This the best you can do for a date?"

"It was coincidental. We both had the same thought."

"And that would be ..."

"That the sniper who killed Gail could have shot from up here." Kit raised her chin. "How'd you know ..."

"Steve Gould," Lincoln said. "He asked Chase where you were."

Kit tightened her lips.

"Come here," David said, drawing Lincoln over to the roof's edge. "Look at this." He handed him the rifle scope. While Lincoln was looking, David turned to Joe. "So what do you do for the mayor?"

Joe cleared his throat. "I'm his chief aide and personal assistant."

"So you basically try to keep him on track."

"I write some of his speeches, review some of his appointments, keep him informed on what the city is doing."

"Right now," Lincoln said, "the city is trying to avoid being shot by a sniper."

"And we're not going to find him jawing up here," Kit said, pulling open her car door. "See you at the office."

✝ ✝ ✝

Reporter Piper Calhoun's assignment was to cover schools' reaction to the sniper, and with at least four jurisdictions involved, she had her hands full.

She'd chosen Philip E. Newberry High School in Norfolk as her target. Yes, she should have gone through the school board's public information officer, but PIOs were usually thick filters, keeping good stories from ever seeing the light of day. She'd take her chances at Newberry.

Climbing out of her old Chevy first thing Monday morning, she adjusted her long denim skirt and shrugged her khaki jacket into place over her Texas bluebonnet print shirt. On her head she wore a black fedora at a rakish angle, a nod to old school reporters, of whom there were fewer and fewer. She happened to know the principal at Newberry used to teach drama, and she thought maybe her attire would pique his interest. Plus, the hat covered the purple dye ("decidedly unprofessional" is what her fussy old editor had called it) she'd put in her hair.

Out in front, the buses were off-loading students. Teachers had moved some portable whiteboards outside, angling them to hide the kids from view as they walked from bus to building.

Classes began at 7:35. Piper checked her watch: 7:26.

She tried at first to blend in with the kids and just walk in, but an alert teacher stopped her. Piper produced her press creds. "Just wanted to talk to Mr. Anderson."

"Wait here," the woman said, frowning.

The last bus off-loaded and groaned away, spewing diesel fumes that made Piper gag. Standing alone in the covered entranceway, she suddenly felt exposed, vulnerable. Fear was in the air along with the fumes.

A uniformed resource officer appeared. Piper explained her mission. Then, behind him she saw a man in a suit, and she recognized him. "Mr. Anderson!" she said, waving.

"Do I know you?" the principal said, moving forward.

"Well, maybe. Not really. I have been in your school." Piper plastered on what she hoped was a "safe" smile.

"I got this, Tom," Anderson said, waving off the school cop.

Piper glanced toward the street nervously. "This sniper's got me spooked," she said, apologetically.

And just like that, she got what she wanted. "Come in," Anderson said, and he led her first into the building, and then into his office. "Now, why are you here?"

"I'm doing a story on the schools' reaction to the sniper."

"You've gone through the PIO?"

"I have called them." Only half a lie. She'd talked to them last year when flu shots were being offered for the first time in schools.

But he bought it. "The students are perfectly safe. We've cancelled outdoor sports practices. There will be no games. And, as you can see, we are obscuring the view from the street." His cell phone rang.

Piper recognized the ringtone, "My Girl."

"Excuse me," he said, and he answered it.

Piper pretended to be absorbed in her notes while he spoke to the caller. "Yes, yes. No, I absolutely do not want them waiting for the bus. You take them. And pick them up. I know, you're low on gas. I'll deal with that tonight."

The conversation must have ended because he clicked off his phone. "I'm sorry." He turned back to Piper.

She cocked her head and smiled. "The kids are perfectly safe, you were saying."

"Yes, and ..."

Before he could finish, the resource officer stuck his head in the door, interrupting. "Sir, we have an alert."

Anderson rose and moved toward the door. Piper watched, then followed as the principal walked into the main office, listening as the officer told him about the strange car seen moving slowly near the school. "Get them away from the windows," the principal responded.

A front office secretary put her hand over the mouthpiece of her desk phone. "Sir, you need to listen to this."

His attention diverted, Anderson took the phone she was handing him and put it up next to his ear. Then his face went white. Piper scribbled notes. Anderson looked at the officer and gestured. He mouthed the words: "bomb threat."

Piper felt a chill. First the sniper, now a bomb threat? Wow! Awesome!

Within seconds, the school staff was scrambling, and in the rush, Piper was forgotten. She got the fear in their voices, the panicked call to the police, the hurried debates over the proper procedure—should they evacuate or not?—the complicated logistics of emptying a school full of teenagers in a world gone mad.

Was the bomb threat a ruse of the sniper? Was he drawing students out of the building to shoot them? Was it a hoax? Was it a student avoiding a test?

No one knew, and no one was willing to take a chance.

In the end, eleven hundred students were herded into the football stadium, ordered to stay in the bleachers, and "guarded" by one resource officer, fifty teachers, a line of parked school buses, and one very nervous principal, while bomb-sniffing dogs combed the building.

Piper got it all, in a story she hoped would do well enough

to be her ticket out of town. "Un-flippin'-believable!" she told her boss later. "It was a madhouse. Panic City." The ten-point newspaper headline the next day would be equally dramatic.

✟ ✟ ✟

Kit put her large skinny vanilla latte, AKA "breakfast," down on a table in the task force room and walked over to her white board. On it were five columns: Five shootings, five victims, a summary of facts.

What was the pattern? What weren't they seeing?

She checked her watch: 7:54. Monday.

As task force members shuffled into the room, a Norfolk PD officer approached her. "We're working a bomb threat at Newberry High School."

She turned to look at him. "Related?"

Norfolk detective Tom Packer standing nearby interrupted. "If you wanted to shoot someone, wouldn't forcing a thousand students outdoors be a tactic?"

Kit called the task force members to order, rapping on the table with her pen. Ignoring Packer's challenge, she focused on the officer who had delivered the news about the school threat. Hank Taylor. That was his name. "Officer Taylor has informed me that they are working a bomb threat at Newberry High School. Officer, would you update us?"

"Call came in at 7:34 this morning. Caller just said there was a bomb in the school. Completely threw off school officials. They had no idea what to do with the kids." Taylor shifted on his feet. "If they left them in the school, there could be a bomb. Take 'em outside, and they'd be targets for the sniper." He ran his hand through his hair. "They made the decision to evacuate. The kids are sitting in the football stadium now. They rolled school buses up close to it to provide some screenage. We've got bomb dogs going through the building."

Kit heard a noise and looked up.

Steve had entered the task force room with someone else, a good-looking, fit man in a tan suit. Who was he? An agent? A cop?

Kit read Steve's demeanor. "Agent Gould?"

Steve stepped forward. "This is Captain Mark Mahoney,

Virginia State Police. He's the head of the governor's security detail." Steve took a deep breath. "The governor is going to be here on Thursday to dedicate the new bridge over the Elizabeth River."

What? Kit felt her blood pressure rising.

"The press is going to be all over that," someone suggested.

Steve continued. "The governor will be present as will the mayor of Norfolk and other local officials at the bridge dedication. It's the kind of thing that will draw more reporters than citizens, but still, those who will be there would make high-profile targets."

"Can it be postponed?" an officer asked.

"Absolutely not," Joe said, piping up. "It's important."

Important enough to die for? Kit thought.

"We'll need someone to take the lead on coordinating with event security," Steve said.

"We got that. Me and Joe," Lincoln said. "We'll get with state police and Norfolk PD. We can handle that." He and Joe disappeared with Steve and the state trooper.

Then Kit asked some of the other task force members to update the group on their parts of the investigation. Chase Carter had found three cameras, so far, disabled at the shooting sites. Investigators would check each one. The Portsmouth PD rep shared what he'd learned by checking Charles Lipscomb's financial and client records: basically nothing.

"Do we have a profile yet?" a task force member asked.

Kit looked to the back of the room, where Candace was standing. She stepped forward to respond to the question. "We want to avoid tunnel vision," Candace said, "and so we will not be releasing a profile until we have narrowed down some facts. Right now, everyone's a suspect."

A chill ran down Kit's spine. The chances of finding the sniper seemed somewhere between "slim" and "none."

☗ ☗ ☗

The Hawk had found a perch high in a parking garage across from Philip E. Newberry High School. His rifle was in a canvas camp-chair bag slung over his shoulder. He took the elevator to the fourth level then walked to where he could see the school, peering over the waist-high concrete wall of the garage.

As a high-school student in West Virginia he'd been very successful in disrupting classes with bomb threats. And why not? It was better than being bored to death and much better than being at home with the old man. Excitement, that's what he craved. Excitement he could control.

Across the street had gone into panic mode, shepherding kids to the football field, trying to protect them with school buses. What a thrill. And all because of him.

He had no intention of shooting that day. He'd just brought his rifle because he thought it would add to the intensity of his feelings. And so it did, pressing into his back, reminding him of who he was and what his mission was.

He'd made the call with the bomb threat from three blocks away using a burner phone he'd then tossed in the trash. The cops would find it if they looked hard enough. Still, they couldn't trace it to him, not without serious investigation. And so far, that seemed out of their reach.

He looked down. The bomb-sniffing dogs had arrived. Two of them. The Hawk grinned. *Go, Fido!*

Focused on the school, he never heard the elevator rising or the doors opening. The officers' footsteps on the concrete floor of the parking garage, however, did register.

Heart pounding, the Hawk turned around. "Something's going on at the school!" he said, feigning concern.

The officers were both tall, both fit, both young. "Yes, sir. Can I see your ID?" one of them asked.

"Sure." The Hawk tried to remember which pocket he'd put the latest stolen driver's license in. He shoved his hand in his back left pocket, pulled it out, and handed it to the officer. "Kids these days," he said, shaking his head. "You'd think they'd appreciate an education."

"What's in the bag?" the second cop said.

The Hawk touched the strap on his shoulder. "This? Camp chair. I'm taking my mother to the park." He took a deep breath. "She's eighty three." He shook his head. "Not doing well. I try to come over several times a week and get her outside. You know how it is with older people." He kept talking rattling on about his mother's ailments and his confusion about what kind of wheelchair he should be buying for her until he saw the cop look away in boredom.

The first cop handed back the ID. "Okay, sir, have a good day."

"Thank you for your service! Stay safe, officers."

Now *that* was exciting, he thought.

CHAPTER 9

AT 11:54 A.M. ON Monday, Kathy Emory sat waiting for the B53 bus on Indian River Road in Virginia Beach. Content with the warm sun on her back, she leafed through a *Woman's Day*. An apple crisp recipe looked particularly good, and she folded down the corner of the page to mark it. Thanksgiving would be here before she knew it, and that meant the kids would be coming home.

Kids. They were thirty and thirty-two, married, each with children of their own. But they were still "kids" to Kathy.

A man came and sat down next to her. Kathy glanced at him, then looked to see if the bus was coming. It wasn't. She looked down at her magazine again. Fall fashions included tall boots, lots of scarves. Maybe for Christmas ...

A shot rang out. The man jumped in alarm. And Kathy Emory slowly pitched off the bench and fell onto the ground, her red blood pooling on the bright yellow maple leaves on the sidewalk.

✞ ✞ ✞

Lincoln and Joe were just outside task force conference room when the call came in. "Let's roll," Lincoln said.

Candace rode with Kit. Fifteen minutes later, the two women stepped out of Kit's Bucar and ducked under the yellow crime scene tape.

Cops and emergency vehicles filled the scene. The body lay on the ground in front of the bus bench. "Do we have an ID?" Kit asked a uniformed officer. Meanwhile, in the back of her head, she was adding another column to her whiteboard.

"Kathy Emory. Driver's license indicates she lives about four miles from here. Receipt in her purse is from a medical office over there." The officer indicated a two-story brick building across the street. "We're checking with them now. Looks like she was just waiting for a bus when he got her."

Just waiting for a bus. How much more mundane could you get?

Lincoln pulled up. Kit noted that he was late.

"Good God A'mighty," Lincoln said quietly. "She is so dead." A leaf fell off an overhanging limb and drifted to the ground, landing on Kathy Emory's still body.

Joe, standing partially behind Lincoln, looked pale.

"Ma'am, we have a witness," a uniformed officer said to Kit.

"Thank you." She followed him to a man standing apart from the rest. Happily, Lincoln remained back at the body.

The witness was about sixty years old, an African-American man dressed in dark pants and a red plaid shirt. "I'm sittin' there," he told Kit, "and I hear this *bang!* and then she fall down. Jus' like that."

"You were waiting for the bus ..."

"Yes, ma'am, and it was late. Went to the doc's 'bout my sugar. Been runnin' too high, he says. Stress not good for it. Then this." He scratched his jaw. "I think I seen her in there."

"In the doctor's office?"

"Yes, ma'am."

"Did you notice anything before you heard the bang? Any cars moving slowly, any people ..."

"No, nuthin' like that. Nuthin' that made me think this lady 'bout to be killed. Nuthin' at all." The man took his Redskins cap off and scratched his head, then replaced the cap, tugging it into place. "She jus' sittin' there and then, bang. She dead. Lord Jesus have mercy."

"Thank you, sir." Kit turned to uniformed officer. "I'd like you and one of my agents to take his statement right now. I'll send someone over." She looked back at the witness. "I'm going to have this officer and an agent talk to you, sir. And please, if you could, don't talk to reporters. We'd like to catch this killer and that will just make it harder."

The old man nodded.

Kit found an agent to take the witness's statement, then walked back to where Candace was standing near the victim. Their eyes met. The profiler said, "It'll be just like the others. No reason she was the victim." She lowered her voice and motioned with her head. "Could just as easily have been him."

As they approached the victim, Kit could hear Lincoln explaining the investigation details to Joe. She tried to warn him with her eyes, but what was the use? Lincoln loved an audience and Joe provided that.

Kit glanced upward at the sound of a helicopter. The press was all over this already. Great. That only fed the panic in the community and the pressure on law enforcement. "Sergeant, can you move that line back a little," she said to the officer in charge of the uniformed police. Her neck felt tight, like a hand was choking her.

"Yes. But ma'am, the press wants to know when there will be a statement."

"I'll handle that," Lincoln interjected.

☦ ☦ ☦

Finally! They seemed to be getting it. The black guy leading the news conference did, anyway.

The Hawk sipped his coffee. Across from him in the hotel lobby sat a young woman, a pretty brunette. Her eyes were fixed on the TV screen. He could see the tension in her face.

She glanced over at him.

"Terrible world, isn't it?" he said, trying to capture her attention.

"Frightening," she replied. She stood up, adjusting the skirt of her business suit. A perfectly manicured hand picked up her leather tote.

The Hawk stood, shouldered his camp chair bag, and began walking with her toward the elevators. "You here on business?"

"Yes. A medical conference."

Why are you giving me information, he thought? *Don't you know who I am?* "Well, be careful out there on the street. Apparently, no one is safe." He gave her his most serious look.

She hesitated. "It's so scary."

The elevator doors opened.

So scary! Ha! You bet it is, sweetheart.

☩ ☩ ☩

Back at the office, Kit tried to shake the tension gripping her. Six shootings. Five murders. And she was no closer to catching the sniper—presumably Gail's killer—than she had been last week.

A week. Had it really been that long ago that she stood on those steps next to Gail? So much had happened, and yet, the most important thing, identifying and arresting her killer, was left undone.

Was she sure these cases were linked? Was she racing after rabbits?

She focused on the whiteboard. Her lists. Still her thoughts flashed in her head.

David called. She grabbed onto his voice, grateful for the comfort it brought. But then he asked her to have dinner with him. "No, I really can't," she said. "I can't get away."

Steve, walking by, stopped.

"Maybe tomorrow," she met Steve's eye.

He signaled a time out.

"Hold on a second," she said to David, and she put him on hold. "What?"

"Is that David?"

She nodded.

"Go spend some time with him."

"I can't."

"I'm ordering you to." He put his hands on his hips. "Look, Kit, you're driving yourself too hard. You're not going to be any use to us if you crash. Go, take a break. You'll be better for it." He gestured. "I'll be here 'til late. I can handle things tonight."

☩ ☩ ☩

Kit pressed the button in her apartment elevator. She checked her watch: 8:43 p.m. Much later than she thought she'd be. She wasn't really looking forward to going out again. In fact, she just wanted to go to bed.

David said he'd meet her at her apartment. When she entered, wonderful smells greeted her. He'd cooked. She wouldn't have to go out. How nice of him.

She pulled off her jacket and removed her gun, placing it high on the bookshelves just inside the door. "Hi, David!"

He emerged from the kitchen, a shock of brown hair falling down over his forehead, a wooden spoon in his hand. "Somehow this just feels right," he said, grinning.

She walked over to him and they hugged. "You need a frilly apron," she teased. "Thank you."

He bent down and kissed her, and his lips felt warm and comforting. "For what?" he asked.

"For dinner. For being you. For being a safe place."

"Rough day?" His eyes searched her face.

"No. I just needed this." She shook her head. "You heard we had another shooting?"

"Yes. I can't imagine the stress you're under."

"It's bad."

"I hope you feel like eating."

She didn't. Not really. "What did you make?"

"I didn't make it. I picked it up: Chicken and gnocchi soup. Fresh bread. And salad."

"Perfect. Just perfect."

While they ate, she told him about the case. All her lists. All the victims. All that they knew.

He nodded, asked a few questions, and let her vent. Then she realized she was forgetting to eat, that she was tight as a tick. The clock in the kitchen read 9:30. It was Monday. "Do you want to finish up in front of the TV? So you can watch the game?"

Of course he did. His eyes lit up. "Sure!"

For him, she pretended to care about the football game. For him, she cheered for the Giants and booed the Cowboys. For him, she protested the referees' calls. For him, she ate half a mug of that delicious soup.

But all the while, in the back of her mind, she was reviewing the sniper case. What were they missing? What was the connection? What didn't they know? Why was Packer so annoying? What should she do about Lincoln?

At the beginning of the fourth quarter, Kit put down her mug and snuggled close to David, trying to relax. She leaned her head on his chest and felt his arm around her. Then he leaned over and kissed the top of her head. "Do you know what I'm thinking?" he said softly.

"No, what?"

"I'm thinking I'd like to spend forever just like this."

"Just like this?"

"Maybe with a couple of kids playing on the floor in front of us."

Kit stayed silent. Her neck had tightened again, the pain radiating to her jaw. Kids. Why did he have to bring up kids?

David squeezed her. "You okay?"

"Sure. My neck is stiff, that's all." That was a lie and she felt guilty immediately. She moved away from him and stretched. "Right now, I can't imagine bringing children into this world." She yawned, pretending to be sleepy. In reality, she felt piano-wire tight.

"Why's that?"

"There's so much evil." And so little love.

He laughed. "If people stopped having kids because of evil, none of us would be here."

A truck commercial played on the TV. Should they check trucks, she wondered? What kind? Panel vans? Box trucks? Then her mind snapped back. David was saying something else about kids.

She interrupted. "Do you ever wonder, with your history, how you'd do as a dad?" Even that was not the real question, but it was as close as she could get, for now.

David grew thoughtful. He rubbed his chin and she could hear his hand go over the stubble of his beard. "I used to. My stepfather was a terrible role model. But I've changed a lot in a year."

That, Kit knew, was an understatement.

David looked at her. "The police cadets look up to me, and it almost feels like I'm a dad. So I think I could do it. I want to, in fact."

Something akin to fear pushed Kit to her feet. On the TV, Dallas intercepted a Giants pass. She made a show of taking her mug to the kitchen. David followed her. She turned. "How do you know that's what I want?" It sounded so selfish. It probably was. She added guilt to her personal indictment.

David looked confused. "Well, I assumed—don't most

women want kids?"

"I'm not 'most women.' I have a career. I'm intense. Look at the hours I work! I can't imagine … how in the world would I be able to handle kids?"

"You don't always work these hours. We'd figure something out."

"Like what? A babysitter who'll work eighteen-hour days?"

"I don't know. Maybe I'll stay home if you don't want to. Look, Kit, people do all kinds of things these days to make a family work."

"I don't see myself in that role! I mean, honestly …

"What, mother? I think you'll make a wonderful mom."

A tremor ran through her, almost an anxiety attack. She turned so he wouldn't see her face.

Too late. David knew her too well. He moved behind her, touching her arms. "Kit, you'll be fine." He kissed her ear.

She turned around. Suddenly, all the pain and fear, all the sorrow and anger and years of frustration, fueled by fatigue, erupted within her. "How do you know? What if I'm not? What if I'm like …"

"Like your mother?"

The TV announcer said the game was tied. Four minutes to go. Giants had the ball. David's eyes stayed fixed on her. "Like your mother, Kit? Is that what you're worried about?"

"What if I get in the middle of it and fail? What if I just cut and run? What if I don't love them? What if I'm not *enough* for them?" The words tumbled out, irrepressible and damning. Kit pounded her fist into her thigh. "I know how to work. I know what I'm doing there, how to succeed. But being a mother …"

"You're not going to fail. You're not like your mother, Kit."

"How do you know? You don't know that." Why was she so angry? Her breath became shallow. Her ribs hurt.

"I know you."

"But you don't know her!"

David hesitated. "Yes, I do. I've talked to her!"

"You've what?" Kit exploded.

David's face reddened and his eyes widened in shock at her reaction. He held his hands up. "Wait. Don't get mad."

"Don't get mad?"

"Kit, honey. Every time I approach the idea of getting married and having a family, you change the subject. I had the idea that you were worried about being like your mom. I wanted to find out who she was, really. So I called her."

"Without asking me? Without considering what impact that would have on me?" Kit's face felt hot. Waves of anger raced through her, like waves slapping a speeding powerboat. And she was about to capsize.

He shrugged "I thought it might help."

"You tracked her down?"

"She has a return address on every one of those cards you've been stockpiling. Every one. I copied the most recent one down and the rest was easy." David cocked his head. "You're not like her, Kit, not at all. She's very quiet, very timid. An artist."

"An artist." Kit spit the words out.

"But you know what? I like her. She's just, well, fragile."

"Fragile? Is that your word for weak?"

"She's married to a guy now who's very low-key. A carpenter. A simple guy. They have three kids, all grown. And she told me the biggest regret of her life was leaving you and your brother." David shifted his weight. "At the time, she thought she'd be able to stay in touch. To see you now and then. As it turned out ..."

"She *abandoned* us!"

"She said she knew your father would raise you well. He was more than competent at everything he tried. And she's so proud of you. Proud of what you've become." David looked down. "Your father has kept her updated."

"My father?" Kit took a deep, shaky breath. A double betrayal. She turned her anger on David. "I can't believe you'd sneak around ..."

"It wasn't sneaking, Kit. I was waiting for the right time to tell you. Then this sniper thing started."

"You went behind my back, intruded on my life."

"If we get married, it won't be just your life. It'll affect both of us."

"Well, maybe that's it, then, maybe we just shouldn't get married!" She saw the anger fuse with hurt and ignite in his face.

He gestured in frustration. "What are you afraid of? Come on, Kit. I love you. I was trying to help. I love you and want to marry you and have kids."

"What if I don't?" The moment those words left her lips Kit regretted them. But she didn't take them back.

"Then that's your choice!"

"Because if you're going to be a control freak," she continued. Why was she saying that? Why? She didn't complete the thought.

David took a deep, wavery breath. She could see his pulse pounding in his temple.

"Kit, here's the deal," his said, his voice tight. "I want to spend the rest of my life with you. I love you. But I can't force you. You want to get married, fine. If not, ... whatever." He raised his hands. "It's your call, Kit. Your call." David grabbed his leather jacket off the coatrack and left, slamming the door behind him.

Kit watched the door close.

The game went into overtime. The Giants lost.

CHAPTER 10

A QUIET DAY. NO SHOOTINGS. Kit thought she should be grateful.

But her coffee tasted bitter on her tongue as she sat next to Candace Stewart and tried to concentrate on geographic profiling.

Her acidic words toward David lay heavily on her mind. But he shouldn't have contacted her mother. He really shouldn't have.

"Here is the output," Candace said, showing Kit a strange-looking map of the Hampton Roads area. "I entered the sites of each shooting. Using the formula, then the program has established the probabilities for the shooter's home or work location, at least so far." She pointed to color overlays on the map. "See here: The brighter colors, yellow and red, are high probability locations, the coolest colors, blue and purple are less likely."

Kit looked blankly at the map, the colors swirling into nonsense. She took another sip of coffee.

"Now here's another output," Candace said, "showing the same information in a different way." The new map on the computer screen looked three-dimensional, its lines bulging upward in the highly likely areas. Candace looked at her. "Are you getting this?"

Kit blinked. "Yes."

Candace sat back and dropped her hands into her lap. "Are you okay, Kit? Because you seem distracted."

"No, I'm fine, I just haven't used these products. I don't know what to do with that information."

"You can't see that you'd want to check convicted felons in the high probability areas, and gun shops? Run wants and warrants? Maybe even do a door-to-door in likely neighborhoods?"

Kit blushed. "I'm sorry, I just …"

"What's going on?"

Candace's voice was soft, almost motherly, and tears sprang to Kit's eyes. She stood up and turned away. How unprofessional. She balled her hand into a fist and pressed it into her thigh, willing herself to get control.

When she could trust her voice, she said, "I'm sorry. I had a fight with my boyfriend last night. He's a control freak." She knew that was a lie even as the words came out.

"This case is stressing you out."

"No, it's not. I'm used to intense cases."

"How many nights have you slept here at the office? When is the last time you had a decent meal?"

"I'm fine," Kit said. "Let's take a fifteen-minute break. I'll get my head back in the game."

✝ ✝ ✝

Steve appeared a few minutes later. "Kit around?" he asked Candace.

Candace smiled. "Taking a short break. She'll be back in a few minutes."

Steve nodded. "Mahoney's going to be here in a few minutes. I'll need Lincoln, or her."

"I'm sure she'll be right back." Candace hesitated, then asked, "By the way, do you know the guy she's dating?"

"David? Sure! Great guy."

"A little controlling, maybe?"

Steve laughed. "If anything, it's the other way around. I'll be back in a minute with Mahoney."

✝ ✝ ✝

Virginia State Police Captain Mark Mahoney didn't look too happy as he followed Steve into the task force conference room. "You remember Captain Mahoney, right, Kit?" Steve said. "He wants to go over the security plan again in light of that last shooting."

"Where's Lincoln?" Kit asked. Lincoln was the one who had worked with Mahoney before. Lincoln and Joe.

"Don't know," Steve replied, "but you're here. So do it."

"Of course," Kit said, feeling off-balance. "Come with me." She smiled at Mahoney, hoping to crack that stony facade.

Kit walked him over to where she had her desk, flipped on a projector, and accessed a file on her computer. In seconds, a smart board displayed a five-mile radius map of the area of the bridge dedication. "I believe this is what Agent Sheffield set up with you," she said, clicking a tab which showed an overlay of the security measures they'd planned for the governor's speech. Blue blocks for police vehicles and personnel. Red for federal agents. Purple for state police. "We'll have two state police choppers and a Bureau chopper in the air. The command center is here." Kit pointed to a large, blue rectangle just off the area where the spectators would be standing. "And the governor's limo will park here." She looked up at Mahoney. "I understand you're providing bulletproof plexiglass shields around the podium."

"Lectern. And yes, we are." He stroked his chin. "What about the buildings around the area? We'll have snipers on the rooftops, but we need to secure the windows. What do we have?"

"We've already arranged that," Kit said. "There are five buildings we felt concerned about, four office buildings and an apartment building. We've arranged to have agents and officers in each one from 6 a.m. until the governor is safely out of there."

Mahoney nodded. "Manhole covers?"

"They've been sealed, and boat traffic on the river will be stopped. Airspace will also be secured." Kit shifted on her feet. She honestly couldn't think of a security measure they'd missed.

Mahoney put his hands on his hips, pushing his jacket back and revealing a strong chest and a flat belly. "I hope that's enough."

Candace walked in. "Good morning." She focused her blue eyes on the captain. "Captain Mahoney, is it?"

"Yes, ma'am."

"I'm Special Agent Candace Stewart. I work in the Behavioral Analysis Unit in Quantico."

Mahoney grunted. "A profiler. You got anything?"

"A partial profile." Candace made him wait for a second. "We believe we're dealing with a white male, former military or possibly a hunter, who is working without an accomplice." She moved over to the computer and began tapping keys. "We plugged in that last shooting." The screen flashed and the odd-looking map of Hampton Roads came up. "You can see, that it falls into the pattern we've been seeing." Candace pointed to the projected image.

Mahoney frowned. He gestured toward the screen. "So, what's this supposed to mean?"

Candace explained the principles behind geographic profiling. "We believe our suspect either lives or works in one of these areas." Using a special marker, she drew two circles on the map.

"And so ..."

"About 200,000 people live or work in the target areas. We're going through the felons, and trying to identify former military snipers. It's a long process," Candace explained.

"We have less than forty-eight hours."

"Since the governor insists on doing the bridge dedication, he'll have to rely on our security measures." Candace leveled her eyes calmly at him.

Mahoney exhaled his frustration.

✞ ✞ ✞

The next day, after leaving work, David ran into Emilio's son Alex in a convenience store near the Academy. "Hey, Alex, David O'Connor, friend of your dad," he said, grabbing the young man's hand. "Good to see you!"

Alex was short and slim. He'd been a machinist's mate in the Navy, and hands were strong. He had his father's dark hair and dark eyes, but not his stature. If he was five foot seven, David would be surprised.

"Yes, sir," Alex said, his eyes darting. "I remember."

David steered him over to a quiet part of the store. "So what's going on? You're out of the Navy ..."

"Yes, sir. Looking for a job."

"As a machinist?"

"Yes, sir." His eyes darted again. "I'd better go, sir. Good seeing you."

David wasn't about to let him get away. "Hold on!" He dug in his pocket and pulled out a business card. Leaning against the wall, he scribbled his cell phone number on the back. Then he handed it to Alex. "Call me. I've had to start over a couple of times myself. I'd be glad to help if I can. Can you work on guns?"

Alex's face reddened. He hesitated before taking the card. "Yes, sir. Thank you."

"You live around here?"

"No, sir. I'd better go."

David watched him leave, moving toward the front of the store to see what car he got into. It was an older model Chevy, a large, dark blue sedan, driven by someone else. He couldn't quite see the tag.

He was still muddling that over when he got home and found a package on his front porch, a large box. It was addressed to Kit, care of him, and by the return address, David knew who had sent it: Kit's mom.

Oh, man. He took a deep breath and put it inside. No telling when would be a good time to give that to Kit. Would it end up in her closet, along with the cards?

Maybe he'd been wrong to contact her mother. Maybe he had intruded. Maybe he should apologize. He certainly shouldn't have brought it up, knowing the stress she was under. *Poor impulse control,* read his fourth grade report card. "Still working on it," he muttered.

For now, the only thing he knew to do was give her space. And pray. Pray for her, pray for them, pray for himself.

He placed his cell phone on his dresser, turned off so he wouldn't be tempted to call her. Being at odds with her was like carrying around a weight. He hated it.

A knock on the door broke his train of thought. He walked out to his foyer, looked through the peephole, and saw his neighbor, Cissy. "Hey!" he said, opening the door. "What's up?"

"Any chance you could help me with my car?"

David looked over her shoulder at the dark blue Nissan Altima. "What's wrong with it?"

"Flat tire. I know how to change it, but I can't get one of the lug nuts off."

"Sure, I can help you with that." He patted his pocket to be sure he had his keys, then he closed his front door and followed Cissy across the street.

She had the car up on a jack, and four of the lug nuts were already off and sitting in the hubcap. David picked up the tire iron, placed it on the lug nut and pulled. On the second tug, the nut released. David finished the job, and stood up.

"Thank you," Cissy said. She smiled. "You want to come in? I've got lasagna just about ready. I owe you a dinner, you know."

Lasagna. He'd been planning on making himself a sandwich. He scratched his head. "Sure. Thanks. That would be great."

All through dinner, Cissy talked about the sniper. About the school children. And about the fear she was dealing with.

David listened, responding with compassion and sometimes advice. He was good at that. But in the back of his mind, he kept seeing his phone on his dresser, and wondering if Kit had tried to call.

Later, when he was helping her clean up the dishes, Cissy's hand brushed his. Was it an accident? By the way she looked at him, he doubted it.

When they were finished, she touched his arm and looked deeply into his eyes. "Thank you, David, for helping me."

"No problem. I'm good at loading a dishwasher," he joked, hoping to lighten things up.

"No," she said, her eyes tearing, "with this sniper thing." She sighed. "You've made me feel so much better."

In his mind, he saw the cell phone on his dresser.

Swallowing hard, he moved away from Cissy. "I'd better go," he said, and he bent down to pat Annie and left.

☩ ☩ ☩

The sun rose on a tense Hampton Roads early Wednesday morning. More car horns than usual seemed to blare their disapproval. On the way to work, Kit saw that some gas station owners had rigged tarps to obscure the street view of their gas-pumping customers. A mom crossing Lexington Avenue with her young child tried to shield him with her body while half-running across the street, anxiety twisting her into an awkward position.

Kit's heart fluttered. She felt it too—the fear of the unknown. Where would the sniper strike next? Whom would he target? What family would be impacted? What community?

She had to get one step ahead of this guy.

Kit had gone over the structure of similar big investigations. Who was in charge and why? How were the units arranged? How were personnel used? What interference did they get from politicians? How did they manage the press?

The 24-hour news cycle made the media hungry. Morning, noon, and night the air was filled with stories and commentary about the cases she looked at. Profiles of the victims. Analysis of the investigation. Scraps of new information gleaned from who knows where. The opinions of irrelevant people. The talking head "experts" shilling for the media were often dead wrong.

The lesson Kit took from that was that a judicious release of information to the general public was crucial. Reveal enough to get all eyes looking for your shooter, but manage the information correctly—that was crucial.

So what ended complicated cases? Some of it was good investigation skills. Some was luck. A good part was teamwork, and that's one thing Kit had been working hard on—keeping all the different agencies and units working together, and not allowing the testosterone-driven investigators to expend their energy butting heads and playing king of the mountain.

So much depended on leadership. So much depended on her.

Inexplicably, her thoughts turned to David. She hadn't talked to him since their fight. Frankly, not seeing him gave her more time to think about the case.

But it also left a big void in her life. It was as though she'd left her part of her heart somewhere. She missed his encouragement. His notes. And the way he looked at her with love in his eyes.

But he'd contacted her mother. Without her permission. She wasn't sure she could forgive him for that. What else would he do?

She didn't want to think about it. She didn't want to think about him. Not now, anyway. Maybe after the case concluded.

✝ ✝ ✝

Cissy Singleton stood before her third-grade class, once again explaining what a topic sentence is. An announcement came over the loudspeaker asking teachers to move students' desks at least six feet away from classroom windows.

Had someone been spotted in the area? Some slow-moving car? A suspicious truck?

The desks began scraping across the floor and the kids moved to comply. A shiver went through Cissy.

Suddenly, Annie got up from her bed at the front of the class. She moved quickly to Cissy's side and nudged her, whining.

Seconds later, Cissy felt it. The dizziness, the weakness, the disorientation.

She stumbled toward her desk, where she kept glucose tablets and candy, but her feet got tangled and when she tried to catch herself, she fell.

Annie whined and nudged her, but she could not move. Her vision went dark. Somewhere in the distance, she heard a child yelling, "Get the nurse!"

✝ ✝ ✝

David sat on a folding chair on the stage in the auditorium facing twenty-seven graduates dressed in blue uniforms seated in the front rows. Spit-shined and polished, they looked good. They were good. And tomorrow they'd be on the street, protecting Norfolk citizens and the highest official in the commonwealth alike.

The kids. His kids. He'd miss them. But they'd be around. After just a little over a year at the academy, David was already developing a cadre of contacts in the police force, connections he knew he could count on.

Emilio leaned over to him and whispered, "I'd give anything if my kid were sitting down there."

David nodded. "I know. But you have to play the hand you're dealt."

"The hand *she* dealt," Emilio responded, speaking of his

former wife. "Who knows what he's doing?"

David didn't reply to that. He felt for what Emilio was going through with his kid. He'd told him about running into Alex at the convenience store, but that didn't help. Emilio wouldn't be happy until the kid was settled.

The speakers on the podium began with the usual speeches. David zoned out. Emilio's problems were one thing; the sniper was something else again. After six shootings, everyone was terrified. The whole population was a walking ball of tension. Personally, he knew he would not be able to fix things with Kit until the case was done.

He'd spent hours going over what he knew about the sniper case. But he was getting everything secondhand. Seeing the evidence from a distance. And he wished he could get up close, find the key, "the odd sock," some guys called it.

What was he doing with his life? Mentoring the kids was good. But was that all? They called him "coach." Truth was, his player's legs were itching.

David began to pray silently. By now, prayer had become a reflex. Like his vest and his gun, he relied on it. *You've promised to direct my path*, he reminded God. Verses played over in his mind as the speakers droned on. Twice he closed his eyes to concentrate.

He had three weeks before the next class entered the academy. He looked up at the stage. NPD Chief Jason Swagger sat next to David's boss, the director of the academy.

He prayed again. And by the end of graduation, he knew what he wanted to do.

CHAPTER 11

THE FIRST THING KIT DID when her alarm went off at four on Thursday morning was check the weather. Fair, becoming cloudy later tonight, high of 73. Good. She had hoped the weather moving in from the south would hold off until after the governor's speech so they would have good visibility and the choppers could fly.

She and Lincoln and Steve had debated how they should deploy during the event. In the end, because she had more tactical experience than Lincoln, they'd decided she would be in the Bureau's mobile command center at the location, Lincoln would be on the stage with the governor and the mayor. Steve, along with Chase Carter, would remain back at the task force headquarters.

Now the plan had been written, conveyed, rehearsed, and reviewed. They were as ready as they'd ever be for a high-profile event in the middle of the most devastating period Hampton Roads had ever seen.

She showered and as she dressed in tactical clothes, her mind flipped to David. She knew the police academy graduation had been moved to Wednesday because of the governor's visit, so what would he be doing? She couldn't pretend, even to herself, that she didn't miss him.

But she was too busy to deal with that now. Kit ate some yogurt, grabbed her briefcase, and left.

On the way to the task force headquarters, she drove by the site of the governor's speech. The platform was in place, and so was the Bureau's mobile command center. Three agents were manning it already, keeping eyes and ears on the ground.

Why did the governor have to be such a news hog? She had leads to follow and data to run. Instead, his visit was absorbing valuable man hours—not only hers, but the whole team's.

The task force team leaders had agreed to meet at seven a.m. for any last-minute instructions. The governor's speech was at eleven. He would arrive at 10:50. The mayor would give a short introduction. The ribbon would be cut at 11:10.

All this planning and energy for twenty minutes.

When she got to the office, she buried her nose in the maps. The site of the governor's speech. Emergency routes to and from. The places where paramedics and the city's SWAT team would be staged. All this, compared to the sniper's victim locations. Was there any correlation?

Kit's stomach felt tight. The task force team leaders filed into the conference room shortly before seven. Promptly on the hour, Kit began the briefing. Lincoln, of course, was late.

Going around the table, each team leader summarized the status of his or her assignment. The agent who was the liaison with the Bureau's chopper pilot questioned the weather coming in. "I think it will hold off," Kit said, "provided the politicians keep to schedule." A Norfolk officer questioned the traffic control plan. Someone else raised an issue with policing in the rest of the area.

One by one Kit addressed the problems. And at seven-thirty, when they were about ready to go, the door in the back of the room opened. Steve, who had disappeared briefly, walked back in. "Before you leave," he said to the group, "I want to introduce you to a new task force member." He stepped aside. "Detective David O'Connor."

Kit's heart seemed to stop. Her face flushed. She barely heard the rest of it.

"David is detailed to us from the Norfolk Police Academy where he babysits recruits and counts push-ups, right, David?" The cops in the room laughed. "Before that he was a homicide detective in D.C. He's partnered with us before and I have high regard for his abilities." Murmurs followed that statement. "He'll be working here in the office until he gets caught up."

Kit's head was swirling.

The others pushed their chairs back and began shuffling toward the door. "We'll meet at four," she called after them. Then she pointedly looked at David. "Detective, could I see you for a moment?"

While the other agents and officers moved toward their assignments, Kit demanded, "What are you doing?"

He shrugged. "I've come to help. Fresh eyes."

She started to retort, but then Lincoln got her attention. "Agent McGovern, let's boogie!"

✞ ✞ ✞

Governor Frank Mancini's entourage was ten minutes late in arriving. Kit thought Norfolk Mayor Jesse Crawford, seated on the platform, looked like a bride left waiting at the altar. Through video feeds in the FBI's Mobile Command Center, she could see him sweating, twisting the ring on his right hand, and bouncing his knee. If her lip-reading skills, developed over hours of sitting with David watching NFL coaches on the sidelines, were accurate, he was also cursing. For once she felt sorry for Joe Langstrom. Seated next to the mayor, he was getting the full brunt of his boss's turmoil.

Turmoil. She had her own. Her stomach was still in a knot, thinking about David joining the task force. She didn't want to deal with him being there. She wanted her life structured, compartmentalized, and he was not supposed to be in this compartment!

It was completely true and utterly selfish. Her face reddened.

She couldn't think about it now. She changed her focus and cleared her throat. "How are we doing?" she said out loud. Two agents and a Norfolk policeman sat crammed with her in the mobile unit.

All good, according to the replies. "I've got the governor's limo five minutes away," one agent monitoring traffic cams reported.

Kit relayed that to Lincoln through his earphone. He stood at the back of the platform. Then she saw him walk forward, lean down, and become the mayor's new best friend.

Five minutes later, the governor's black SUV rolled into

place and Captain Mark Mahoney opened the door and escorted Mancini to the platform. "Show time," Kit said as the dignitaries on stage shook hands.

She'd heard there was no love lost between the mayor and the governor, although both were from the same political party. Kit didn't care. She hated politics. Today her job was about scanning the windows of nearby buildings for the glint of a rifle, observing the crowds for a clown with a gun, and being prepared to act should the worst happen.

Mayor Crawford stood up to the microphone and began the usual yada-yada about what this new bridge would mean for the citizens of Norfolk and how long his office had fought for money for the structure. The mayor was up for re-election this year and he would take every opportunity to remind the citizens of Norfolk just what he'd done for them. Even if it was mostly a lie—he'd been in office three years; the bridge had been planned for a decade or more.

As he droned on in the background, Kit scanned the crowd. A couple hundred people were standing in the open under a partly cloudy sky along a street and in a grassy area in front of the podium. Looking at the way they were dressed, Kit decided they were mostly city workers, released from their offices to applaud the mayor. The real audience, she knew, were the cameras, and getting the prime spots on the evening news was the goal.

Kit spotted a familiar hat in the gaggle of reporters near the front of the stage. A large man moved slightly and Kit confirmed her suspicions: Piper Calhoun was reporting on the event. But Piper wasn't watching the mayor. Dressed in a black blazer, pink shirt, and denim skirt, she was turned to watch the spectators. Smart girl, Kit thought.

Lincoln's voice sounded in her earplug. "How we doing?"

"So far so good." Kit watched as the mayor introduced the governor. Crawford waited while the governor walked to the lectern. "Photo op," she said, watching the grip-and-grin on the stage.

"Kit, check out this guy," another agent said, pointing toward the screen he was monitoring.

Kit turned. A man dressed in scruffy clothes pushing a shopping cart had moved to the back of the crowd.

Something long rose out of the cart. "Homeless man," Kit said. "Zoom in. Okay, it's just a broom. Still, let's have NPD move up behind him." The agent relayed that to their contact with the police department, and on the screen, they watched as an officer casually changed his position to be close to the guy.

The governor began speaking. Kit began to feel the tension in her neck as she hovered over the monitor. He was only supposed to speak for ten minutes. Ten minutes, then three to get back in the limo, and then it would be over and she could get back to her real job.

"Okay, you're done, governor," the agent sitting next to Kit said. But Mancini wasn't going to be constrained by his ten-minute timeframe, apparently. "Time to shut up," the agent coached.

"Here we go, he's winding up," Kit said. Could it be? Could it be they'd get through this without incident? "Shake the mayor's hand, wave goodbye to the crowd, good, good …"

"Shots fired, shots fired!" the NPD officer yelled.

"Where?" Kit's adrenaline surged. She scanned the stage, the crowd, the street. Everything looked normal. No one was reacting. "Where?"

The NPD officer pressed his headphones to his ear. "Wait. Not here. Virginia Beach. Outside a shopping mall. Rifle fire. One civilian down. Units responding."

Kit looked into her monitor. Outside, the SUV's door closed as the governor seated himself. The mayor began making his way off the stage. Members of the crowd drifted away. "Give me an address. I'm on my way."

✝ ✝ ✝

Even with the blue lights, Kit knew she'd have trouble making progress through the traffic mess around the bridge dedication site. She'd barely moved from her parking place when she heard a rap on her passenger side window. Lincoln.

She unlocked the door and he climbed in. "Can I hitch a ride?"

"You know where I'm going, right?"

"Shooting. Heritage Mall."

"Right. Where's your buddy?"

"Joe? Mayor needed him. Said he'd catch up later." Lincoln adjusted himself in the seat and clicked the safety belt into place. "So, what do you figure? The sniper was counting on the diversion?"

"Possibly." Kit maneuvered up onto the sidewalk, sounded her siren, and slipped past a chain of cars. Then she pulled right, onto an onramp, and accessed the relative freedom of the HOV lanes on the Interstate. "It's weird, though. This is a little out of range, I'm thinking."

"Based on what?"

"The geographic profile."

Lincoln rolled his eyes. "Anybody tell the sniper?"

✞ ✞ ✞

A woman dressed in strappy sandals, a short, khaki skirt and a bloody white cardigan lay on her face in the parking lot of the Heritage Mall, a pool of blood spreading out from under her on the black asphalt. Pink packages from Naughty 'N Nice, an upscale lingerie store, lay scattered around her. Uniforms had roped off the crime scene and the medical examiner was squatting next to the body, gently examining the victim.

Dr. Sullivan's bald head looked red in the sunshine. "Looks like you got another one," the ME said, glancing up at Kit. "A through-and-through this time."

"Well, then, we ought to find the bullet," Kit said squinting in the bright light. "She was coming out of the mall, right?"

The medical examiner nodded. He stood up. On his jacket was a shield imprinted with the words, *Mortui Vivis Praecipiant.* May the dead teach the living. "You're looking at the exit wound," he said.

"So we should have a bullet over there somewhere." Kit gestured toward the mall.

"I'm on it," Lincoln said, and he began jogging in that direction.

"Who is she?" Kit asked.

"Julia Rankin, 23." A Virginia Beach officer held her driver's license in his hand. "Lives at Orion Towers, looks like."

"That's pretty upscale," Kit said. "Let me see that for a

second." She used her secure phone to call the address in to the task force office. "Have someone go over there and talk to the neighbors," she told Chase. "Let's see if we can link her with any of the other victims. Oh, and make sure Candace is in on this, okay? That she has the address of this shooting."

Kit clicked off her phone and looked around. The mall was a two-story structure with anchor stores in three locations. The parking lot was studded with islands planted with mature trees. Where would a sniper hide? She turned her back on the victim and stared at the possibilities. In a tree? Across the perimeter road stood a six-story office building. Had the sniper hidden there to take his shot?

She turned to the officer: "I need you all to check all the trees in this section of the parking lot. Look for fresh scars on the trunks."

"Who are you?" the officer asked, frowning.

Kit flashed her creds. "Special Agent Kit McGovern, Sniper task force." She pocketed the leather case. "Any questions? I'll be happy to have your chief answer them for you." Irritated, she turned back to the victim and forced herself to refocus. What had caused Julia Rankin to decide to shop that day? Why this mall? What bizarre sense of timing had caused her to emerge just in time to walk into the crosshairs of a sniper's scope? What family had she left behind now to grieve her death? What future was lost?

Kit shivered involuntarily."Got nothing," Lincoln said. "No bullet."

"Let's let the Evidence Response Team have a go at it," Kit responded.

She crossed her arms in front of her chest. All this started with Gail. Then Charles Lipscomb in Portsmouth, Shirley Bailey in Norfolk, Ralph Ellis and Mitchell Silverman in Chesapeake, Kathy Emory in Portsmouth, and now this young woman. And no connection between them, none at least that Kit could see. All dead in a flash. Removed from this life with the pull of a trigger, blood staining the ground.

Whirring sounds pulled her from her thoughts. She turned around. News photographers were standing on cars parked just outside the yellow crime scene tape, snapping shots of this latest victim. Of the police officers standing around. Of the medical examiner. Of her. "Move them back," she ordered.

"Yo, Lincoln!" one of the photogs called out. "Give us a break, man!"

"You're on a first-name basis with them?" Kit asked.

"What can I say? They like me!" He grinned at her. "That's far enough!" he yelled to the officers moving the press back.

Kit glanced over her shoulder. "Not really," she said, under her breath.

"So what's next?" Lincoln asked. "Do you need me? 'Cause I thought maybe I'd go in there and get me some lunch."

She blinked. Lunch? "Go for it." One less irritant. Then she saw one reporter had broken out from the herd and was following Lincoln inside.

Great.

The medical examiner's staff zipped the victim into a body bag and began loading it into the van. Kit strode over to it. "Thanks, Doc," she said.

He grunted. "Here we go again."

"Let me know what you find."

As the ME's van pulled off, the Bureau's Evidence Response Team pulled in. Good. Soon, Kit could release the scene to them and get back to the office.

A Virginia Beach representative on the task force arrived next. From what she'd seen, Tim Reynolds was a stand-up guy. "How's it going?" he asked.

"We need a couple of teams to go check those buildings over there," she gestured, "and get security cam footage from the mall. And maybe traffic cam footage as well."

"You got it," Tim said.

"I don't know where he took his shot from," Kit said. "Do any of those buildings have rooftop parking garages?"

"No."

"Check the rooftops anyway."

The leader of the Evidence Response Team approached. "What we got?"

Kit explained what they knew. "It was a through-and-through, so there ought to be a bullet somewhere."

"What was the angle of trajectory?"

Kit drew a blank. "The ME didn't tell me."

"All right. We'll see what we can find."

Kit glanced at her watch. One-fifty. The task force would meet at four and she wanted to check in with Candace before that. And collect her thoughts. Kit looked up. Lincoln was jogging out of the mall, a soda cup in one hand and his cell phone in the other. "What's up?" she asked him as he drew near.

"Mayor wants to hold a news conference," he wheezed.

Simultaneously their cell phones went off. They both answered. She stared at Lincoln as the unbelievable news registered. Another shooting. Downtown Norfolk. Lincoln for once had no jokes. He clicked off his phone. "Let's go."

As Kit edged her car out of the parking lot, she caught a familiar figure out of the corner of her eye. Piper Calhoun was waving madly at her.

Kit hit the accelerator, hard.

CHAPTER 12

"LUCKY, LUCKY, LUCKY," LINCOLN SAID. The eighth shot had missed a cashier by inches after penetrating a convenience store's front window and then shattering a glass case near the back.

The cashier, Patrice Sweeney, was shaken but unhurt. "I'm telling you," she told Kit and Lincoln, "I was just ringing this customer up when I heard a *crack!* and the cases exploded. Glass everywhere. I dropped down and hit the panic button. Seemed like forever before the cops showed up."

Kit looked across the street. Where could the shot have come from? She walked toward the shot-out refrigerated case.

"Hey, look at this!" A customer wearing a plaid shirt, open, over a white T-shirt and jeans held up a can. Beer still dripped from a hole in the side.

"That's evidence," Kit said. "Where did you get it?"

"Back there." He motioned with his head toward the case.

"Show me exactly," Kit said. "Lincoln," she called over her shoulder. "I need uniforms back here, please."

The customer led Kit across broken glass to the refrigerated case. "What shelf?" Kit asked. He showed her. "Okay, put it back just like you found it."

The can came from the second shelf from the bottom. "I'll need your name and contact information," Kit told the customer.

After gathering that information, she walked toward the front of the store, to where the bullet hole pierced the front window. Then she looked back at the refrigerated case. The trajectory was slightly down. Turning again to stare across the street, she saw it: the low, flat roof of an auto repair shop across the street. Was that the sniper's location?

But first, was this shooting even connected to their sniper case?

"This don't look like the same guy to me," Lincoln said.

"Why do you say that?"

"He missed. Not only did he miss, but this shooting happens, what forty-five minutes after Miss Strappy Sandals? How'd he get across town that fast? We had trouble even with the blue lights!"

Kit had to agree. "We should be able to find a bullet. And we need to check that building over there." She pointed to the auto repair shop.

A familiar car pulled into mix of cruisers in front of the convenience store. Steve Gould emerged, and with him, David.

Kit's stomach tightened. She wanted to feel his arms around her. And she wanted him away from her job.

"What do we have, McGovern?" Steve asked, striding up to her.

She filled him in on the details. Over his shoulder, she saw Lincoln walking toward where the news media had been corralled. "Sir, someone has to have seen something."

David was looking across the street. "Gail was shot from a rooftop. The guy in Portsmouth could have been shot from a car, and so could the two women. Others are unknown. So, yeah, we could be looking for a car or a van, or we could be looking for a sniper's perch, in a building, up a tree or whatever."

Steve's cell phone rang. "Gould. Yes, sir. Yes, sir." He turned his back to David and Kit.

Kit turned to David. "I thought you were working back at the office?"

"I am."

"You seem to be *here*."

"Steve wanted to see this. He told me to come." David grinned at her, and Kit wondered just how many people he'd charmed with that grin. "Do we even know this is connected to the sniper?" he asked.

"Not yet."

Steve returned. "That was the SAC. Pressure's on."

"Let's see what we can see," David said. He spotted the hole in the front window, then walked to the back of the store. Using his arm, he estimated the trajectory. "I'm going across the street," he said to Kit.

"I'm right behind you." She hated to admit it, but as a homicide detective, he'd done a lot more of this sort of thing than she had.

Mack's Auto Repair occupied a 1950's-style cinderblock building which used to be painted white. The closed bay doors echoed the evidence of the fading sign: Mack's was out of business and had been for a long time.

Weeds grew in the narrow opening between the closed shop and the building next to it. David and Kit made their way over the rubble—rusting cans, old newspapers, rags, and one single tennis shoe—in the narrow opening, broken glass crunching under their feet. In the back of the building, a metal ladder affixed to the building provided access to the roof.

David looked around at the ground in the back. "These could be relevant," he said, pointing to fresh tire tracks. Then he pulled plastic gloves out of his pocket and put them on.

"You're going up?" Kit asked.

"Yes."

They climbed up the ladder. The roof lay covered with leaves and spotted with rainwater. They made their way to the front and looked toward the convenience store. "Check this out," David said, handing Kit the rifle scope he had pulled out of his belt.

Looking through it, she could see the clerk. "Now raise it just a little," David pulled the scope up, "and you can see the beer case."

"Yes, so he missed? Is that it?"

"That's my guess."

✞ ✞ ✞

The Evidence Response Team would take hours to go over the convenience store, the parking lot, and the roof of the auto repair shop. They were dusting the ladder for

fingerprints and casting the tire treads when Kit left. She had
to make it back to the task force office in time for the four
o'clock meeting.

As she entered the room, she saw David standing there
talking to an NPD detective. She took a deep breath and laid
her notes down at the end of the table. Lincoln entered the
room, and she could tell, even from a distance, that he was
agitated. He turned as if responding to a sound, and then
Kit saw Joe Langstrom catch up to him.

Langstrom was back.

That's when the fatigue hit her. She stood quietly for a
moment, gathering her thoughts. "Gentlemen!" she began,
and the task force members shuffled into their seats. "We
have updates."

"Excuse me," Lincoln said, interrupting. "The mayors of
Norfolk and Virginia Beach are insisting on holding a joint
news conference at five o'clock. These latest shootings have
everyone in a panic."

"Calls are coming into the tip line like crazy. People are
scared."

"Okay, so everyone's panicking. What are we doing to
solve the case?" Kit said, bringing the group back to the task
at hand.

"What's this guy's point? That's what I want to know," one
officer said.

"Fear. No one's safe. He's exercising power over the whole
community." An agent who'd spent time at Quantico leaned
back in his chair.

Candace walked into the room and sat in a chair near the
wall.

Chase Carter was over at the sniper wall, adding
information on the latest victims.

"Can we go over the specifics of these last two shootings?"
someone asked.

"Of course." Kit turned to Chase, who was just then
posting a driver's license picture of victim seven. "Chase, can
you give us the summary?"

The young agent turned, and, using the victim wall as a
visual, he began. "We had a strong police presence, as you all
know, at the bridge dedication. Within moments of its

conclusion, Julia Rankin, age 23, was shot coming out of a shopping mall in Virginia Beach. She is a graduate student at ODU, lived in Orion Towers, and has no family in the area."

"Either her folks are rich or she has a sugar daddy," someone muttered.

Chase continued. "She took one shot to the chest, a through-and-through, and we are still on site looking for the bullet or other evidence. Victim number eight escaped injury." He detailed what they knew about that.

"Thank you, Chase." Kit turned back to the group, she saw Langstrom had left the room. She guessed he had to get ready for the news conference. "Candace? Your perspective?"

"Shooting number seven is out of range according to the geographic profile. However, we may simply need to adjust our areas of likely connection."

Kit nodded.

Ten minutes later, after listening to reports of one blind lead after another, Kit dismissed the group. Candace approached her. Over her shoulder, Kit saw Lincoln approaching.

"I'm doing that news conference," he said.

Kit responded, "Fine. Just don't reveal the young woman's identity yet." Why did she even have to tell him this? "We don't want her name out there. Locations are releasable and the basics—single shot, and so on. And emphasize the reward money."

"We're already overloaded on the tip lines," Lincoln countered.

"Even so," Kit said, "we may pull in some mope with good information if the public thinks money's involved."

Steve appeared. "McGovern, tell me you've got something new."

"No, sir, we're just pressing on."

He frowned. "I just got a call from the SAC. He wants to see us, right now."

"Us?"

"You, me, Lincoln."

"What about the mayors' press conference?" Lincoln asked. "I think I need to be there."

Steve hesitated. "Okay. McGovern, it's you and me."

✝ ✝ ✝

The office of the Special Agent in Charge of the Norfolk division occupied a good chunk of the level that topped the FBI's new building, which was actually in Chesapeake. Washington had decided to move the office but retain the name, "Norfolk Division." Typical, Kit thought. And confusing.

She stepped into the office behind her boss. Steve was tightening and untightening his fist at the side of his leg, over and over. The back of his neck looked red.

The window wall in the SAC's office let in plenty of light. Off in the distance, Kit could see the Atlantic edged by its sandy beach. What she wouldn't give to go stretch out there for an afternoon.

Instead, she was standing on a dark blue rug in a light blue office, waiting for Samuel L. Jones, special-agent-in-charge of the Bureau's sixth smallest division, to show up. In front of her sat a walnut desk and behind it, a credenza holding the requisite family pictures and more than one golf trophy. Over to the right was the SAC's "me wall" featuring grip-and-grin shots of him with a senator and other dignitaries.

Jones hadn't been SAC for long. None of them seemed to stay long. The way Kit saw it, the helicopter pad outside was actually a launch pad for big-wig wannabes. They could come here, check the box, and go on to a bigger office. Jones was just the latest in a long line.

Still, she liked working in Norfolk, especially after the crazy politics of the Washington Field Office. And then, there was that beach out there, the one she could get to in half an hour if traffic wasn't too bad. If she looked hard now, she could almost make out the waves breaking just offshore. She was about three hours from her favorite place in the world, Chincoteague Island. And then there was David.

"Gould!" The booming voice of Samuel L. Jones cut into Kit's thoughts. He strode in, all six foot four of him.

"Yes, sir."

"Tell me you've got a strong lead."

Kit snapped to attention.

"Not yet, sir, but ..."

The SAC's short-cut hair was edged in gray and his blue eyes flashed. He turned to Kit: "And you are Katherine..."

"McGovern, sir. Special Agent Katherine McGovern. Kit."

Jones nodded almost dismissively. "I don't have to tell you what the stakes are in this case. Seven civilians shot. That's unheard of." He paced behind his desk. "I've got three mayors calling me demanding a resolution. Their people are scared, they say. Well, I'm scared. I'm scared *my* people—you —are dropping the ball." He didn't bother sitting down nor did he invite them to. "The director's asking for daily updates. Senator Crandall has called three times. Congressman Wendell, the delegates from this area—all the politicians are breathing down my neck. The Bureau's reputation, *my* reputation is at risk. I don't intend to spend the rest of my career in some backwater resident agency because you guys messed up this investigation. Six people dead. Now tell me you've got good news." He stared straight at Kit.

"Sir, we have no suspect yet." Kit realized she was sweating.

"Over a week and no suspect." He turned to Steve. "What do you have to say for this Gould? This is the second major case since I've been here that you've failed to resolve."

Steve didn't deserve that blame. Jones was alluding to a drug case another agent worked with DEA. The judge had thrown it out. It wasn't Steve's fault.

Kit's heart felt like a hammer in her chest. That's when she realized she was just tired enough and just frustrated enough to do or say something stupid. She tightened her mouth into a thin line to keep the words from shooting out.

She saw Steve straighten his back. "Agents McGovern and Sheffield have been doing a great job. The task force just needs a break."

"You can't wait for a break, Gould, you have to *make* the break!" Jones threw his hands up. "Jesse just called me."

He was talking about the Norfolk mayor.

"His aide tells him there's a lot slipping through the cracks."

"Sir, that is not true!" Kit said, her face burning. "We have followed thousands of leads, rousted half the felons in Hampton Roads, tracked down every purchaser of .223 ammo, all while successfully protecting the governor at a completely unnecessary high-profile event."

The SAC turned to her. "And what about Gail Massey's husband, Brian. What about their financials? The big life insurance payout he got?"

How did he know that? Was Joe Langstrom revealing evidence? Kit got even madder. "Sir, we chased that rabbit as far as it would run. He is not a suspect." Kit crossed her arms. "Besides, what reason would he have for these other shootings?"

"We're working with CIRG, with a geographic profiler," Steve said, "Homeland Security is on board, and we will find this sniper." He shifted his jaw and played his trump card. "Don't worry. You and the mayor will be able to host your golf tournament in three weeks."

Zing! Kit half-smiled and looked down, impressed with her boss's chutzpah.

Jones' face flushed. His eyes narrowed. He picked up a pen on his desk and began tapping it on the blotter while he looked at Steve and Kit, his eyes flashing. "You get this guy, you hear?" he said. "ASAP. No excuses. Or you'll be working cases in Juneau this winter."

"A golf tournament?" Kit said and she and Steve rode down on the elevator.

He rolled his eyes upward.

That's when she noticed the security camera. So she waited until they were in Steve's Bucar. "Did he bug this, too?" She spat out the words. "What right does he have to blast us like that? We're working so hard. Honestly, Steve…"

"Honestly? He's just a guy who knows how to manipulate, how to pull strings, how to advance in an organization, without really having the management skills or the personality to have earned his job." He turned a corner. "The Bureau has them just the same as any other organization."

She exhaled loudly. "And Lincoln? Is he one of them?"

"Jury's out on Lincoln. He may be a manipulator, or it

could be he's gotten by on his charm for so long he doesn't think twice about using it at any level. I told you someone's backing him. That someone is higher than the SAC."

⭑ ⭑ ⭑

The Hawk paced. How could they think he shot that girl! Those idiots!

He'd been happy at first, watching the mayors at the news conference. They talked tough, but he saw their nervous tics. Then, the FBI guy spoke and he got it all wrong!

No way could he take that girl down at the mall, then get back to Norfolk that fast. No way!

And of course he didn't have a partner! This was his mission, his alone. Couldn't they see that?

He'd have to make it clear to them. Very clear.

Something else bugged him: Who was horning in on his mission? Who was trying to pull the focus away from him?

That girl was not his shot. They should know that. He'd have to up his game, make it clear.

What do I have to do, get one of them?

⭑ ⭑ ⭑

David had begun to develop some ideas that he wanted to pursue. He had one hand on the driver's door of the unmarked police car he'd borrowed from the academy when he noticed Cissy, across the street, with her car's hood up.

He really needed to get going. But how could he ignore her?

"Hey, what's going on?" he asked as he jogged across the street.

"My stupid car won't start. I'm supposed to pick up my friend at the airport in half an hour!" Tears ran down her face. Cissy wiped a cheek with her sleeve.

David didn't have time to deal with it. But he couldn't just walk away. He looked at the engine, jiggled a few wires, and climbed in the driver's seat. Annie, in the back seat, licked his ear. "Hey, girl," he said, gently pushing the dog's head away. He tried the ignition and got nothing.

He got out. "Look," he said, "I'm in a rush. I don't see what's wrong. You can call somebody, or you can take my car."

"Really?"

"I don't need it today." He dug in his pocket for the keys to his Jeep. "Here, take it."

As he drove away in his cruiser, he realized he'd forgotten to tell her that the car was okay for gas. When the gauge read "empty" it still had a quarter of a tank.

What could he say? It was old. David thought about calling her, then rejected that thought. "She'll be okay," he said to himself.

✞ ✞ ✞

"How's it going with David working with us?" Candace asked Kit, setting a cup of coffee down in front of her. They'd just finished the morning task force meeting and were ready to delve into some profiling work.

How should she answer Candace's question? Kit wasn't used to baring her heart, especially at the office. "It's okay," she said. "I'm too busy to really notice." That was a lie. She noticed every time he was in the room. She could smell his aftershave. She could hear the way he made a soft noise in the back of his throat when he was thinking. She could feel his very presence, and it ignited her senses the way it always had. Still, she wished he wasn't on the team.

"He seems like a nice guy."

"Yes, he is."

Candace continued to leaf through a notebook of some kind, then turned toward Kit. She had a wistful expression on her face. "I'm sorry I wasn't wiser when I was younger."

"What do you mean?"

"I let this job kill my marriage."

"Yes, well, when criminals work nine to five, we'll have time for other things."

Candace's voice grew quiet. "You know, I'm fifty-five. I have had a wonderful career. I have enough money to live on. I have my health. But you can't snuggle with any of those things at night when the winds are howling outside. And you can't hold hands with them and walk on the beach on a warm September day." Candace smiled softly. "I miss those things, Kit. I really do."

Kit frowned and laid a piece of paper in front of her. "Why don't you show me how to incorporate these facts into a profile?"

✝ ✝ ✝

At 7:58 a.m., the call came in to the task force office. Driver shot at a gas station near Old Dominion University.

Kit was headed for the door when Lincoln intercepted her. "Kit, look!" he said, holding up his cell phone with a picture of a car on it. "Recognize it?"

A green Jeep. Old. With the driver's side back seat window covered in cardboard.

Kit froze. Her heart leaped to her throat. No, no, no …

"What?" Candace appeared at her side.

"Victim's car looks like David's," Lincoln said. "How many green Jeeps have that back window covered in cardboard?"

The air seemed to get sucked out of the room.

"Come on, I'll drive," Candace said, after a pause.

Kit tried calling David. Texting him. But he was not answering.

A thousand images ran through Kit's mind.

Finally, her phone rang. David! Her heart jumped. "Where are you?"

"What's wrong?"

"Are you all right?"

It took them both a minute to calm down. Then Kit told him about the shooting.

"What?"

She repeated the information.

"I'll meet you there."

Before she could respond, he'd hung up.

CHAPTER 13

"I THOUGHT IT WAS YOU!" Kit said, and she and David ducked under the crime scene tape.

"I loaned my car to my neighbor. Was she the one shot?" His voice sounded clipped, tense.

"White female, 29," a cop said, overhearing him. "Here, I scanned her license."

David looked at the image on the cop's phone. Cissy. His mouth went dry.

He'd told her she'd be fine. He'd told her not to worry. He'd practically told her to trust God.

Now, was she dead? And the station was one that had erected a tarp to shield the pumps.

Why didn't he tell her about the gas gauge?

He swallowed hard. "How'd it happen?"

"Witnesses say she had just gotten gas and was exiting the station," the cop said, gesturing toward where David's car sat in the road. "She got shot, lost control. Another car hit her." The Jeep was definitely totaled.

"Is she alive?" Kit asked the question.

"She was when they transported her."

"Where'd they take her?" David said.

"Sentara."

David looked at Kit. "Go," she said. "Pick up what evidence and information you can."

He started to leave then stopped. "Where's the dog?"

"What?" the cop asked.

"She had a dog with her. A yellow Lab. Annie."

The cop looked at him carefully. "I'll ask if anyone saw

her."

"You get someone to find that dog!" David yelled as he jogged off.

Kit watched him go.

"He's upset," Candace said. "Did he know her well?"

"I'm not really sure," Kit responded.

"Do you need to go with him?"

Kit shook her head. "He'll be fine." Right now, she had a crime scene to process.

✞ ✞ ✞

He could see them from the woods, see them all! So amazing!

First the cops came. Then the rescue squad. Then the FBI.

He knew them now. The black guy from the news conferences. An older woman. A younger woman with sandy blond hair. All with FBI raid jackets. And then the other guy, the one built like a rock. No jacket. He was not FBI?

He'd memorized their faces; now if he could get their names! Which one should he target? Whose death would count the most?

The Hawk reached down and petting the panting dog standing next to him. "Sorry you got scared," he said.

When he looked back at the scene, he saw the younger woman—*what was her name?*— standing with some cops gesturing toward the woods. His woods!

"Gotta run," he said to the dog. He thought about taking her, but what would he do with a dog? He slipped off her collar. A souvenir. "See ya!"

✞ ✞ ✞

David stood next to the window in Cissy's room in Sentara Norfolk Hospital. Her head was bandaged, her eyes were closed, and medical instruments documented that she was barely clinging to life. The doctor had told him she was brain dead. They were maintaining her life until her family could get there from Northern Virginia. And in his pocket was the bullet that had killed her.

Once the doctors had retrieved the bullet, he'd been free to go. Truth was, he couldn't stand the thought of her lying there alone. Of her family coming in and finding her by herself.

If only I hadn't loaned her my car. If only I had remembered to tell her about the gas gauge. If only …

The beeping of the instruments seemed to catalogue the "if onlys."

He sat down in a chair. What Cissy had feared had come about, after he, David, had encouraged her not to worry.

He dropped his head into his hands. Suddenly, all the doubts he'd ever had rushed in like a flood. They swirled through his soul, sucking him deep into a whirlpool. *Why?* He felt like he'd lied to her. Told her she'd be safe. He shouldn't have. Life was so unpredictable!

But what was he supposed to do? Tell her the stark naked truth? That every day could be her last? That was true for everybody. Especially now.

He felt a hand on his shoulder. He looked up. A nurse stood next to him.

"Sir, are you all right? Can I get you something?"

The compassion in her deep brown eyes drew him to her. He tried to respond, but felt his throat close up.

She sat down next to him. She was wearing green scrubs and she had a stethoscope around her neck. Her hair was braided and he could see a small, gold chain around her neck. "My name is Tonisha. My friends call me Toni." She took David's hand. "Did you know her?"

"My neighbor." Emotion charged him like a bull. He drew in a deep breath, trying to calm himself. *In for four seconds, out for eight.*

"You're a police officer? Working the Sniper case?"

He nodded. "Yeah."

"So it just got pretty personal for you, then, didn't it."

He wasn't sure he could speak, but then words spilled out. "She was so scared. Just a few nights ago, I told her that her chances of being a victim were very small. Today, I loaned her my car. I feel like somehow I helped this happen." He gestured emphatically as he sat up straight.

Toni put her arm around his shoulders. "She died because of the sniper, not you." She squeezed David gently.

He dropped his head into his hands again. "I feel like I failed her."

"Why?"

"I could have told her to stay off the street. Not loaned her my car."

"People have to keep living."

"But she died."

"And who are you? God? To keep every bad thing from happening to people you know?"

That struck a chord with him. He most certainly was not God.

"Are you a believer?" she asked.

He nodded.

"You need to release it to God. I have to, every time we have a patient die. I've got to bow before the Almighty God and accept his will, even if I don't like it."

David looked up at Toni. She had high cheekbones and her brown skin glowed. Years of law enforcement had made him a pretty good instant judge of character. He felt nothing but trust for this woman. "I don't feel God right now."

"That's understandable," Toni said. "Tell me about her. What was she like?"

"A teacher," he began. He told her about Cissy's bad breakup. About the diabetes. About the dog. "They can't find the dog," he said. "I don't know what happened to her."

"She'll come home," Toni said, rubbing his back. "She'll find her way home and you will, too. And when she does, you remember this: You may have lost track of God, but he has never lost track of you."

✞ ✞ ✞

An hour later, Kit felt able to leave the crime scene in the hands of the evidence techs and other investigators. "Ready to go back?" she asked Candace. She felt a stab in her gut.

"Don't you want to go to the hospital?"

Guilt. How could she ignore David? "Maybe later."

Candace was having none of it. They got in the car, but she didn't start the engine. "We need to talk."

"What?"

"David needs you. You know that, but you're refusing to go to him?"

"I have work to do."

"And being gone for an hour will ruin everything."

A mixture of resentment and anger rose in Kit's heart.

"Kit, what happened?"

Her back stiffened, right there in the front passenger seat of the Bureau car. Why should she tell Candace anything?

She opened her mouth to object to the question but then her jaw tightened and tears came to her eyes. She caught her breath, tried to stifle the emotion, and utterly failed.

What emerged from her mouth was her story and their story, ending with the fight. But as she described it, her anger seemed overly intense, even to her. "He shouldn't have contacted my mother!" Kit glanced over, looking for affirmation. "That was controlling behavior."

"Really?" Candace let her disagreement hover in the air. "Kit, did you ask yourself why you were so angry you were willing to let David walk away?"

That was the question, wasn't it? She truly did love David. Yet she was quick to hold him at arm's length.

Candace waited for her to answer. Kit remained silent, staring at her own hands. Candace continued, "He challenged your truth."

"What?" Kit looked up sharply.

"He challenged the truth you'd created about your mother."

She shifted in her seat.

"We build emotional maps in our minds, certain presumptions that form a grid through which we view life. Yours included an analysis of your mother. David challenged it, disrupting your view of reality. That made you angry." Candace reached over and touched Kit's hand. "I understand that. But you know, in the long run, I think he did you a favor."

Kit looked down at her hands again. Tears welled in her eyes.

"Sometimes emotional grids become bars that trap us. I think David may have unlocked the bars, giving you the freedom to walk out, if you choose to."

"And what? Pretend she didn't abandon us out of her own selfishness and weakness? Just forgive all that?"

"How much have you been forgiven?"

Her statement dropped in Kit's soul like a bomb.

Candace started the engine. "Now, how about I drop you

at the hospital?"

✟ ✟ ✟

Kit walked into the hospital at a little after four o'clock, just as David emerged from a hallway enclosed by two double doors. Even from twenty feet away, she could see the stress in his face.

"Got it," he said as he approached, patting his pocket.

He was talking about the bullet that had killed his friend, now evidence in her death. He had had to watch it being removed, receive it from the doctors, and catalogue it. Hard enough to do under any circumstances. Very difficult when you knew the victim.

"I'm sorry about your neighbor," she said, falling in stride with him. "How are you doing?"

"Rough." He started to say something else, but stopped as a couple of orderlies walked by.

They walked together in silence toward the elevator. Words of comfort stuck in Kit's throat.

The elevator came. They both got on. The doors closed. They were alone.

Kit touched his arm. He turned and reached for her, wrapping her in his arms. She yielded to his embrace. He kissed her and she felt his breath on her cheek. "I'm so sorry," she whispered, and he kissed her again.

"We have to find this guy, Kit. I'm sorry for offending you by calling your mom. I should never have told you that night. I'm truly sorry. I don't want to fight with you."

"I know. I'm sorry. I overreacted. I love you, David. I really do."

"We worked well before. Can we do this ... together?"

"Yes," she whispered.

✟ ✟ ✟

After he'd turned the bullet fragment in, Kit made David go home. "Get some rest. We'll need you at your best tomorrow," she'd told him.

He was tired, and hungry, but first he drove back to the site where Cissy was shot. He parked, walked around, and called for Annie, but no goofy yellow Lab came racing to him.

The officer had left him a voicemail assuring him all of the shelters, rescue organizations, and vets had been alerted. "If she's here, we'll find her," he said.

Maybe, David thought, when he got back home, she'll be on Cissy's front porch. The murder site was less than five miles away. And dogs have good instincts.

He went through a drive-thru and grabbed a burger, then drove home. But there was no dog on Cissy's front porch. He walked around her house, just in case, but Annie was not there.

He took a shower, threw on some sweats, and tried to watch a game to dispel the gloom. About nine o'clock, he heard a noise at his front door. Annie? He jumped up.

But when he opened the door, on his porch stood Piper Calhoun, the reporter. "Piper? What are you doing here?"

She stood there dressed in boots, a flowered skirt, a white peasant blouse, and a black blazer. A battered black fedora crowned the outfit. "Hi, Detective O'Connor."

"Why are you here? How did you find me?" A cold wind blew through the open door.

She glanced around toward the street, like she was nervous. "Can I come in?"

"What?"

"It's creepy out here, you know, with that guy. Can I come in?"

David exhaled softly, moved aside so she could enter, and shut the door behind her. "You can't stay, Piper." His eyes fell on her reporters notebook and iPhone clutched in her hand.

"This will only take a minute." She looked around. "Wow, this is nice. You have good taste." She picked up a duck decoy from a small table.

"What do you want?"

"Just to talk." She moved a few steps into his living room and gestured toward the waterfowl art on the walls and the conch shells on the end tables. "This is so beach-y!"

"Talk about what? How did you find me?"

Piper turned to him, hugging her chest. "Remember when we ran into each other at that coffee shop downtown?"

"No."

"It was like, mid-August, maybe. You told me you'd bought a house. So I checked the public records of real estate transactions."

David ran his hand through his hair, trying to understand what she was saying. What was this girl up to? He turned back around. "So are you stalking me?" He sounded a little aggressive. He meant to.

"No!"

"Piper ..."

"That last shooting ... earlier today. I thought I recognized your car. From Chincoteague, you know? When we worked together."

Piper had provided crucial information in a human trafficking case the year before. Still, David resisted her characterization of their relationship. "We didn't 'work together.'"

"So it's your car, but it was a woman who got shot, right? Still, how awful. How are you feeling, anyway?"

"That's none of your business. I need you to leave."

"Okay, okay, but first, David, can I ask you some questions?"

"About what?"

"The sniper." Piper looked up at him, eyes begging, her pen and notebook poised.

"Of course not."

"But Detective, you're a victim, well, your car is anyway, and the public wants to know what it feels like to be targeted like that."

"I wasn't targeted. And no comment." He took her arm and began guiding her back to the door.

"But it was your Jeep, right? So clearly you knew the woman who was shot. In fact, wasn't she a neighbor?"

His anger flared. "Leave it alone, Piper, I'm not talking about it."

She grew pensive, tapping her pen against her lip. "What about the dog? It belonged to the woman right, this," she looked at her notebook, "Cissy Singleton? People saw the dog running across traffic. Did he shoot her, too?"

David took Piper's elbow. Grabbing the doorknob, he pulled the door open. Cold air and darkness flooded in. "I'm not talking about it!"

Staring into the dark, she said, "Does it make you afraid?

Like afraid to go out? To take a run? To fill up your car? To go to the store? Do you worry, now about being in public?" Piper looked up at him, her brown eyes wide under that ridiculous hat. "And if you, a cop, are afraid, Detective O'Connor, what is the rest of the community supposed to do? All those mothers. All those children. All those people just trying to live their lives. Terrified, now, that each breath could be their last."

Rage filled him. "There's only one person in Hampton Roads who should be afraid," David said, his jaw clenched, "and that's the scumbag doing these shootings. Because we, the law enforcement community, are coming after him with everything we've got. Cops, FBI, ATF, Marshals … everybody. We will find that son of a …" he took a breath, "when we find him, he'll discover there is a hell on Earth. And it's a lot worse than a single-shot, instant death." He clenched his fist, never noticing Piper was scribbling madly on her reporter's pad.

"So you're saying …"

"I'm saying nothing," and David gave Piper a little push and marched her out to her car. He opened the driver's door, and guided her in. "Go home. And don't come back."

Back inside, he sagged back against a wall and tried to quiet his pounding heart. He went over to the sink, filled a glass with water, and gulped it down. Then reality struck.

What had he done? Would she quote him? What had he given up?

David cursed softly. He opened the refrigerator. A friend had left a beer. He picked up a Coke instead, and went into his living room, sat down on the couch, popped the can and took a long drink. Then he set the can down on the coffee table and dropped his head in his hands. "Why am I so impulsive?"

☆ ☆ ☆

First thing the next morning, Lincoln came striding across the room. "Hey, Ms. Kit!"

She looked up and saw he was wearing a gray suit, a plum-colored shirt, and a gray-and-plum tie. Amazing, she thought. He must spend a fortune on clothes.

In his hand he carried a newspaper, and from the swagger

in his step, Kit figured he'd gotten some pretty good coverage.

"Your boyfriend got better play than me," he said, plopping the newspaper in front of her. "And in the Sunday paper. Tell him, game on!"

What? Kit picked up the paper. Her eyes fell on a picture of David's crushed car after the shooting and accident. Next to it was a story … oh, no. Piper Calhoun. Her heart clutched.

Lincoln's words slurred in her ears as Kit began reading. *There's only one person in Hampton Roads who should be afraid …* Oh, David. She tore her eyes away and looked up at Lincoln. "I'll speak to him."

"No, hey, it's all good. Man's gotta blow off steam once in a while. I was just surprised is all."

When David walked in a few minutes later, she said, "Did you see the paper?"

"What?"

"The newspaper."

"Oh, no."

Kit handed him the copy Lincoln had left with her.

David read the article. "I'm sorry," he said when he was done. "She came to my house."

"How'd she find you?"

He told her.

"They're like rats, these reporters."

"Did I do any damage?"

"I don't think so." She straightened her back. "Let it go."

✝ ✝ ✝

Chase came in, looking for Kit. "We got a break," he said. "Across the street from the mall where Rankin was killed, we found this hotel room key card." He handed her a plastic evidence bag.

The card's design featured a drawing of colorfully striped beach chairs on sand. Kit looked at it and turned it over. "There's no hotel name on it."

David joined them. She showed him the card.

"I have uniforms checking with all the hotels in the area of the mall."

"How about prints?"

"It was clean."

"That's suspicious," said Kit. "What normal hotel guest is going to wipe off their key card? How many hotels do you suppose there are in Hampton Roads?"

"Thousands," Chase responded.

"You have officers at the beach?"

David handed Chase the card.

"There is one more thing," Chase said. "They also found a small white pill, or half of one, really." He showed her a picture of an oblong pill on the ground. "We're testing it now."

"Let me see that," David said. He took the picture. "It's Xanax. The anti-anxiety pill."

Kit looked at him. "Why Xanax?"

"Professional snipers sometimes take half a Xanax to calm themselves down before they shoot. Counteracts the adrenaline."

Kit frowned.

David continued. "That's interesting, though: I've been thinking we were dealing with a psychopath—someone who could look into a scope, see a real, live, person, and calmly kill them. But when psychopaths are doing their thing, their blood pressure goes down, their pupils dilate—they are calmer when killing. So why would he need a Xanax? He wouldn't. Maybe our sniper is not a psychopath. Maybe he's a pro with a grievance."

Candace had joined them. "I have to say, though, that that shooting was an anomaly, geographically. Maybe it's not even the same shooter."

Kit looked at Chase. "Let's get on this."

CHAPTER 14

SIXTEEN HOURS LATER, OFFICERS AND agents found the hotel: The Sunrise Inn and Suites, nestled in a quiet part of Virginia Beach.

Management cooperated immediately. No one wanted the sniper incident to end more than the merchants whose businesses took a hit with every shot. The manager helped the FBI access the room number off of the magnetic stripe on the card as well as the day the card would expire—Tuesday, the day Julia Rankin was shot and killed. The name of the guest in that room that day was Clifford Moore. He paid in cash.

"Of course it's a fake name," Kit said, frustration edging her voice.

"No driver's license, car tags were fake—the dude's not traceable," Lincoln added.

"We're getting the hotel security cam footage. And I want to talk to the desk clerk on duty that night again."

"But we don't even know Moore is our man." Lincoln put his hands on his hips. "I mean, just a dropped key card. And a pill. That ain't much."

"But right now," Kit said, "it's all we've got."

☦ ☦ ☦

The motel manager let Kit and Lincoln use his cramped office to interview Susan Bondurant, the clerk who checked in Clifford Moore.

"Honestly, he seemed just like a normal white guy. He had dark hair and kind of an expensive haircut. Sort of a George Clooney look. He had sunglasses which he put in his shirt like this," she slid one finger down the front of her shirt. "I'd say he was probably five foot eleven or so, and he looked pretty fit. He had on a leather jacket, which was kind of heavy, I thought, but then it does get cold at night this time of year." The fifty-something clerk pushed her hair back. She had on her uniform top and black slacks, and her fingers twitched as she spoke to them.

"Did he have any kind of accent?" Kit asked.

"Accent? No, I don't guess he did."

"What kind of car was he driving?" Lincoln asked.

"I never saw it. He didn't pull up front. I guess he wrote it down, though, on the registration form. We require that."

Kit glanced at Lincoln. Chances are the guy lied there, too.

"How about ID? Did you ask for a driver's license?"

Susan frowned. "I suppose I did. That's routine." She rubbed her chin. "I mean I always do, right?"

Kit's impatience grew. "Mrs. Bondurant, is there anything else, anything at all that you can tell us about this man?"

The clerk frowned. Lincoln exhaled in exasperation. Then Mrs. Bondurant spoke. "Well, now that I think of it, there is one thing," she said. "I noticed that this man had a tattoo on his right arm." Her eyes brightened. "Maybe that's why he was wearing the jacket."

"What kind of tattoo?" Lincoln pressed. "What did it look like?"

Mrs. Bondurant grimaced. "Well, let's see. It looked like ... like the tail of a snake. That's it, a snake, like one of those Indian snakes. A coiled snake."

"Can you draw it?" Kit said, pushing a sheet of paper toward her.

The woman bent over the paper intently. She seemed to take forever, and Kit noticed Lincoln was bouncing his knee. But when Mrs. Bondurant looked up and shoved the paper back, Kit's eyes widened in surprise.

"Holy smokes!" Lincoln said.

On the paper was an amazing drawing of a hooded cobra ready to strike. "Of course, I only saw this much," Susan said, drawing a faint line just above the tail, "but I imagined what the rest looked like."

✟ ✟ ✟

"Well, that was a surprise," Kit said, and she and Lincoln left the motel.

"No kidding! With that talent, what's she doing working as a clerk?"

Kit shrugged. "She's an artist who never got a break, and never had the chance to express her talent." She climbed into the driver's seat of her Bucar. "The question is, do we go with her idea of what the rest of the tat looked like?" she asked Lincoln as he settled in his seat.

"We got nothing else." He tapped the dashboard. "Let's go, girl!" He grinned sheepishly. "Sorry. Didn't mean to say that."

Oh, but you did, Kit thought.

Within an hour, they'd faxed both the part of the tattoo Mrs. Bondurant had actually seen and her conception of the complete design to the FBI section that managed the tattoo database. Kit put copies of the picture up on the murder board. After the four o'clock task force meeting, several people remained clustered around the board.

"I think it could be a military sniper's tattoo," David said, stroking his chin. "You say the name he used is wrong and you couldn't ID his car? That sounds like a pro."

Lincoln said, "We got the security footage from the parking lot. He walks out of the motel, a ball cap low on his head, and steps through six-foot high bushes. He'd parked in the next lot over, so we couldn't see his car."

"And what about that place's cameras?" David asked.

"Broken," Chase replied.

"Broken or obscured?"

"Definitely broken," Kit confirmed, "and they have been for a month or more. It's the parking lot of a grocery store that closed."

"Clever guy," David said. He crossed his arms.

"What?" Kit said. "I can tell you're thinking something."

"I don't think this is your shooter," he confessed.

"Why, man? It's the best lead we got," Lincoln said.

David took a deep breath. "First off, we don't know the person who rented that room had anything to do with the shooting at the mall. We only know we found his key card near there. Secondly, even if he DID that shooting, things don't match. We didn't find a Xanax at any other place. The cameras at the mall where this victim was shot were not obscured. Shootings seven and eight were only, what, forty minutes apart? Travel time would have been more than that. And this guy, whoever he is, has traveled from out of town."

"He's right," Candace said. "He doesn't fit the geographic profile. The site of shooting seven is an anomaly."

"But hey, that stuff's a guesswork anyway," Lincoln said. "It's educated, maybe, but guesswork all the same. I say we go with this guy."

"I think we have to," Kit said. "His behavior is suspicious. That's enough to pique my interest."

An agent approached. "We have CBS News looking for a comment."

"I got that!" Lincoln said, and he left, his arm around the other agent's shoulders.

Kit put her hand on her forehead.

"Hey, let's get some dinner," David suggested.

✞ ✞ ✞

David took her to a steak place that, ironically, also served great salads.

"You knew this is what I'd want, didn't you?" Kit asked him, toying with her Cobb.

He grinned. "Nah. It was all about the red meat." He cut into his steak.

The restaurant was half-empty and Kit couldn't help wonder if fear of the sniper was keeping people at home.

"How long will it take that database unit to respond?" David asked.

"I don't know. I haven't used it before. And a lot of what we're going on is supposition. I mean, David, we couldn't believe that hotel clerk. She was this older, kind of lower-class, not-well-educated woman, but her drawing—it was amazing."

"But like you said, it's supposition: her idea of what the rest of the tat looked like."

Kit stabbed a piece of lettuce and tried to chew it. "You still think we're headed the wrong direction."

David sat back. He shrugged. "I think you have to pursue

it, just like you are."

"Thank you! That's what I think, too." Kit moved a slice of hardboiled egg out of the way. "And it gives Lincoln something to blurt out to the press."

David laughed. "He still bothering you?"

She lowered her voice. "The man is like a ten-year-old who ran out of Ritalin. He's all over the place. Schmoozing people, running his mouth. Talking about stuff he has no business talking about. It's ridiculous."

"I kind of like him."

She felt her face turn red. "Of course you would! He's a man. And a jock. And that's the ticket in this business."

"And that really bugs you."

"Yes, it does. I mean, I like sports, but …"

"You'll never get into the locker room."

"Right."

David put down his knife and fork. He reached over and touched her left hand. "You know, Kit, you're doing a great job in what is still a macho profession. You lead men! And they're okay with that. But Kit, it's okay not to *be* one. In fact, I kinda like it that way." He grinned and withdrew his hand.

"I know. It's just that …"

"You're afraid there's no way to compete with him."

She narrowed her eyes. He was right. Why was he so right? "You creep me out. You're like a profiler who specializes in one person—me."

"That's my job." David began cutting his steak again. "Be patient with Lincoln. He'll either blow up on his own or succeed and help you out someday."

She smirked at him. "Or he may just run me over. Some day, if you find me lying in an alley with cleat marks on my back…"

"Then I'll know who my suspect is."

Kit's phone buzzed. She clicked it. Her eyes widened and she stood up, her napkin falling to the floor. "We need to go. We may have an ID on that tat."

✝ ✝ ✝

The man who called himself "Clifford Moore" may or may not be Cliff Tryon, a former Army marksman wanted for his association with organized crime figures in Philadelphia. The tattoo could be a match, based on what they knew of it. Kit, Lincoln, and David spent hours huddled around computers trying to determine if Cliff Tryon's size and general body type on file with the FBI might match the man in the little bit of motel security video that they had.

But what would he be doing in Hampton Roads?

"And that kind of blows the idea of the geographic profiling," David pointed out. "If he's not from here, those maps are useless."

"I've said that all along. By the way, the *Norfolk Times* is doing a major story tomorrow," Lincoln said. "A lot of it is on these special methodologies."

"What have we told them?" Kit said. Her voice, she realized, sounded demanding.

"Me? Nothing. But they go after these retired agents and cops, and suddenly, they got a story."

Kit rolled her eyes. "I hope they're not onto the geographic profiling. It could skew our results."

"If Tryon is the guy, though, that's irrelevant," Lincoln pointed out. "I said from the beginning that stuff was bogus."

"We'll have to find Tryon and bring him in to figure out if he's our guy."

"We have a BOLO out on him. We're trying to get a warrant to track his phone and his credit cards."

"That could take a while."

David stretched. "In the meantime, I'm going home. Kit?"

"I'll call you if we have anything."

✟ ✟ ✟

Rain obscured the windshield of David's unmarked police car. The blue lights on the dashboard panel announced the time: 10:08. He drove down his darkened street and glanced reflexively at Cissy's front porch, hoping to see Annie. He didn't. Every day he had someone check with the shelters, the rescue groups, vets, and every day the answer was the same: no Annie.

As he pulled into his driveway, though, his lights swept his front porch and there huddled a dark figure. The person, obviously a woman, sat next to his door, her arms resting on her bent knees, her head cradled in her arms. The headlights made her look up.

David jerked to a stop, unholstered his gun, and pulled his flashlight off of his belt as he got out. Then the light illuminated her face. "Piper?"

Yes. Piper Calhoun sat on his porch. She stood as he approached.

"What are you doing here?" David asked. "I thought I told you not to come back!" Anger thumped in his chest. "I'm done, Piper. I'm arresting you for trespassing." He pulled his cuffs off of his belt. "Turn around. Put your hands behind your back." She complied, and that's when he noticed she was soaking wet, and shaking in the cold.

"You wouldn't answer my calls, you or Agent McGovern. I had to push it. You had to know."

"We've both told you we're not talking to the press. And you're the press. You're on my property and that's trespassing. So come on, I'm taking you downtown. This is over, Piper." Clicking the cuffs shut he turned her and began walking her to his car. He jerked open the back door and guided her in, covering her head with his hand so she wouldn't bump it. When she sagged into the back seat and looked up at him, he saw her lips were blue. Empathy gnawed at his gut. He shoved it away.

"Is this bugged?" she whispered, nodding toward the interior of the car, as he got in. "'Cause I really, really need to talk."

"But I don't need to listen," David said, as he got in and slammed his door. "Where's your car?" he asked, glancing into the rearview mirror.

"I took a cab here."

"Your car in the shop?"

"I didn't want anyone to know I was here."

"So you sat on my front porch." David turned the ignition. "How long have you been here?"

She peered over the front seat at the dashboard clock. "Two hours and twelve minutes."

"Why in the world would you spend two hours sitting on my front porch?"

"Because I know something that blows this sniper case wide open. And I'm scared to tell anyone but you or Agent

McGovern."

CHAPTER 15

DAVID SIGHED. HE LOOKED IN his rearview mirror at the soaked young woman. He muttered something under his breath. Then he turned off the car, got out, opened the back door, and said, "Come on."

Fifteen minutes later she sat on his couch, dressed in his ludicrously big sweats, and wrapped in a blanket. She huddled over a cup of steaming tea. "Thank you," she whispered as he sat down across from her, "for the hot beverage." She grinned as if he should know the reference.

He didn't. "Piper, you know ..."

"I know, I know. But David, Detective O'Connor, I mean, I just had to tell you."

"What? Had to tell me what?"

"These shootings—they've been so random, you know? They've sent me out to cover them because, well, I'm on the city beat now. I cover the mayor, the city council, pretty much everybody who has something going on."

"And ..."

"But with the shootings, it's like, 'all hands on deck,' you know what I mean? So I've been all over the place. I covered the governor's speech on Thursday, and then, when that other shooting took place at the Heritage Mall, well, my editor sent me over there. Had an awful time getting there, and then ..."

"What?"

"I saw her on the ground. The victim. I looked at her and I couldn't believe it."

"Believe what?" David drummed his thumb on his knee.

The clock on the wall behind Piper read 10:45.

"I even walked around, tried to push past a cop, anything to see her closer." Piper took a big drink of tea. "Finally, when they put her in the body bag, I could see her face." She put down the tea and picked up her iPhone, accessed a picture, and showed it to David. "I'm sure of this. Absolutely sure. This woman is the mayor's mistress."

David blinked. He stared at the picture. He cleared his throat. "Wow," he said.

✞ ✞ ✞

"You know, I've got to tell my editor," Piper said to David as he drove her back to her apartment.

"I understand. Will it be in tomorrow's paper?"

She glanced at her watch. "Nope. Sorry. Just missed the deadline." She grinned, and by that, David knew her delay was intentional. "It's okay. He won't let me run it until we verify it somehow."

"Online?"

"Not even there."

So what did it mean that Julia Rankin was having an affair with the mayor? David pondered that thought after he dropped Piper off. It probably was coincidental—like Gail, she was simply a random target. But what if … what if the sniper had a grudge against the city or the mayor or government? He shoots a government prosecutor, then the mistress of a government official—but then, why didn't he take down the governor?

That didn't fit.

Kit wasn't answering her phone. And David knew now he wouldn't be able to sleep until he'd dropped this piece of the jigsaw puzzle onto the table. So he drove to the task force office. Candace was the only one there.

"You holding down the fort by yourself?"

"I went home for a while, but then came back when I heard about this potential suspect," she responded. "I'm just trying to connect the dots."

"Here's another one for your collection: Victim Number Seven was having an affair with the mayor."

"The Norfolk mayor?" Candace stood up and faced him.

"Yes."

"Oh, my," she replied. "That puts a wrinkle in things. I suppose it could just be coincidental. How'd you find that out?"

"A reporter." He looked around. "Where's Kit?"

"Kit and Lincoln are on their way with a SWAT team to pick up this suspect, Tryon."

"Seriously?" David checked his phone.

"Yes, just south of Fredericksburg. Tryon used his credit card at an Interstate 95 motel."

"When did they leave?"

She told him.

He checked his watch. They were ninety minutes ahead of him already. And he'd have time to check out Cliff Tryon when they brought him in. Common sense said he should just go home and get some sleep. But then, in his mind's eye, he imagined Kit, with a SWAT team, taking down Tryon. "I'm headed up there," he told Candace, and before logic had a chance to engage, he dashed out.

✞ ✞ ✞

By 2 a.m., the rain had stopped, and for that, Kit gave thanks. Gathering her troops behind Maggie T. Brower Elementary School in Clearview, Virginia, she mapped out the plan: Cliff Tryon had checked into the Sweet Dreams Motel just a mile away at around 8 p.m. Apparently, Tryon felt that it was safe using his real ID, now that he was away from Hampton Roads.

An alternative view was that he wasn't their suspect at all, that this was a false lead that would end up simply distracting them from their primary goal: catching the sniper before he killed again.

Kit didn't want to think about that.

"Don't matter," Lincoln had said on the way up when she'd expressed that thought. "Dude's a convicted felon. Time somebody brought him down."

But Lincoln, it turned out, had never been on a raid, never made a serious arrest of a violent criminal. So Kit would take the lead and that was fine with her.

Calling ahead, she'd asked an agent from the Fredericksburg office to check the place out. He'd gone dressed as a civilian and reported it was an older, U-shaped motel, with a pool in the center courtyard and breaks between the wings of the building. The owner must be a frustrated Floridian, the agent reported, because there were lots of plantings—ferns and bushes and small trees in large pots—all around. "It looks like something you'd see at the beach," he said. "There's a lot of mood lighting—colored lights and all that. It's weird." Of the thirty rooms in the one-story motel, eighteen were rented out. "The manager said it was a good night," he said.

"Okay, so here's the plan," Kit said, after she'd absorbed the report. She held a clipboard so that everyone gathered under the streetlight in the dark parking lot could see it, hoping the adrenaline charging through her system would not make her hand shake. "Tryon is in Room 13, here." She circled the room on the drawing of the motel. "These rooms, here and here and here, are occupied. Lincoln, you and I will be here," she drew an X, "in this corner, taking the overview.

"That's good. There's a little rise there," the Fredericksburg agent said. "You'll be able to see everything."

"I want you two," she pointed to two men, "to pop through the front door of his room, the side near the parking lot. His natural impulse will be to run out the courtyard door, so you three," she pointed to three other agents, "will be waiting for him there. That leaves two spots," she drew Xs on the map, "for you two."

"What about this?" Lincoln asked, pointing to the egress near the front left of the main building.

"Steve is working on getting some local support. He'll be here before we launch. They'll cover that as part of the outer perimeter." Kit looked at the group. "Any questions?" The men were silent, and she was wondering if it was nerves or annoyance at having her, the only woman, leading the team. "Okay, then, remember: Tryon is armed and dangerous. He was implicated in the murder of a security guard at a bank in Philly. He was the driver of the getaway car. We can't assume he'll go quietly." She checked her watch. "Time is 2:20 a.m. Steve Gould has asked that we wait until he gets here. If he can't make it by 4 a.m., we have authority to go. Please, take a break, stay dry, and if you have any questions, please come see me. Or Lincoln." She added the afterthought.

David. She probably should call him. On the other hand, maybe he didn't get her text, and maybe he was asleep, and maybe, if she just did nothing, he wouldn't come charging up here to put his bullet-magnet body in the line of fire.

That was her preferred outcome. So she tucked her phone in her pocket.

⚜ ⚜ ⚜

David was halfway up Interstate 64, between Williamsburg and Richmond, before he realized he didn't know where he was going. So he called back to the task force office. Candace answered. David checked his outside mirror and moved into the left lane to get around a truck. Thankfully, traffic was light tonight. "Hey, I need an address," he said.

He heard Candace rustling papers. "Here it is," she said. "They're going to the Sweet Dreams Motel in Clearview. Just off Exit 106. But they're staging at the Maggie Brower Elementary School half a mile away."

"Got it!"

⚜ ⚜ ⚜

A cool front coming in from the northwest triggered a layer of fog over the rain-soaked ground, shrouding the night in a gray mist. "This isn't going to help visibility," Kit muttered.

"Hey, you only need four feet, right? Enough to read the number on the door of Tryon's room?" Lincoln nudged her with his elbow. "This dude's goin' down."

Kit saw an unmarked police car pulling into the parking lot. She frowned.

"Hey," David said, emerging from the driver's seat. "I can't believe I wasn't invited to the party." He grinned.

"Gate-crashers welcome, man," Lincoln said, extending his hand.

"What part of 'get some sleep' don't you understand?" Kit said.

"Hey, I'm good. What can I do, besides catch bullets in my teeth?"

Kit pulled out her clipboard. "Okay, Superman, here's the plan." She went over the arrest plan with him, secretly happy when he clearly approved. "Why don't you station yourself here," she said, pointing to the southwest corner of the motel, near the office. "That way, if he gets past the rest of the team, you'll have him."

"Awesome," David replied. He looked around. "Steve here?"

"He's on the way."

"There's a work zone near Ashland on northbound I-95," David explained. "Just one lane getting by. They had a five-mile backup when I came through. Took me twenty minutes." Lincoln strolled away. David glanced around again, as if to ensure he could speak without being overheard. "Kit, I need to tell you something," he said in a low voice. "Something Piper told me."

"Piper? You've been talking with Piper?" Kit's eyes flashed.

But before he could respond, Kit received a text. "The light's come on in the room next to Tryon's," Kit said. "We need to go. Now."

Kit called the team together, carefully explaining to the deputies and state troopers their job as outer perimeter, and going over the arrest plan once more with the agents. Then she led the team to the motel.

David took his place near the front of the building. Kit positioned herself next to Lincoln on the landscaped rise at the northeast corner, looking into the courtyard pool area and at the courtyard door of Tryon's motel room. She watched as everyone moved into place. The fog shrouding the motel hung even thicker around the pool, softening the colored lights illuminating the courtyard and forming clouds like pink and yellow and blue cotton candy. "I can barely see anything," Kit whispered.

"You'll see it in a minute when that dude jumps out the door," Lincoln responded. "He comes our direction, I will be ready for him."

Kit ignored the bluster. "All ready?" she whispered into the radio. When the answers came back affirmative, she counted down. "Three, two, one…"

A loud *boom!* signaled the ram hitting the door and shouts echoed through the night. Then Kit heard it get quiet. Was Tryon in custody?

"Did we get him? Did we get him?" Lincoln asked.

Gunshots told a different story. Both she and Lincoln had

their Glocks out, and out of the corner of her eye, she saw Lincoln sighting his gun, his arms outstretched. But what was he sighting on? Gunfire echoed through the courtyard. The muzzle flashes looked like lightning in the colorful fog. Kit strained to see what was happening.

"Runner!" someone shouted.

Suddenly, the back door of Tryon's room burst open and a figure, backlit by the light in the room, appeared. "It's him!" Lincoln shouted.

Kit's heart jumped. She saw Lincoln's arm move as he aimed. "No, stop!" she yelled suddenly and she pushed his gun arm up before he could fire.

"What the ..." Lincoln turned to her.

"Look!" she said. The man turned, and the orange letters on the back of the raid jacket identified him as FBI. "He's an agent."

"Holy ..." Lincoln said, cursing. He lowered his weapon.

"Suspect is down," a voice said on the radio. "We have him in the parking lot. Bring the ambulance around."

Kit stood up and holstered her weapon. Next to her, Lincoln sat staring at the gun in his hand. "We got him," she said. Then she realized he was trembling. "You okay?"

Lincoln looked up at her, his eyes big. "I could have killed him."

"But you didn't."

"Oh, man." Lincoln lurched to his feet. "I could have killed an agent."

Kit kept her voice level. "You didn't kill him. Put your gun away. I'm going to see what went down."

But Lincoln just stared at her.

"Lincoln! Put your gun away."

He complied.

"Come around back when you're ready."

"I didn't know. I didn't see the jacket."

✝ ✝ ✝

How could he not have seen the jacket? "Remember, guns can't see or think—that's your job," her firearms instructor at the FBI Academy had always said. Apparently, Lincoln wasn't either seeing or thinking.

Kit tried to shake off the adrenaline as she jogged around

to the parking lot side of the motel. A cluster of agents and officers stood around a body on the ground.

"He's dying," an agent said, moving to block her.

Was he trying to protect her from seeing death? Kit glared at him and moved past. Tryon lay on the black asphalt, a glistening pool of blood spreading out from underneath him. Could she get a dying declaration from him? Close the case?

"Mr. Tryon, help is coming." Kit pulled on plastic gloves. "We're going to help you. But Mr. Tryon, we need to know, did you shoot a woman at a mall? Mr. Tryon?"

The man's mouth moved, but only enough to allow a trickle of blood to flow out.

Suddenly David was at her side, snapping on gloves. "Tryon," he said, bending down, "look at me!"

But their urgent calls had no effect. Tryon's eyes rolled back.

Kit stood up. "What happened?"

"I shot him." Special Agent Frank Leonard raised his hand.

"Let me have your gun, please." Kit held out her hand. It was a routine request. Ballistics had to be checked. "You take mine until I can give you a replacement." She handed the agent her Glock. Psychological recovery from a shooting incident demanded the presumption of innocence. The agent would stay armed.

"Now, from the beginning," she said.

"We popped open the door to his room. It was empty. Then we heard shouts back here, in the parking lot. Tryon had come out of the adjoining room, saw us, and opened fire."

"He fired first?"

"Absolutely."

The others nodded assent.

Kit saw Lincoln walking toward the group. His face looked strained. She saw David clap him on the shoulder then react as he, too, saw the look he wore.

"Okay, who else fired a weapon?" Kit counted two hands. "You will need to spend the next rest of your life filling out paperwork. Lincoln, will you help me with this?" The ambulance had just pulled up. Over Lincoln's shoulder, Kit saw EMTs pull on gloves as they approached the body. "The shooting-incident investigators will need statements from everybody," Kit said. "For now, just relax, please."

Steve arrived. "What happened?"

She told him.

"Call the field office."

"I've done that, sir."

Steve put his hands on his hips. "The boss is not going to like this."

"Sir, Tryon called the play, not us."

David appeared. "Can I see you two for a minute?" he asked

"What's up?" Steve said.

"Over here." David led them to the corner of the parking lot.

"What's going on?" Steve asked.

David's eyes were bright. "I tried to tell you this before, Kit. When I got home at 10:30, that reporter, Piper Calhoun, was sitting on my front porch."

"Piper? What a pest!" Kit responded.

"That's trespassing," Steve said.

"Yeah, and I had her cuffed and in my car. I was going to take her in. But something made me stop. I decided to hear her out."

"Why would you do that?" Kit asked, irritated.

"Listen to me." David raised his hand, imploring her. "She told me that Julia Rankin ..."

"The one killed at the mall," Steve said.

"Yes, the young woman killed at the mall, was having an affair with the mayor."

"What?" Kit exploded.

"Listen, listen. Piper's been on the city beat for a while. She's followed the mayor all around to different events. She's seen her with him several times, once coming out of the Omni Hotel." David glanced over his shoulder. He lowered his voice. "Do you get it? If the mayor or his wife or someone close to him wanted to get rid of the mistress, what better time to do it than when some idiot is going around killing people?"

Kit's heart beat hard. "And that could be why that

shooting doesn't fit the geographic profile."

"Wait. These are serious charges," Steve said. "Serious charges!" He turned away and stared down, obviously thinking. "Look," he said, turning to David. "We need to verify this woman's relationship to the mayor. Privately. Before this goes any further." He raised his eyebrows. "Will it be in the paper?" He checked his watch. "Today?"

"No. Piper told me she had to tell her editor, but it was too late last night to make their deadline. They won't even run it on the web until she's able to verify it. So I'm thinking we've got maybe twenty-four hours before news gets out."

Kit felt a sudden surge of anger. "Sir, the mayor's aide has been in on all of this. He could have tipped the mayor off." She took a deep breath. "Joe Langstrom cannot continue to have access to the task force!"

Steve swallowed hard. "You're right," he said. "You were right from the beginning." He cursed. "Blast it all!" Then he looked hard at Kit. "What about Lincoln?"

"Sir?"

"Was he in on it?"

"Lincoln?" Kit's mind raced. Lincoln? In collusion with Langstrom and the mayor? One word even hinting of his guilt and she could be done with him.

But David stood right next to Steve, his eyes on Kit. And his face was so trusting, so honest. She just couldn't do it. "No," Kit said. "Honestly, Lincoln may be many things, but I don't believe he'd be part of any conspiracy."

"No," David said in agreement. "Think about it: He's openly ambitious. Being part of a conspiracy would work against that." He crossed his arms. "In fact, if all this is true, I think it's possible Langstrom was duped."

"That may be why he left the task force room as soon as I announced Julia's name," Kit said, her mind returning to that scene.

"Okay, look, change of plans." Steve said. "I'll stay here. David you go back and see what you can find out about Rankin and the mayor. Kit, you go get some rest. Oh, and take Lincoln with you. We'll meet at noon and see what we've got."

Kit started to leave but Steve's words called her back.

"One more thing," he said. "Don't say anything to Lincoln. Just in case." Kit and David started to leave. Steve called them back again. "Wait, wait," he said, motioning for them to come close. "Ordinarily, with a high-profile subject like this, I'd tell the SAC. Keep him in the loop. But Jones is tight with the mayor … very tight. What do you think?"

Was Steve really asking their advice? Kit saw David turn to her. She thought carefully, then responded. "Sir, I don't think I'd do that this time." David's nod confirmed his assent.

Steve's square jaw tightened. "I agree. So that's the game plan, then. Just the three of us know."

"At least until Piper's story hits the news," Kit said.

ቸ ቸ ቸ

Samuel L. Jones might be unhappy with the death of Clifford Tryon, Kit thought as she steered her car onto I-95 and headed south, but it could have been a whole lot worse if an agent had been shot.

Lincoln was too subdued, too quiet. Kit glanced over at him. He sat staring out of the passenger side window.

She knew she should just enjoy the peace, but as she drove, images played over and over in her head: the sound of gunfire, the flashes of light, the shouts. What made her push Lincoln's gun up? She had no idea. But thank you, God, she prayed silently. Thank you, thank you.

Lincoln should have been paying attention to where he was aiming his weapon. But it was also true that the lighting was bad and the agent emerged unexpectedly from the motel room, just as they expected Tryon to, and there was gunfire and adrenaline pounding in a dozen chests.

She glanced over at Lincoln as she swung east from I-95, onto Interstate 264. "You're quiet," she said.

She saw him turn to look at her. "You should be yelling at me."

"Yelling? Why?"

"That was a boneheaded thing I did. Completely wrong. Against all our training. And you should be angry." Lincoln slid his hands down his thighs, as if his palms were sweating. "If you hadn't been with me, Kit, if you hadn't yelled and knocked my hand up, I could have shot that guy. I could have killed an agent!"

That was the first ounce of humility she'd ever observed in the man.

"I'm glad I could stop you." Kit took a deep breath. "It's true: we're trained to think before we shoot. But look, the lighting was bad, all that fog and those weird colored lights. You're not the only one who might have made that mistake."

Lincoln shifted in his seat. "What did Steve say when you told him?"

"I didn't."

"You didn't tell him?"

"No. Why should I?"

"You saving it for the investigators?"

Kit took a deep breath. "Look. You made a mistake. I caught it. Nothing happened as a result. That's it."

"You're kiddin' me, right?"

Kit just looked at him.

⚜ ⚜ ⚜

News of the take-down had gotten out to the press. There'd be no time for sleep for Kit. After dropping Lincoln off at his apartment, she drove to her place and showered. She cradled her cell phone on her shoulder as she pulled on fresh clothes. "You're going after Joe Langstrom?"

"Absolutely," David replied, "if I can find him. His wife said he didn't come home last night, and he's not at his office."

"So he disappeared?"

"I'm thinking he's running scared. He could just now be waking up to the fact that he's been involved in a criminal conspiracy."

Kit mulled that thought.

"But he's our best bet to confirm Julia was in an affair with the mayor. We need that before we confront the mayor."

"Or face the SAC," Kit said. "The news conference is scheduled for eleven o'clock." She hopped on one foot as she slid on her black dress pants. "Lincoln asked me to take it. I'm not sure why, but I'm happy to do it."

"Yeah, he looked a little shaken up after the shoot out."

Kit started to respond but decided to hold her tongue. She glanced at her clock. "I've got to leave in ten minutes. I'll call you later." She clicked her phone off and dropped it into her jacket pocket, she faced the antique mirror in her bedroom. The phrase, "What would Lincoln wear?" popped into her mind. That made her smile. They were such opposites!

She turned and found a white silk shirt in her closet, along with a stunning turquoise crop jacket she hadn't worn since her marriage days. She pulled her honey blonde hair back into a low ponytail. At the last minute, she added a bow. It was TV, after all.

Her mission was to say something without saying anything. After all, many on the team, on the task force in fact, were under the impression they'd caught the sniper. The news media were jumping to that conclusion as well. Only she, and Steve, and David had doubts.

Steve was waiting for her when she arrived at the task force office. He blinked when he saw her. "You look nice."

"Thanks!" she responded.

⭐ ⭐ ⭐

Unbelievable! The Hawk cursed as he processed the news he'd just heard. They'd caught the sniper? Killed him? Really?

They didn't get it. They weren't giving him the credit he needed.

What if he failed because of them?

No! Failure was not an option.

When was their news conference?

He checked his watch.

He'd show them. He had to.

⭐ ⭐ ⭐

"I'll introduce you," Steve said. "And then you take it from there. You okay to do this?"

"Absolutely. How's the boss?" Kit asked.

Steve rolled his eyes. That said it all.

A few minutes later, Steve called her to go outside to where over two dozen reporters waited by the gate. Their mics looked like snakes, Kit thought, waiting to strike. She straightened her back as Steve introduced her. She couldn't help but notice Piper was nowhere in the crowd. Was she, even now, writing up her story?

"Last night," Kit began, "the Sniper task force received information indicating that a person of interest in the

Hampton Roads sniper shootings had checked into a motel in Clearview. Because this person was a convicted felon wanted in the shooting of a bank security guard in Philadelphia, we assembled a team and proceeded to the motel. At approximately four this morning, the team attempted to take this man into custody. He opened fire, and subsequently was killed. Information as to his identity will be released once notification of next of kin has been accomplished."

"What evidence links this man to the sniper?" a reporter shouted.

Kit turned to look at him. "We believe he was recently in Hampton Roads. That's all we can say for now."

"Is he former military?" the reporter asked Kit.

"We'll be releasing more information later."

"What was his motive?"

Kit ignored that question, and pointed to a reporter in the back.

"Did an officer kill him or did he shoot himself?" he asked.

"The autopsy will confirm that but all indications are that one of the team members fired the fatal bullet."

"Would that be considered a justified shooting?"

"All indications are that the person of interest initiated the fire fight. The FBI's standard review process has already begun."

"Agent McGovern, the people of Hampton Roads have been terrified now, for over a week. Can they now resume normal activities? Are you confident this is the sniper?"

David walked into her field of vision. He approached Steve and handed him a slip of paper. Then David looked at her, and the look on his face sent chills down her spine. She knew, without being told, that the sniper had struck again. She tore her eyes away from the two men and re-focused on the reporter.

"… are you confident that you have neutralized the Hampton Roads sniper?" the reporter repeated.

"Of course," she responded, her mouth like cotton, "that would be our hope. But we need hard evidence to connect this man with the shootings in Hampton Roads." She cleared her throat. "Until we have that evidence, everyone should remain vigilant."

CHAPTER 16

"THIS IS UNREAL," KIT SAID to David as they arrived at the scene of the latest shooting. This time, the victim was a teen. Tomas Mathus was taking his younger brother to the doctor when a single gunshot rang out in the Park Place area of Norfolk. By the time Kit arrived at the crime scene, the teen had been taken to the hospital.

David had insisted on driving, even though he had been up all night as well. All the way to the shooting site, he'd listened patiently as she vented her frustration. "I was still hoping Tryon was the guy and this could be over. I can't believe this!"

"The problem is, with Tryon dead, we don't have assurance that he killed the mayor's mistress. All we know is that he was in Virginia Beach. So for all we know, we got the wrong guy. Or this latest is a copycat."

"Or Tryon was the copycat," Kit said. "Look, we've got the gun that was in his car. Now, what we really need is the bullet from that shooting, the one Lincoln couldn't find." Kit picked up her cell phone and called Chase Carter. "Send somebody back to Heritage Mall, somebody with really good eyes. Or one of ATF's dogs. We need the bullet that killed Julia Rankin." She clicked off her phone.

"Maybe the ME will help us out after he does the autopsy," David suggested. He parked the car. Before they got out, he reached over and took Kit's hand. "You okay?"

She nodded. She wasn't—she was exhausted and stressed and even a little scared—but she couldn't afford to acknowledge that right now. "I'm okay."

He squeezed her hand. "You're doing great. You're a natural leader. I'd follow you anywhere."

"How about following me over to that crime scene?"

They got out and threaded their way through the police cars and ambulances already clogging the street. "Over there," David said, pointing toward a cluster of cops.

Kit's head was spinning as she approached the scene, the now-familiar blood on the pavement, the tension in the air. Cops moved aside to let her and David through. Her stomach clenched when she saw who had taken charge: Tom Packer.

"Shot in the back," Packer said. "He was alive when they transported him." His eyes narrowed. "You know, shooting adults is one thing. Shooting kids, now that's totally over the line." He put his hands on his hips. Off to one side, a little boy of about eight huddled next to a policewoman, clinging to her legs. Packer frowned at Kit. "I thought you got this guy!"

His tone was accusatory. Kit fought to ignore it. "Why was Tomas bringing the brother here? Where were his parents?"

The detective shifted his weight and crossed his arms. He looked irritated at her refusal to address his challenge. "Single mom. Dad's MIA. She's working. Has a hard time getting off. So the kid was helping out. And this is what he got." The detective shook his head sadly.

"What's that?" Kit gestured toward a black backpack on the steps.

"His backpack. Tomas was wearing it. Those school books may have saved his life."

Oh, the irony. Kit looked around the scene. Park Place was one of Norfolk's poorer neighborhoods. The doctor's office was in an old Victorian Row house on a street that also held a barber shop, and a small grocery store. A green neon sign advertising the Virginia lottery glowed in a liquor store window.

The NPD had closed off the entire block. Still, Kit could see reporters gathering, even a couple of news trucks with their giraffe-neck antennas rising in the air.

She turned her back to the crime scene, vaguely aware of the ongoing conversation between David and Packer behind her. She was looking for places the shooter could have hidden. The street was wide, four lanes. Across it to one side was a green area, sort of a pocket-sized park with a few pieces of equipment for kids. Straight across was a parking garage. Was that the shooter's lair? How did he get away? Why didn't anyone see him?

Kit turned back around. "We need uniforms to go door-to-door over there," she gestured, "as well as on this street. We need to find out if there are any security cameras. This guy is not a ghost. Someone must have seen something."

Packer's eyes flicked over to a couple of cops escorting a young Latina down the street. "Who's this?"

Kit's chest tightened. "The mother." She glanced at David, then spoke to Packer: "Please keep overseeing the scene. You know what we're looking for."

"Someone wearing a T-shirt that says 'Sniper' on it, right?" he said, sarcasm dripping.

Kit ignored him. "I'll take care of the mom."

Of all the things Kit had to do in the course of her job, talking with a victim's survivors was the one she hated most. She could handle arresting bad guys, staring down punks, and outthinking defense lawyers. Tedious days spent bent over financial records weren't fun, but she'd take any of those options over swimming through the emotions of a survivor interview. At least in this case the kid was still alive. So far.

The mom had swept her younger son into her arms and, tears streaming down her face, was holding him tightly. She looked up as Kit approached.

"Miss ...?"

"Juanita Mathus."

"I'm Special Agent Kit McGovern," she said, squatting down next to her. "I'm so sorry about your son."

"My son, he is just a boy! Why he get shot?" The question emerged as a sob.

David had followed her. "Why don't we go inside," he said. "Let's see if the doctor has a room we can use."

Smart. Why hadn't she thought of that? Kit led the woman and her young boy through the door David was holding open. A nurse guided them to a small conference room.

"Ms. Mathus, I need to ask you a few questions, then we'll take you over to the hospital. Is there anyone Tomas had been fighting with? Did he have any enemies?"

"Tomas is a good boy," the woman answered. She clutched the gold crucifix on a chain around her neck. The patch on her green overshirt read "TSP Cleaning." Fatigue lined her eyes. "My boy, he get good grades, and help me with Marcos. He even learning to cook."

"To cook?" David asked.

She nodded. "He watch those shows on that Food Network and he tell me he want to be a chef. My boy, he make wonderful food."

David squatted down. "Marcos, did you see anything before your brother got shot?"

The little boy was about eight, Kit figured, with big brown eyes and short-cut hair.

"No, sir. Tomas walks up the steps and then, *bang!* He falls down." His eyes filled with tears. "Now he's dead!"

"No, son," David said, touching the boy's knee. "Listen: He's not dead. He's in the hospital. The doctors will fix him. I've been shot before and I'm not dead."

"But all those others, they are dead now, right?" Ms. Mathus reasoned.

Kit hoped her soft voice would calm the woman down. "The medics said he was alive and conscious. So let's hope …"

"No hope." The mother suddenly clutched her necklace. "The Lord. *Jesucristo.* Perhaps he will help." She looked at Kit, her eyes bright. "I need to see my boy. Now!"

"Of course." Kit dispatched a uniformed officer to take Tomas's mother and brother to the hospital. As she emerged back outside, into the October sun, she felt suddenly sick. They were back at square one.

☩ ☩ ☩

Bing! He got 'em. Feeling victorious, the Hawk eased his white van into a parking place several blocks away, got out, and locked it. Then, shoving his hands in his pockets, he crossed the street, rounded two corners, walked a few blocks, and casually strolled toward the yellow crime scene tape. He craned his neck like a tourist, his navy blue baseball jacket flapping open in the wind. "What's going on?" he asked a cop. The officer looked to be about forty-five years old. His gut spilled over his broad, black belt and the seams of his blue shirt stretched uncomfortably. *He has no business being a cop,* the man thought. *He's a heart attack waiting to happen.*

"Another shooting," the cop responded. "A kid this time."

"There've been others?" he asked. He fingered the dog collar in his pocket.

The cop looked at him incredulously. "Where have you been? This is like the tenth one. Stuff's been going on for over a week."

The man plastered on a smile. "I'm from out of town."

"I could tell. Nobody from here'd be walking around as lackadaisically as you."

Lackadaisically. Oooo … big word! "They got a handle on the guy yet?"

The cop sniffed. "They said they got him. Now this." He glanced around to see if anyone else was close. "You ask me, we'd do a better job at this than that fancy FBI team. Streetwork. That's what it takes to close this case."

"The FBI's investigating?"

"You know they are. But all that money won't make any difference."

The man rocked back on his heels, nodding toward the cluster of agents and cops a block away. "You see the ones in charge?"

The cop actually looked. As if he would actually answer that question.

"I don't know. I know it's a broad. Female FBI agent. That one down there, I think." He pointed.

"What's her name?" the Hawk asked.

"How should I know?"

It's Katherine McGovern, idiot! Even I know that. Watch the news!

He couldn't resist one more question. "Who's that?" he asked, nodding toward the woman rushing toward the police line. She was young and was wearing a long denim skirt, flowered blouse, and a rakish fedora.

"That one? That's Piper Calhoun. Reporter, works for the *Norfolk Times*." The cop looked at him. "Better get along, now, sir. That shooter could still be around. Don't want a tourist getting hit."

☩ ☩ ☩

Still at the scene of Tomas's shooting, David pulled out his phone. "Yes?" he said.

Something in his tone of voice made Kit turn his direction.

"Where?" David caught Kit's eye and repeated what the caller was saying. "1175 North Beach Way. Got it. I'll be there in twenty." He clicked off his phone. "Langstrom's conscience has kicked in, big time. He's scared to death."

"He wants to meet with you?"

"Me and another cop he knows. Oh, and his lawyer." David had pulled a small pad out of his pocket. "What was that address?"

She repeated it.

"Thanks. You can get a ride back?"

"Of course."

"Be careful," David said.

☩ ☩ ☩

Joe Langstrom sat in a brown hotel room chair twisting a handkerchief in his shaking hand. "I swear, I had no idea," he said.

David tended to believe him, but just in case, he'd provided a back-up. On the way to the hotel, he'd swung by the task force office and picked up Candace. She would pick up on any deception David missed. He was sure of that.

And he knew he needed help. Fatigue hung like lead in his body. He was getting too old for all-nighters. His joints ached. And although he felt sharp mentally, he didn't want to take a chance on missing something because of tiredness.

"The mayor just told me to follow the task force," Joe said. "And of course he asked me questions. I thought he was interested in the progress of the investigation! Who wouldn't be?"

"What exactly did you tell him?" David asked.

Joe rubbed his hand down his thigh, like his palm was sweating. "He asked me lots of things, like what kind of weapon the shooter was using, and did the task force think he was shooting from a vehicle, and whether a former military man might have been involved, and did they find the bullets.

He asked who was on the task force, and how the meetings worked. I told him everything ... I didn't know it would lead to this."

"How long have you worked for the mayor?" Candace asked.

"Ten years! When he was on the city council I was his legislative aide. Now that he's mayor, I'm his go-to guy for everything."

"Loyal," Candace suggested.

"Yes, absolutely loyal." Joe whispered it, almost like a prayer.

"Why'd you run?" David asked.

"What?"

"We looked for you. You didn't show up at work. Your wife didn't even know where you were."

Langstrom rubbed his beard. "I ... I was scared. I mean, it looks bad."

"What looks bad?"

"The mayor. My involvement with the task force. I didn't know who to trust." His eyes pleaded for understanding. "If I went to you, you might think I was involved. Or maybe I was involved, by telling him so much about the investigation." He crossed his arms in front of his stomach like he felt sick. "If I went to him, if I confronted him, I could end up ... like her."

"So when did you put it together?" David asked.

Joe blinked.

"When did you realize the mayor might be involved in the shootings?"

The aide shifted in his seat. "When it was Julia. I ... I knew about Julia, of course. I even ordered flowers for her, from the mayor. I thought, you know, it was just one of those things that great men are susceptible to."

Great men? Over the years David had heard all the excuses for infidelity, probably been tempted to use some of them himself. Life looked so different now. "How long has the affair been going on?" David asked.

"Two, maybe three years. I want to believe her death is coincidental. But here's the thing: Jesse said it was time to end it. So when I saw she'd been killed, I felt scared."

"You believe he killed her? Or ordered her killed?"

Joe shivered. "I think he could have."

"Did he talk about it? Threaten to do it?"

"He wouldn't. He's cold like that. He'd just ... do it."

"But he didn't do it himself. He was on stage with the governor," David said.

"Oh, he doesn't do his own dirty work. No, he wouldn't do that."

"So you think he contacted Tryon? To do the hit?"

"Yes! He must have. Or he could have."

"What makes you think it was the mayor, and not one of his aides, that ordered Julia shot?" Candace asked.

Good question. David leaned forward.

Langstrom's brow furrowed, like he was struggling to pull some thought out of his mind. "I'm his closest aide. The others ... why would they risk it? They aren't so connected, so joined-at-the-hip. Their future wasn't so tied up with his." Joe's right knee bounced. "Why would they risk getting caught?"

"So they didn't have as much to lose if the mayor's political career ended when the affair became public."

"Right."

"Did the mayor ask you to arrange the hit?" Candace asked the direct question.

"No, thank God."

"Joe, why kill her? Why not just tell her to get lost?"

The aide stood and walked over to the window, staring as if he'd find an answer written in thin air. Then he turned back and looked at David. "I don't know. I can't imagine killing anyone. Especially a woman."

"Did the mayor's wife know about the affair?" Candace asked.

Joe turned to her. He shrugged. "Maybe, maybe not. She doesn't like me much. I'm too close to the mayor. She wouldn't open up to me." His eyes widened. He looked at Candace. "You don't think he's involved in the other shootings, do you? 'Cause I don't see that. I don't see that at all." He looked down. "Then again, I didn't see any of this." His basset-hound face drooped as he sagged back down into his chair.

"What's she like?"

Joe stared at her, uncomprehending.

"What's the mayor's wife like?" Candace asked again.

"Oh, Karin? Gosh, let's see: Very bright, a lawyer by training but she stays home with their kids. The mayor's youngest, Peri, has cerebral palsy."

Candace looked at David. "Not likely the mother of a handicapped child would risk jail."

"Right."

"But would he?" Joe said, his voice rising. "Would a dad? I mean, maybe this is all conjecture, maybe it's just a coincidence. Maybe I'm imagining things."

"How involved was he with his kids?" David asked.

Joe's demeanor sagged again. "That was one of my jobs—trying to keep him connected. Buying their birthday presents. Getting tickets to the Tides games so he could take them. Reminding him of important events coming up—events that he blew off most of the time." He sighed. "The mayor's family definitely came second to his career. They were for show. And Karin knew that. She didn't bother telling him when his son was graduating from sixth grade. She told me, so I could make sure the mayor was there."

"But she accepted his behavior because …"

"Because she wanted to be able to stay home and care for the kids. Peri especially." Joe rubbed his hand through his hair. "Karin put up with a lot."

"So what was the mayor's connection with Clifford Tryon?" David asked.

"I don't know. I mean, we run into all kinds of people in this business but a felon like that? From Philadelphia? I don't know how … wait!"

David saw Candace react.

Joe looked from one to the other, then to his lawyer, who gave a slight nod. "Jimmy Carter had Billy, Jesse has Travis."

"Travis?" David cocked his head.

"His brother, Travis. Five years younger. He's done time. He's been in prison. But not for anything big—cocaine, distribution, I think. Nothing violent, I don't think."

David looked at Candace. "But that could mean he knows people."

She nodded.

"Where does he live?" David asked.

"West Virginia. In their hometown." Joe leaned forward. "Travis is an idiot. If I were Jesse I would have put a wall in between him and me. A wall! He's a drug and alcohol abuser, married three times ... a loser. I tried to tell him."

David pulled out his phone and sent a text message to an officer on the task force. Time to check out Travis Crawford. "Joe, we're going to need a list of everyone who works in the mayor's office, including volunteers," he said as he replaced the phone.

Langstrom nodded to his lawyer, who pulled a stapled document out of his briefcase and handed it to David. "I thought you would."

David looked down at the list. He'd given them names and contact information. "Thank you." He and Candace stood up to leave.

"Wait," Joe said. "What do I do now? I mean, if I don't show up at work, he'll know something's up. What if he guesses I turned him in?"

"Go back to work," David said, "and watch your back."

"One more thing," Joe said. He looked at Candace, then David. "The story about the mayor's affair will break tomorrow morning. I want you to know I was the source for that reporter, Piper Calhoun."

David's eyebrows raised. "Why are you telling us?"

"I want you to know I had nothing, absolutely nothing, to do with ending Julia's life. I was already tired of buffering the mayor's bad behavior. That pushed me over the edge. I will not cover for him any more."

Driving back to the task force office, David asked Candace, "What did you think?"

"I think he's a political operative who's in over his head," she responded. "He wasn't being deceptive. The mayor used him."

"Why would a man with as much ambition as Jesse Crawford risk it all by killing a woman?"

"Because he thought he could get away with it. She was expendable. And he was invincible. That's the way these guys think."

"Until something breaks them," David said.

✞ ✞ ✞

The story crashed like a wave over Mayor Jesse Crawford's head the next morning. "Victim No. 7 was Mayor's Mistress" screamed the *Norfolk Times's* headline. What followed was a thirty-inch story written by Piper Calhoun outlining the mayor's relationship with Julia Rankin and citing a "source within the mayor's administration." Included were pictures dug out of the paper's own files showing shots of the mayor with Julia. In some, she was just part of the crowd; in others they were side by side. In every one, a circle highlighted Julia's face.

On Page A5, a sidebar listed all of the shooting victims, their ages, occupations, and where they were killed. A shorter story gave information on Clifford Tryon. "Authorities have not commented on any connection between the mayor and Tryon," the story concluded, successfully posing the question without actually accusing the mayor.

The morning task force meeting buzzed with tension. The mayor had been no friend to the law enforcement community, trimming budgets and placing inordinate demands on his personal security detail. "I've been hearing for months about hinky stuff going on," an NPD officer said. "I knew the mayor was breaking bad."

Kit stood at the head of the U-shaped table. Six hours of sleep had taken the edge off of her fatigue; she could have used twice that much. Off to the left, she saw David talking to Lincoln. He had his hand on Lincoln's shoulder. Had Lincoln talked to him? Told him about the terrible mistake he'd nearly made when they were arresting Tryon? Somehow, she knew he had. Her heart turned: David's compassion was evident from thirty feet away.

Time to start. She tapped her pen on the table. "Gentlemen," she said, "I know this is a hot story, but we need to re-focus on the sniper."

"The mayor's news conference is at nine this morning," one investigator said. "We need to wrap up before that."

"Then let's get going."

Before Kit could call on the first contributor, before one word could be expressed, Steve walked into the room. "Kit, let's go. The boss wants to see us."

Kit's heart sank. What now?

"Lincoln, you, too."

CHAPTER 17

NAUSEA MADE THE RIDE TO the main office miserable. Kit sat in the front passenger seat of Steve's car, silently working on a game plan. But what was the game? What could the SAC want?

If it was more information on the mayor and his connection with Julia Rankin, she could give him that. If it was the Tryon connection he was looking for, no such luck. They hadn't developed anything yet.

Maybe the SAC was trying to cover his own bases. After all, he was friends with the mayor. Maybe he had to answer to the people above him about that. Assuring them that the mayor was innocent in regard to Rankin's death would help him maintain his own position as an independent law enforcement official.

Kit tried to reassure herself with these thoughts, but a nagging fear kept tugging at her heart. The approval-seeking sixth grader inside her hated being called on the carpet. But here she was, riding up the elevator with two silent men, that carpet nearly in sight.

Right now, Lincoln should be telling Steve a football story or laughing about a dopey criminal's mistake or recalling his mother's home cooking. Instead, he stood staring at the lighted numbers as they ascended, his face a study in solemnity.

Minutes later, Kit found herself standing in the light blue office, staring longingly at the beach visible in the distance. Again, she sensed Steve's tension. Again, adrenaline sparked through her body.

It felt like going on a raid, except they had no body armor and there were no weapons except for their wits.

Samuel L. Jones did not ask them to sit down. He did not offer them coffee, or water, or a bullet to bite—he just launched in. "Gould, I'm not happy. This whole Tryon thing, including going Hollywood with that takedown at the motel, is a distraction." Jones shoved his chair back and stood up, pacing behind his desk. "The real issue here is not Tryon, it's ten people shot and eight people dead! And an entire region is looking to us, to the Federal Bureau of Investigation, for answers."

Kit could see Jones' scalp redden through his close-cropped hair. The blood vessels on his forehead stood out like worms.

"And what answers do we have? None."

Steve remained silent, his square jaw impossibly angular, his eyes narrowed. He shifted forward, on his toes, and Kit felt his suit coat brush against her arm. Was he trying to reassure her? Or just moving? Her heart drummed.

"And you," Jones said, pointing at Kit, "you give a news conference reassuring the press that you'd gotten your man, and before you're done, another shooting happens! How embarrassing was that?"

Kit's throat tightened. Before she could speak, Steve jumped in.

"It was not embarrassing at all, sir," Steve said. "She gave the press only the facts, not conjecture about Tryon being the sniper. In fact, she cautioned everyone about remaining vigilant."

"Look at this," the SAC responded, pushing a button on a remote. The video screen to the left of his desk activated and a shot of Kit's interchange with a reporter played.

Are you confident that you have neutralized the Hampton Roads sniper? the reporter asked onscreen.

Of course, Kit answered.

"It was ridiculous!" the SAC yelled, clicking off the clip.

"That was edited!" Steve said. "She never said or implied Tryon was the sniper."

"All I know," the SAC seethed, "is that now I have to answer to Washington about it." He paced again. "Don't think I'm going to sacrifice my career to defend you," Jones said, gesturing. The SAC turned his back on the three agents, placed his hands on his hips, and dropped his head. When he turned suddenly, Kit jumped.

"I want you," he said, pointing to Kit, "off the investigation."

Kit's eyes widened. Cold, icy fear mixed with fury raced through her. Off the investigation?

"Sir, that's ridiculous," Steve said.

Kit choked down the stomach acid rising in her throat.

"She knows more than anyone else about this case!" Steve said.

Jones stiffened. "I will not have her embarrassing this office any longer."

Embarrassing? That is so unfair, a voice screamed in Kit's head. But her mouth felt full of cotton and she could utter no words.

Then Steve started yelling. "What are you doing? She went after Tryon exactly as she should have. She had no idea there was a second sniper!"

"Her press conference gave the public the impression it was safe."

"No, sir, it did *not!*"

"Gould, enough!" Jones's face was red.

Steve's gone out on a limb, Kit thought.

"It's the connection with the mayor, isn't it? That's what's embarrassing! To you, anyway."

Kit's eyes widened. Steve hadn't just gone out on a limb, he was sawing it off! She realized her hands were shaking. Her head felt like it would explode. She closed her hands into fists, trying to calm herself.

Jones came around his desk and stood toe-to-toe with Steve. "You're on the bricks, Gould, for ten days, for insubordination."

"I protest!"

"You have no grounds." Jones turned. "McGovern, you're done. Go back to," he waved his hand, "whatever you do. And you," he said, pointing to Lincoln, "you take over. Run the task force and be the face of the investigation."

Lincoln? The guy who'd truly screwed up? Lincoln? Kit's

heart pounded. She opened her mouth, then thought better of it.

"Do it right, Sheffield, you understand? Because I will be watching you, too! Now get out of here, the three of you."

If the ride up in the elevator was silent, the ride down was like being entombed in ice.

☩ ☩ ☩

The three agents rode silently back to their office. Rage in Kit's heart felt like a wildfire snapping and popping through pines, out of control, a fierce firestorm. She couldn't remember ever being so angry.

Everything is broken, she thought. Everything is broken. Even her beloved FBI.

"I need some time," she said to the two men as they got out of Steve's car. Neither of them tried to stop her.

She turned away from the building and jogged toward her Bucar. She got in, slammed the door, started it up, and jerked the car out of its parking place. Driving too fast, she exited the lot. The guard at the gate saluted her—a kindness, not an obligation, that she would remember later.

☩ ☩ ☩

"Hey, hey, hey, why so fast, Ms. McGovern?" The Hawk sat in the parking lot of a convenience store around the corner from the task force office.

By now he knew her name, where she worked, and what car she drove. Next, he'd decided he'd try to follow her to see where she lived.

But why was she speeding off like this? His curiosity kicked in. So did his adrenaline. He jerked his van into gear and took off after her, the Voice urging him on.

☩ ☩ ☩

Chase Carter burst into the task force room. David rose to his feet, reacting to his energy.

"Did you hear?"

"No, what?"

"Steve's on the bricks. Kit's canned. Lincoln's in charge."

Kit, canned? "Where is she?" David asked.

"In the parking lot, I think. Headed home."

David ran to the parking lot, but she was gone. Reentering the building, he overheard something that set his blood boiling.

"It's about time," Tom Packer was saying to another task force member. "She didn't know what she was doing." He used an expletive to describe Kit.

David grabbed Packer's shoulder, turned him around, and slammed him up against the wall. He could smell the alcohol on Packer. He cursed him, eyes blazing, fist clenched.

"David!" Candace grabbed his arm.

Her voice cut through his anger. Slowly, David released Packer. He took one step back. His heart beat hard.

"What's the matter? You afraid to fight?" Packer said, rising on his toes.

"You'd better shut up," Candace said to Packer, keeping one hand on David. Then she turned and put her arm through David's. "Let's go."

✞ ✞ ✞

"Come on," Candace said, tugging David's arm.

He jerked his arm away, chafing at the restriction. "I need to talk to Steve," David said, striding off.

"Stay away from Packer," she called after him.

Steve was packing up some things from his desk. He relayed his version of the story to David. "He hasn't heard the last of this," Steve said.

"How did Kit take it?"

"She didn't say anything, not to me and not to Lincoln. But I could tell she was angry."

Chase stuck his head in the door. "Sir, the mayor's press conference is on. I'm watching it with Candace in the small room."

Steve looked at David. "Go for it. I'm leaving."

✞ ✞ ✞

Off the task force! All her work. All her leadership. All her investment of time. Gone because one man, one possibly corrupt man, could end her role.

The air was thick with humidity. A front coming up from the south had brought warmer temperatures. A rumble of thunder announced an approaching storm.

She drove automatically, without thinking, her foot hard on the pedal, her hands jerky on the wheel. Her mind stayed snared by the SAC, by his accusations, by words seared in her mind. Again and again, she heard Jones say, "You're off the task force!" Anger gripped her, a terrible, mouth-drying, heart-aching, fury mixed with hatred.

She'd worked so hard. And now it had all become ashes in her hand. Everything she'd worked for. Everything she'd fought for. In less than fifteen minutes, gone. She'd been demoted and disrespected. Once word spread in the Bureau, her future would be destroyed.

She found herself on I-64, headed north. Brake lights up ahead announced a wreck. Kit crossed three lanes, ignoring the horns that blared behind her, and exited. She could not sit still in traffic. She couldn't!

Her phone vibrated. She looked down. "Not now, David," she said without answering it. She flipped it over so she wouldn't see his picture.

✝ ✝ ✝

Man, she was hard to follow! Wow! He shouldn't risk a ticket. Still, the Voice drove him forward.

For a moment, the Hawk wondered if the Voice was trying to destroy him!

He shivered and pressed down on the accelerator. *No*, he said to himself. *Follow orders and you'll be free. He promised!*

✝ ✝ ✝

On the way to watch the press conference, David tried calling Kit. Of course, she didn't answer. David figured she needed some space. How much space? And for how long?

"Ladies and gentlemen, the mayor will make a brief statement but will not take questions at this time." The press secretary, a man dressed in a funereal black suit, white shirt, and red tie, stepped away from the cluster of microphones.

David sat down next to Candace. She was a profiler by profession. He was just an old homicide detective, upset and angry, looking for motive, means, and opportunity. Did the mayor have anything to do with Julia Rankin's murder? Or were they spinning wheels?

It was time for this blasted case to end.

As Mayor Jesse Crawford stepped up on the podium, David pointed at the screen. "No wife."

"He's in trouble," Candace said, agreeing. The loyal but grim-faced wife had become an all-too common feature of these *mea culpa* sessions for political figures with zipper problems. However, Karin Crawford was clearly not standing by her man, not this time, anyway.

"As you all know," the mayor began, "my name has been linked with one of our recent sniper victims. Julia Rankin was, indeed, a friend of mine. More than a friend: she was my apprentice."

"Who says 'apprentice'?" David asked.

"He's trying to avoid the word 'intern.'"

The mayor took a deep breath. Short, stocky, he filled out his gray suit. David figured he must dye his hair—the color was too flat.

"Karin and I both thought Julia was a lovely young lady," the mayor continued. "She was about to graduate from one of the state's finest schools: Old Dominion University. When she told me she wanted to learn the political ropes from me, I was flattered."

Crawford took a handkerchief out of his pocket and wiped his brow before continuing. "Some in the media have reported I was involved in a romantic relationship with Julia. It disgusts me that they would suggest that. She was a beautiful, innocent young woman, and now she is gone. My heart goes out to her family."

Candace said, "He isn't actually denying it. That indicates deception."

On the screen, the mayor blew his nose. "I'm grateful to have had the opportunity to work with Julia, and I hope my daughter grows up to be just like her."

Candace groaned, "Oh, please!"

"Mr. Mayor!" A newsman tried to get Crawford's attention.

"No questions," the press secretary said, leaning into the microphone.

The newsman persisted. "Are you categorically denying having an affair with Miss Rankin?"

"No questions!"

But the mayor couldn't resist. "Are you doubting my word?" He grew misty-eyed. "It's amazing to me the lengths you guys will go to in sullying the memory of a young woman. But that's media for you." Then he turned and walked away.

"Did the mayor ever do community theater?" David asked.

Candace agreed. "What a performance. So from this we can gather two things: One, that the mayor did have an affair with her, and two, that he thinks we're all idiots."

✞ ✞ ✞

Kit drove north, anger fueling her as surely as gas fueled her car. She reviewed the scene in Jones' office over and over.

It was bad, so bad. But she'd never forget Steve standing up for her. Now he was on the bricks—suspended—an action that could seriously affect whatever future he'd hope to have in the Bureau.

Still, in her experience, men landed on their feet. Women, on the other hand …

She could imagine the talk in the task force office. Steve getting suspended would make him a hero. The discipline inflicted on her would be an "I told you so" with many of the men, despite her good work. Packer would be chortling. Her stomach clenched. She took a right at the next corner a little too fast.

Hitting the accelerator, her father crashed her thoughts. She imagined telling him what had happened and hearing his questions, his challenges to her assertions, his logical, analytical critique of her actions, the SAC's actions, Steve's actions. Just like a trial. He was so good at it.

The outcome of their discussion would be the same as it always had been: There'd be something she could have done better, some words she could have said, some response she could have made, some logical retort that would have elevated her position, perhaps even won the day.

"I'm never enough, am I?" she cried out, hitting the steering wheel with her hand. She could never do enough or be enough to make anyone happy.

Rain started falling, gently at first, then with more intensity. Ahead, a light turned yellow. She thought about running it, but her foot hit the brake instead.

She flipped on her wipers. The rain began pounding the roof of her car like so many angry fists.

The light turned green and she took off. Images crashed

into her mind, a virtual album of family disasters. She wasn't enough for her mother to choose to stay and raise her. She wasn't enough for her father to stop challenging her actions. And she wasn't enough for the FBI. Her best work was not enough.

Her throat felt tight. It was so unfair.

Blindly she drove, furiously moving toward an unknown destination. She had to get away. That's all she knew.

Ahead, a light turned green. The road was clear. She accelerated. As she entered the intersection, she glimpsed something out of the corner of her eye. Instinctively, she jerked the wheel to the right. There was a tremendous crash. She felt the car shudder. The airbags deployed. She heard a terrible grinding of metal on metal. She couldn't see. She couldn't breathe!

Then the car began rolling, rolling. Her head slammed against the side window over and over. She gripped the wheel with every bit of strength that she had.

✝ ✝ ✝

"No!" the Hawk screamed as he saw the SUV hit McGovern's car. "She's mine!"

He hit his brakes as McGovern's car went through the guard rail and over the bank. The brake lights on the four cars ahead of him flashed bright red in the rain. Two cars pulled over, the others went on.

As he passed by the crash, his heart beating hard, he saw one of the stopped drivers on his cell phone.

They'd be here soon. The cops, the ambulances, everybody.

He wanted to stop, to take it all in. But he realized he was shaking! And what if they noticed? Would they realize who he was?

The Hawk hit the accelerator, fishtailing a little on the wet street. No. He had to leave. Before they saw him!

He cursed his luck. Now he had to pick another target! Because Katherine McGovern, FBI, was surely dead.

✝ ✝ ✝

Three rolls and then the car stopped. Kit groaned. What happened? Her door was bowed in, pressing on her leg. Her head hurt. She closed her eyes. I'm tired, she thought.

She heard someone calling her name. David.

"No, no ..." She felt herself drifting away. He called her again.

Her feet ... her feet felt wet.

What? Why were her feet wet?

Kit forced her eyes open. Through the rain splatting on the windshield she saw water. The front of her car was tilting down. And now she could feel water rushing in around her legs.

It was so cold. Why was she in the water? She closed her eyes. Her head hurt so much. She felt her hand move and unbuckle her seatbelt, but it was as if someone else was moving it. She heard David calling her again, more urgently now.

She opened her eyes. Water covered her lap. She was freezing! She heard David telling her move to the back seat. She didn't want to. "I'm tired," she said. But he wouldn't be quiet.

Irritated, Kit pushed herself out of the driver's seat and moved into the back seat.

Now, David said, *grab the shotgun. Break the window!*

What? Water, water was everywhere. So cold!

The shotgun.

Kit reached up, fumbled with the latch, and removed the shotgun secured on the interior roof. The swirling water splashed around her face. She inhaled some and choked.

Knock out the window!

Oh, he was so demanding. She struck the window with the gun butt. On the third blow, the window gave way.

Out, out, get out! Now!

The water in the car was up to her neck. She knocked out the shattered window, took a deep breath, and pushed herself through the broken glass, then used her foot to shove herself away from the car.

Swim up!

Where was up? Kit moved her arms and legs. She felt herself moving through the water. She was so tired. Everything seemed to be in slow motion. She just wanted to sleep.

Kick! David yelled.

She gave it one more kick, then everything went black.

CHAPTER 18

SHE FELT TWO HANDS GRABBING her, lifting her. She opened her eyes. Her face broke the surface of the water. She saw a badge. "FBI. Gun," she tried to say. Her eyes closed again.

"I got her, I got her." Officer Darius Washington began swimming back to the edge of the pond, holding the woman's head above the water.

"I'll check the car," his partner yelled, splashing through the pond.

The water felt cold, stiffening the officer's limbs. He hadn't taken the time to remove his shoes, not once he'd seen the person in the water, and he was being weighed down.

But he was almost to the edge, and the rescue squad had arrived.

Then two more officers waded in and grabbed the woman, pulling her to dry land. "Gun!" he heard one of them say.

Officer Washington sat down on the grass, breathing hard. Somebody draped a blanket over him.

"No ID," a voice reported, "but she's carrying."

"Check her pockets."

Officer Washington stood up. He shook the hand of his partner. "Good work," he said.

"You, too, man. Wonder who she is?"

✠ ✠ ✠

David's mind stayed on Kit as he worked the rest of the day. Would she want to talk that evening, he wondered? Or would she still be too angry?

His first job that afternoon was checking in on Tomas Mathus, the young victim shot while taking his brother to the doctor. But as David was starting his car to go see him, he got a call from Emilio's son, Alex.

"Alex! What's up?" he said, surprised.

The boy needed to talk. Could David meet him at a park?

Ten minutes later, David pulled into the parking lot. The normally busy park was empty, another impact the sniper was having on the community.

Alex stepped out from behind a restroom, jogged to David's car, and slid into the passenger seat.

David could feel the kid's fear. That put him on high alert. He felt for the backup gun he had slid down between his seat and the door. "You want to go somewhere?" he asked.

Alex took a deep breath. He curled his hand into a fist and put it near his mouth, exhaling in a long, shaky wave. "No. I just need to tell you something."

"Okay."

The kid shivered. Whatever it was had been eating him alive, David could see that.

"After I washed out, I needed money. So I've been dealing a little." He glanced at David. "Nothing serious. Just weed, I promise."

"All right."

"This kid, his father left. So he traded me his father's hunting rifle for some weed." Alex looked over at David. "The gun was worth a lot more than the weed I was giving him, but his dad really ticked him off, leaving like that, so," Alex shrugged, "I got it."

"What kind of a gun?"

"AR15. Bushmaster."

David shifted his jaw. "Where's the gun now?"

"I sold it. For $300. Well, it was supposed to be $500 but I got ripped off."

"Who'd you sell it to?"

Alex shook his head. "I didn't know him. Friend of a guy I was in the Navy with. Called himself The Hawk."

David's heart quickened. "Describe him."

The kid did: white guy, forty-something, thin hair, short. "The guy creeped me out!"

"When was this? And where?"

Alex told him. The timeline fit. And the location—was it in a red zone? David would have to check.

"So you sold him an AR15. You sell him any ammo?" David asked.

"I gave him two boxes. Remington .223 cartridges."

"What was he driving?"

"A ratty old van. White. But I didn't get the tag."

David tapped his leg restlessly. "What do you think you should do about this?"

The kid drew in a breath. "Tell the FBI. But I can't ... I mean, the pot."

"You got any on you right now?"

"No, sir."

"With the information you've just given me, I doubt they're going to be much interested in pot."

"I'm so messed up!" The kid was on the edge of tears.

"You haven't gone so far down the road that you can't come back."

"My dad's ready to kill me."

David shifted in his seat. "Your dad will be very proud of what you're about to do." He started the car. "You ready?"

Alex closed his eyes and took a deep breath. "Yes, sir."

David drove him to the task force office, and ushered him into an interview room. He had every intention of sitting down with the kid and listening while he was interviewed, but just then, his phone rang. The caller ID said it was Kit's father, Robert McGovern.

That's odd, he thought, quickly leaving the room as he pressed the answer key. "O'Connor."

"David!" Kit's father's voice boomed. "Are you with Kit?"

"No, sir."

"Is she all right?"

"Yes, sir." David frowned. Where was he going with this?

"Well, look. The Bureau called me about her accident, but I'm in the middle of a trial and I can't get down there. So I'm hoping you ..."

"An accident?" David pressed the phone to his ear. "What accident?"

Mr. McGovern hesitated. "She was in a car accident.

Transported to a hospital, but they didn't know anything about her condition." Mr. McGovern hesitated. "You don't know about this?"

"No, sir!" David's heart had already begun racing. "I haven't seen her for a few hours. Did they tell you what hospital?" Where could she be? Why hadn't anyone called him?

"Center something?"

Sentara. "Yes, sir. Got it. I'll go check up on her. I'll let you know."

"Okay, thanks. And tell her I'm sorry I can't come." Mr. McGovern hesitated. "Let me know if I can do something, okay?"

"Yes, sir." David clicked off his phone and yelled for Chase. "Who in the FBI would notify next of kin?"

Stunned, Chase just blinked. David quickly filled him in. "Track it down. I'm headed for the hospital." David turned to leave. "Call me!" he yelled.

☦ ☦ ☦

David found her lying in a bed in a room on the West Wing of Sentara hospital. Her eyes were closed. Her face was bruised. But he saw no casts and no bandages, just as the doctor had said. Relief poured into his heart.

He sat down in the chair next to the bed, took her hand, and cradled it in his. He'd talked to the investigating officer, and in his mind he could see her car in that pond. In his mind he could see her in the water. In his mind he could see what might have been. He shivered, then he began praying, thanking God she was alive, praying for whatever injuries she had, praising God for his mercy.

Her eyes fluttered. "David." She raised herself partway off the pillow and reached for him with her other hand.

"Shh, shh," he said. "You're all right." He leaned over her and kissed her on her cheek. He inhaled her smell, which right now was some mixture of pond water and hospital chemicals. He stroked her cheek and kissed her again.

"What happened?"

He sat back down. "You had a car accident. Someone hit you."

She nodded. "There was water."

"Yes." His heart trembled. He lifted her hand to his lips and kissed it. She closed her eyes.

Seconds later, her eyes popped open again. "Are you hurt?"

David frowned. "No."

She nodded. "I'm glad." She touched his face. "Thank you for saving me."

What? "I didn't save you, Kit. I wasn't there. A Norfolk officer pulled you out of the pond."

Kit frowned. "No. Before that. You made me get out of the car."

He cocked his head.

"Don't you remember? You told me to move."

What was she saying?

She pushed herself upright as if to make herself clear. "You made me get in the back. Use the shotgun to knock out the window. That's how I got out." She settled back on the bed. "I was so tired. The water was so cold. I just wanted to sleep. But you kept saying, 'Use the shotgun! Swim! Kick!' and … and I did. You saved me, David. It was you." She smiled. "I was mad at you. I just wanted to sleep."

He let her statements ride for a minute, unsure what to do, and then he said softly, "I wasn't there, Kit."

She rose on one elbow. "I heard your voice!"

David saw the agitation in her face. The doc said she needed to stay quiet. Avoid stimulation. Let her brain rest. He backed off. "I love you, Kit. I'm so glad you listened."

David sat with her while the sky outside her window grew dark. A few FBI people came by: Steve, Candace, Chase. Kit slept through most of it. The nurses came in and woke her every two hours to make sure she didn't slip into a coma. Twice David had to remind them.

David stayed by her bedside, eating candy bars, crackers, and soda out of the vending machine. He thought about what she said.

What had she heard? Was it her training kicking in, with his voice added? Was it an angel? Was it God?

He loved this woman and would do anything to protect her. Anything.

Trouble was, he knew he couldn't.

✝ ✝ ✝

David left the hospital briefly the next morning, drove to Kit's apartment, and picked up some fresh clothes for her. When he got back, the doctor was running her through a series of tests to gauge her coordination and mental acuity.

She looked so much better. There was bruising on her face, and an actual lump on the side of her head, but the sleepiness was gone.

When the doctor finished, he heaved a big sigh. "I can't justify keeping you," he said to Kit. "I think you've had a mild concussion but you seem to be recovering quickly. I'm going to release you, but I'd like you to take it easy for a few days." He turned to see if David was listening. "No driving. Minimal screen time. No sports or motorcycle riding. Don't even jog. I want to see you at my office in a week. Otherwise," he shrugged, "you're good to go."

"Work?" David asked. He expected Kit to shoot him a look, but she didn't.

"Just take it easy," the doctor replied.

✝ ✝ ✝

Kit stayed quiet on the ride home. She had so much to think about. Her head still hurt, and her body ached all over. The doc had given her a prescription for pain meds, but she knew she wouldn't even bother getting it filled. Mostly she wanted to rest and think.

The sky was brilliant blue and the sun blazed down on the streets like it was July. David had brought her a pair of sunglasses along with her clothes. So considerate. She looked over at him as he drove. Since he'd spent the night at the hospital, he hadn't shaved. She smiled softly.

"What?" he said, glancing over toward her.

"Nothing." Then she reached over and stroked the stubble on his face with the back of her hand. "I kinda like Scruffy Dave."

A little smile bowed his lips. Then he pursed his lips and nodded. "Yeah, most women do." He snapped a glance at her.

She laughed.

The other driver, she'd been told, had died. He was a young man. He'd been texting his girlfriend, racing to her because she thought she'd heard a shot and was afraid of the sniper. So sad.

She, Kit, should have died as well. She knew that. The thought of it made her shiver.

Kit felt her eyes relax a little as David drove into her underground parking garage. He carried everything for her and kept one hand on her elbow as they entered the elevator. Her gun, rendered safe, was in her bag along with her creds. Everything else—her wallet, her shotgun, the papers she'd been carrying, was MIA, either in the pond or in the car.

David opened her apartment door and held it for her as she went in. She caught a faint whiff of orange and cinnamon from an unlit candle on a table near the door. Colors, smells, textures—she seemed to be noticing everything.

The door closed behind her, and she heard David put something down. She turned to him before he could speak, folded herself in his arms, and kissed him on the neck.

"I love you," David said.

"I know." She kissed him gently on the lips. "I think that's why I heard your voice in the car."

His lips found hers again, and she responded, hungry for his kisses, for the feel of his skin. She stroked his cheek, caressed his ear, and kissed him again. Then she pulled back. "I need to sit down. Will you hold me for a little while?"

"Sure."

He sat down and she snuggled next to him, resting her head on his chest. Scenes played over and over in Kit's head. She seemed to be remembering more about the accident every hour. The sound of the metal, the frigid water, the voice telling her to move. She remembered coughing. She remembered the shotgun. She remembered the dark and cold.

She could have died. She *should* have died. And she knew, beyond a shadow of a doubt, that God had saved her.

Why? She'd been holding God at arm's length for years, living on her drive to achieve, and cradling her bitterness toward her mother like a beloved child.

But as the water swirled into that car, God's grace had enveloped her, lifting her up to life. Undeserved mercy.

Unconditional Love.

Nothing would ever be the same.

✝ ✝ ✝

Late that afternoon, the security system buzzed announcing a visitor on the first floor.

David and Kit looked at each other. "I'll get it," he said, rising from a dining room chair. Kit's gun was in pieces on the table. He'd been cleaning it for her while she slept.

He pushed the button on the intercom. "Yes?"

"Hey, it's Lincoln. Can I come up?"

Lincoln?

A few minutes later, David opened the door and Lincoln walked in, dressed casually for once. A fishing vest, one that assuredly had never known a splash of water, covered his gun.

"Kit, how are you?" he began. Concern modulated his voice.

"Doing pretty well," she responded. "Sit down." She gestured toward the armchair. David sat down next to her.

"You scared all of us," Lincoln said, rubbing his hands on his thighs. "Seriously." He shook his head.

"I'll be fine." She felt a shiver.

He nodded. "Look, I came to say I am sorry." He put his palms together and touched the tips of his fingers to his lips, almost like he was praying. Closing his eyes momentarily, he dropped his hands to his lap. "I am so sorry about what happened in the SAC's office. You didn't deserve that. And I just wanted you to know," he took a deep breath, "that I had nothing to do with that scene, nothing at all. You've been doing a great job."

Kit bit the inside of her cheek. She nodded. "Thanks."

David squeezed her hand. "The doctor told Kit to take it easy for a few days," he said pointedly. "She went through quite an ordeal yesterday."

Lincoln nodded. "I understand." He pressed his hands on his thighs. "But whenever you're ready, I'd like to talk to you about continuing to work on this case." He raised both hands, editing his words. "No, I *need* you to work on it. I can't do this. I'm good at some things—football, connecting with guys. But you are a much better investigator. And I need you if we are going to find this sniper."

Kit swallowed the lump in her throat.

"What Jones did to you was totally unfair." Anger webbed Lincoln's voice and pushed him to his feet. He paced. "I stood there shocked. I didn't know what to say. So of course, I did nothing." He sat back down and rubbed his hands together. "I'm not proud of that. But here's what I realized later: The night of the raid, you gave me a break, Kit, by not telling anyone. Jones dealt you a bad hand. That's not right." His eyes glistened with emotion. "But the way you handle things ... honestly, Kit, next to you, I feel shabby."

Kit smiled. "Shabby? With your clothes?"

Lincoln laughed. "Now, let me finish!" He held up his hand. "You got a boot to the backside you didn't deserve. If I can make it right, I will. In the meantime," Lincoln looked from David to Kit and back again, "I really need you guys. Will you keep working with me? To find this sniper?" Lincoln asked.

David looked at Kit.

"The SAC banned me," she said.

"He's been called to D.C. I don't know why. So I went to the ASAC. Updated him on the case. He asked me who my top people are. I told him. He asked why you weren't on the case. He must have called the SAC, because he called me this afternoon and said, as long as you're not the face of the case, you can work it."

Kit shifted her weight on the couch. That was insulting, in a way. "I'll think about it. Let me talk to David. I'll call you in a little while."

"You take what time you need. Me, I'm headed back to work. I've got a lot of catching up to do."

After Lincoln left, Kit looked at David.

"That break you gave him?" David said. "That was grace. And grace changes everything."

"I know," she said softly. She moved over to the front window. The sun was declining in the west. She stepped out on the balcony. David appeared next to her. He put his arm around her.

Kit suddenly took a quick breath.

"What?" David asked. "What's wrong?"

"Look," she said, gesturing toward the beautiful sunset. "Remember I told you Gail said something as she was dying?"

"Right. One word: Gordon. We thought it was a clue."

"No," Kit whispered, "it was *golden*. That's what she said, 'Golden.' I wonder if she was seeing ..."

"Heaven?" David said, finishing the thought.

She squeezed him.

CHAPTER 19

CANDACE GREETED KIT WITH A hug when she walked into the office two days later. "Are you okay?" the older woman asked, cocking her head.

"I will be," Kit responded.

"She needs to take it easy," David interjected.

Kit rolled her eyes. "And stay in the office. I know. I'll be good, I promise."

David smiled. "I turn custody of this woman over to you, Candace. Good luck. And may God have mercy on you."

Both women laughed. Kit touched his arm, silently conveying her love.

David left and Candace turned to her. "You gave us all quite a scare."

"I know." She closed her eyes and saw herself in the water again. She shivered.

Candace put her arm around Kit. "You want to talk about it?"

Kit shook her head. "I'm still processing it."

"You can't just stuff it down."

"I made an appointment with the counselor. Today at one. David's coming back to take me."

Candace smiled.

"I won't stuff it, I promise. But this morning, I want to get an overview of the case again. Take a fresh look at everything. Begin at the beginning. Maybe I've missed something."

Candace pulled up a broad map of Hampton Roads on a laptop hooked to a large monitor. "So here we are. The shooting locations are marked by red dots."

Kit nodded.

"David came up with a promising new lead," Candace said, filling Kit in on Alex's statement. "Now, these are the questions I'm asking myself: Why did he choose these spots? How did he get there, and also, how did he leave? Are there obvious escape routes? What is he thinking?"

"We cannot link the victims, except by the shooter. So, the victims are random."

"Right," Candace said, agreeing. "So, how did he choose the locations? Was it access and egress?"

"Or did each provide a place for him to hide?" Kit mused. "Did he just wait for a victim to come along?"

"Was he shooting from a vehicle?"

"We think that shootings one and eight originated from buildings: Gail was shot from a parking lot on a roof, and the shot that entered the convenience store came from a garage roof." Kit stood up and began pacing, one arm in front of her supporting the elbow of the other while she touched her hand to her chin. "The others? We're not sure."

"So they could have come from a vehicle."

"If so, was he parked or did he have an accomplice driving him?" Kit plopped down in a chair.

"There's a key. We just need to find it."

"The guy Alex sold the gun to called himself 'The Hawk.' Isn't that a comic book character?" Kit pressed her forefinger to her lips.

"I have no idea." Candace returned to the spreadsheet. "Look, in shootings one, four, and five, he was relatively near an interstate."

"Right. The first shooting came out of the blue. He could have driven down from the parking lot and away. No one was looking for him then, and we weren't stopping cars."

"He used cooking spray on the cameras, which showed organization. He isn't doing that any more. Not in these last few."

"But he knows we're going to respond quickly now, so how does he get away?"

Kit's eyes widened as a possibility came to mind. "Maybe he just slowly leaves the area. He's got a vehicle that looks like it belongs in the neighborhood. A cab, or a utility truck ..."

"Or a white van, like Alex saw," Candace said.

Kit's mouth twisted as she stared at the screen. "Show me that chart again, that spreadsheet with all the facts." Candace projected that sheet. "Something's there, I just don't see it." She looked at Candace. "Maybe he doesn't get away. Maybe he just watches from the area."

Candace's face lit up. "So we need to have someone check the crowd shots at the shooting scenes."

"Okay, so what else?" Kit tapped her chin with her finger. "Let's look at the choropleth map again."

♱ ♱ ♱

On the corner stood a hotel. Rooms by the hour. *Perfect,* he thought. He walked to his van, removed his rolling suitcase, and strolled back to the Park Place Hotel. Pulling a handkerchief out of his pocket, he draped it over his hand, grasped the metal door handle, and pulled it open. No prints. No way. "Got a room?" he asked the old guy at the desk.

The guy, scrawny and bald with a fringe of gray hair, looked at him over his rectangular glasses. Wordlessly, he shoved a registration form toward him.

No computer? Oh, this is way too easy!

The Hawk filled out the form. "Jack Black," he wrote, and then he made up a fictitious address.

"How long?" the desk clerk asked.

"Let's see: I need to roll out of here by nine tonight." The man smiled.

"Fifty dollars," the clerk said. "Can stay all night for that."

"Won't need to," the man responded. "I got to be in Raleigh tomorrow." He pulled out his wallet and removed fifty bucks.

The clerk took a metal room key off of the rack and slid it across the battered wooden counter.

"Streetside, right?" the man asked.

"Didn't ask for that, now, did ya?"

The man's eyes narrowed. *I could kill you with one hand,* he thought.

The clerk sighed and picked up the key, replacing it with a different one off the rack. "Three-o-one."

The man smiled. "Thanks."

Up in the room, the man flopped the suitcase on the bed and hurried to the window. Yes, a good view of the police station. And below him, on the street, a cluster of people waiting for a bus. "Want to see something?" he muttered.

The room was what he expected. Dirty wallpaper. A bare bulb overhead. Cheap art.

He checked his watch: 10:40. Better hurry. He needed a place to brace the rifle. He found it, pushing the table near the window and sighting downward. Needing a bit more height, he jerked open a drawer, found a phone book and a Bible, and stacked them on the table. Then he unzipped his suitcase.

The M16 knock-off had served him well. He stroked its barrel. It was becoming part of him.

Laying the rifle on its side, he went to the window and carefully raised it. No screen. Good. The man returned to the rifle, propped it on the books, and cradled its barrel on a folded pillow. Then he sighted through the Nikon scope. So bright. So accurate. So perfect for finding the target.

Thirty yards. Forty maybe. Easy pickings either way. The lot was full of cruisers coming and going. And police officers everywhere. Walking to and from their cars. A cluster of three of them were hanging out talking.

About what? About him?

He hoped so.

He put the crosshairs directly on a woman with blonde hair. His trigger finger quivered as a tremor went through him. He started to squeeze and then inexplicably she dropped down, squatting and pointing to something on the street. The man cursed and stood up, easing his back.

Again, he bent over and eyed the group through his sight.

But he jumped at the sound of knocking at the door and a key—in the lock! He jerked the gun off of the makeshift stand, shoved it under the bed, and turned just as a Latina dressed in a housekeeping uniform and carrying towels came through the door.

"*Lo siento! Lo siento!*" she said, her face registering shock. She glanced up at the number on the door. "He give me wrong room number!"

The man hunched up his shoulders and started toward her. "Idiot!" he said as the door closed behind her. "You idiot!" He kicked the door. He looked at his watch: 11:03! Too late, too late! He ran to the window. The cops were gone! The bus riders were gone!

Then the shaking began. The man cursed. He raised his leg and kicked the table over, sending it crashing to the floor. He picked up the pillow and began flailing the bed with it.

Still, the shaking wouldn't quit. Stupid maid!

✝ ✝ ✝

The counseling session brought a flood of tears. So much pain. So much hurt. Such grief! Kit had no idea all that was bottled up inside. A few well-chosen questions from the counselor had sent her tumbling into her whitewater past. At first, it felt terrifying. Then exhausting. But after a while, hope emerged, like a flower pushing through a crack in the concrete. A tiny, fragile, vulnerable hope.

Afterwards, she slept on the cot in the back room at the office for a couple of hours. David brought her coffee and a sandwich, then briefed her on the investigation. She asked him to pray. When she felt ready, she returned with David to where Candace, Lincoln, and Chase sat reviewing evidence and batting around ideas.

They were stuck.

"Has anyone tracked back the sale of that weapon? Who was the kid who sold it to begin with?"

David shrugged. "He's been interviewed but he doesn't know much more about The Hawk than Alex."

"Hawk or no hawk, what's this guy's motivation? What hurts people the most?" Kit asked.

Everyone turned to look at her. "We're motivated by pain, by greed, by a lust for power, by love, by anger. What's pushing this guy?"

"The worst calls we get are domestic disturbances," David said. "The people closest to us hurt us the most."

Kit nodded, biting her lip to keep tears back.

"Discrimination," Lincoln suggested, "but this guy is shooting people of all colors."

"Men and women," Candace said.

"Even kids," Lincoln responded. "Who shoots kids?"

"The victims are diverse, so what's the common thread?" Candace projected a spreadsheet, a summary of all the shootings.

They all stared at the screen. After a while, Lincoln muttered a curse word and began to pace.

David's knee bounced with tension.

"Wait!" Kit said. "Look at the time. Every shooting except Julia Rankin's took place between fifty minutes past the hour and the top of the hour."

They all began scrolling through the times of all the incidents. "You're right," Candace said.

"What's up with that?" Kit asked.

David frowned. "What's happening at the top of the hour that he's trying to stop?"

✞ ✞ ✞

Kit stared at the numbers. The fact that the shots were clustered just before the hour told them two things: First, there was a reason for the clustering. Second, the shooting of Julia Rankin, which occurred at approximately 11:26 a.m., was an anomaly, both in timing and location. All of the other shootings were fitting into a pattern. That one was an outlier. The odd sock, David called it.

Kit crossed her arms. "Could we draw the sniper out with a carefully worded press statement?"

"Now we're talking," Lincoln said.

"I wonder," David said, "if we mentioned time, or high noon, or at the top of the hour if this guy would call us."

"That's a great idea," Candace said.

They began wrestling with words.

"What happens at a specific time?" Candace said.

"Judgments are pronounced, like in a courtroom," Kit said. "I can't get past Gail's shooting. Maybe some traumatic judgment came down just before the hour."

"Like getting court martialed," David suggested.

"Or divorced." Kit still could remember the terrible finality of that reality.

"Or die. People die," David mused. "Maybe someone he knew died just before the hour, and now he's trying to kill in revenge."

"That's a good one." Candace started making a list.

"What else? Some things happen once, like death or divorce. What else happens every day?"

"People leave for work, and get home from work." Kit said. "Leave for school and get home from school."

David rubbed his chin.

Lincoln ran his hand through his hair. "When I was little," he said, "I remember getting tense every day at five-thirty knowing my stepfather would be home at six." He shook his head. "I had this Pavlovian response: five-thirty meant trouble was on the way."

They turned to look at him. "Why?" Kit asked.

"My stepfather was an alcoholic." Lincoln stared at his hands. "He'd get off work at five. If he was home by five-thirty, it meant he hadn't stopped at a bar. If not ... he'd come in that door about six o'clock, drunk, looking for trouble. Mostly it was me he found." Lincoln shook his head. "I don't know if it was because I was a boy and he thought I could take it, or if he saw me as some kind of rival, or what. But he'd find something I'd done, anything, and," he hesitated, "it was bad." He looked at Kit. "So, yeah, my anxiety would start triggering at five-thirty every day. I learned to tell time very, very young."

Kit sensed something very real had just happened. "So maybe," she said softly, "some traumatic event occurred at the top of the hour that this sniper is trying to process."

"And maybe by mentioning time in your press conference, we can draw him out," David added.

Lincoln straightened up. "Okay, I'm game. Tell me what to do."

Half an hour later they had a statement Lincoln could read. Ninety minutes later he was doing just that, in front of TV and radio news microphones. Kit, David, and Candace sat watching him in the office.

Lincoln had changed out of his suit and was dressed casually, in khakis and a yellow shirt, open at the neck, no tie. The idea was to look and act non-threatening, sympathetic, in fact. He walked up to the microphones and began speaking: "As we approach the top of the hour, we wanted to update you on the investigation into the rash of sniper attacks in the Hampton Roads area." His voice sounded calm. He checked his watch, for effect. "It's a few minutes before five. It's time we know why these shootings are happening. What does the shooter want? Why is he hurting people? Human behavior is a mystery. But we'd like to help solve this one."

"He's even modulated his voice," Candace said.

Lincoln continued, "The reward fund has grown to $50,000. Anyone with information should contact the number on your screen."

"Yes," Kit said, "good tone, good demeanor."

"There she is!" David said.

"Who?"

"Piper." He pointed to the screen. "I texted her and told her she should be there."

"So now you're using the press?"

"Why not?"

The press conference continued as Lincoln said he would accept a few questions. "Are all these shootings related?" a print reporter asked.

"We believe all but two are connected." Lincoln purposely gave false information in an attempt to draw the shooter out.

"What about Clifford Tryon?"

"We think he is responsible for one or two of the shootings. Beyond that, we're not sure. Maybe he did them all."

Kit cheered. "Okay, so if the real sniper isn't mad now, he'll never be. Imagine! Tryon getting credit for his kills!"

Two more questions, and Lincoln stepped down, but not before mentioning time again. "It's time," he said, "to talk. The clock is ticking. It's time to start the healing process. It's time for the shootings to end."

"That went well," Candace said.

✟ ✟ ✟

Piper Calhoun chewed on her lip as she typed, the background buzz of the newsroom at the *Norfolk Times* providing a platform for her thoughts. Her desk was in a corner, at her request, and faced the wall, also at her request. Large piles of source material created a channel through which anyone wishing to speak to her had to navigate.

Her desk was her safe place at work.

Why had David O'Connor alerted her to the news conference? He'd never done that before. Why now?

The guy who spoke, Lincoln Whats-his-name, seemed low-key, almost professorial. In other press conferences, he'd been much more animated. Why? Were they managing the news somehow or trying to communicate with the shooter?

She continued to type, setting the scene, quoting the agent, then reviewing the facts about the sniper shootings so far. Shootings so far? Or facts so far?

Someone in the newsroom shouted something. Her stomach clenched. Ever since she'd broken the news about the mayor's mistress, she'd felt on guard. Her personal phone number was unlisted. No one knew where she lived—not even the newsroom contact list contained that information. But the bottom of every story she wrote contained her work email and her cell phone number—necessary, if a reporter hoped to get information from the public.

Yes, they knew how to reach her. Maybe even find her.

Laughter signaled the all clear. Piper turned her mind back to her story. Should she create another sidebar? Or run the bulleted list of the victims again? She has already posted an update on their online addition.

"Hey, Piper!"

She turned to see who was calling her. Another reporter stood outside her channel. He had a small brown envelope in his hand. Great. Another collection. "What's it for this time? A baby? A wedding? A funeral, for crying out loud?"

Before he could answer, her cell phone rang. She smiled at the reporter and shrugged sheepishly as she picked up her phone. As she spoke into it, the reporter walked away. "Piper Calhoun."

Breathing. Just breathing.

Piper's senses went on high alert. "Can I help you?"

"It's about time," the voice said.

Male white middle-aged drunk? Piper scratched notes on a pad. "What's about time, sir? How can I help you?"

Time! *TIME!* screamed a voice in her head. Her eyes fell onto her computer screen, where Lincoln's words stood out. *It's time to start the healing process. It's time for the shootings to end.* The shooter? Piper trembled. She stood at her desk and waved her arm, trying to get someone's attention. Anyone. *9-1-1 people! 911!*

"You got it right. You knew." The caller cursed as he spoke of the shooting of the mayor's mistress. "Why would I do that there? At that time? Those idiots!" The man's breathing was heavy.

Piper sat down again. She shifted her jaw to try to relax. "You have information, sir, on the shootings?"

The caller laughed, a weird, almost cackling laugh that sent chills down Piper's spine. "Look. I know who you are. I've seen you, with that weird little hat. Who do you think you are, Sam Spade? You think this is a game? No, this ain't no game. I'm the hunter. I'm in charge. No one can stop me. You put that in your story."

The call ended. Adrenaline drove Piper to her feet. She looked around. Her editor's desk was empty. A couple of reporters stood around the Life Section desk laughing about something. The obit clerk stared blankly at her computer.

"Omigosh, omigosh," Piper said. She fumbled with her phone, found the "recent" list, almost deleted it, then wrote the number down. Then she called David O'Connor. "Answer, answer! Don't ignore me!" She felt like she was going to throw up.

Then she heard his voice. "O'Connor."

"He called me!"

✞ ✞ ✞

"What we'd like," said David, "is permission to put a tap on Ms. Calhoun's cell phone. I understand it belongs to the paper." He was sitting in a small conference room with Piper, the editor, Buzz Reynolds, and an associate publisher, Mary Knowles. The fluorescent lights cast a greenish tint on everything, even Reynolds' bald head. "If he calls her again, we'd like to be able to trace it."

Reynolds turned to Piper. "Did you already show it to him?"

"Sir?"

"The number. On your phone."

"No, sir." Piper shifted in her chair. Technically, she hadn't. She did, however, give David the second piece of paper on her steno pad, which happened to bear the number's imprint, a "coincidence" David had acknowledged with a subtle nod as he tucked it into his pocket.

"I'm not comfortable with this. Our people are trained to report events, not participate in them," Reynolds said.

"On the other hand," David countered, "it would make a heck of a story. Think of it: Woodward and Bernstein wrapped up in one young woman. With you, of course, guiding her." David smiled at Piper.

Reynolds looked over at the associate publisher.

"I have just three words to say," she said, tapping her pen on the table, "'single copy sales.'"

Reynolds exhaled and rubbed his hand over his head. "How do we protect Piper? I can't afford to lose her."

"We can put her up in a hotel," David said, "with a female cop. We'll make it a suite, so Piper has privacy. That way, if this guy has scoped out where she lives, he won't find her."

"And she can report stories from there and the office?"

"Absolutely," David said. "All we really want is access to her phone in case this guy calls her again."

Reynolds turned to Piper. "How do you feel about this?"

Piper straightened her back. "Sir, I think we have a civic responsibility to help the police stop this guy."

"You trust these people to keep you safe?"

"They're fairly competent. I think I'll be okay." Piper nudged David's foot.

✞ ✞ ✞

"I don't want a cop with me. Or an agent," Piper Calhoun told David when they'd left the office.

"Why not?" David raised his eyebrows.

"I'm used to being by myself. It'll feel weird."

"Your editor just agreed to that."

"My editor is not my keeper." Piper stopped walking and put her hands on her hips. "No babysitters."

David frowned. "No deal. I won't risk you going at it alone."

"It's my life! I'll cooperate on my terms, or not at all."

He shook his head. "No, you won't. You're going to do it my way. I've already got a cop lined up. She's meeting us at the place I've arranged for you."

David had booked her into a two-bedroom suite at the

best extended-stay hotel in downtown Norfolk. Apparently, the classiness of her temporary surroundings changed Piper's mind about the babysitter. "Oh my gosh, this is so nice," Piper said, her neck craning as she looked around.

"This is Officer Cara Burns," David said, gesturing toward a woman dressed in jeans and a pink tunic top emerging from a bedroom.

"Just call me Cara." The officer shook Piper's hand.

Piper offered no resistance.

"There's a pool here, and a spa, and they even have a grocery shopping service," David explained. "Use it. The tab's on us."

"Us as in U.S.? My rich uncle? But look, I didn't expect a vacation!"

"Just don't go wandering off on your own."

"Okay, right."

"We've got your phone tapped, and here's an extra one." David handed her a burner phone.

"What's that for?"

"Emergencies if your phone is dead."

She tossed it in a tote bag.

"And one more thing, Piper. Just in case the shooter is watching your place, don't go back to your apartment. We'll send someone over to get some clothes for you, or whatever you need. Make a list. We'll take care of it."

"Gosh. Fine. This is great."

"And remember, your phone is live. Someone's listening all the time. So be sure you say only nice things about me." David winked at her.

On the way down in the hotel elevator, David thought, *I'll need all the nice comments I can get.* Tom Packer had filed a complaint against him and was threatening to file assault charges. "Why am I so impulsive?" he muttered, looking toward the ceiling.

CHAPTER 20

FAILURE TO COMPLETE A SHOT was unacceptable. Unacceptable! And yet, it had happened when that hotel maid interrupted him. How had he let it happen?

The shot that had missed the convenience store clerk had left him hungry, unnerved, itchy. Failure to complete the next shot was totally outrageous. He had cops in his sights, and he had failed.

So many missed opportunities. The clerk. The cops. And watching McGovern get killed *by someone else!*

Every hour, when the big hand moved past the six and up toward the top of the hour, he could feel it mocking him. He knew his mission: He had to stop the clock. Stop the pain. Stop the fear. Stop it.

Stop it by shooting. Sweet relief. But only for a time. Then it would build, build again, like a summer storm.

Now, the Voice had said, it was time to end it with a really big, spectacular move.

So far, he'd failed. Another miss would kill him. Send him screaming into darkness.

No, he would make this next one. Make this shot. If he planned it right.

He sat in his white van watching, his eyes half-closed, like a plumber on a break. The woman with a stroller. The man with a briefcase. The kids skateboarding.

Should they be next?

Rousing himself, he sat up straight, turned the ignition, eased into traffic. He drove down the street, past the MacArthur Memorial, past the Tide light rail train, past

Nauticus with its massive destroyer.

Destroyer. He was the Destroyer. He had come to steal and destroy.

Like his childhood had been stolen. And his life destroyed.

The only way to get it back was to keep stealing and destroying until ... until he was free.

Free. One day. When enough had been killed, he would be free. That was the promise the Voice made.

That's what kept him going.

Then he spotted it. A ridiculously painted liquor store, the kind the Old Man would have come stumbling out of on a Friday night, bottles in hand. The store held down one corner of an intersection. Someone had painted the stone around the windows black, the door a bright red. Bright red! Ha! Like taunting a bull.

His fingers twitched. Someone blew his horn. The light had turned but he didn't care. The store, the store. That was the place. Maybe one good shot would end it—one good shot once the reporter showed up.

"All right, jerk!" the man said out loud to the impatient driver behind him, and he slowly proceeded across the intersection. He'd drive around the block, looking for a spot, looking for his place.

He'd done parking garages, a park, a rooftop, and he'd shot from his own truck. What would be next? What would do it?

Because he wanted to be free. He would be free. The Voice had promised.

He would call the reporter. The press needed to know. Needed to know how much he was in control. *She* needed to know.

Tomorrow, then. He'd do it. And they'd all know.

✟ ✟ ✟

At the task force meeting that afternoon, ATF Agent Brick Bresner reported that the bullet from the shooting of Julia Rankin was not a match for the bullets found at three other sniper shootings. However, it did match the gun found in Clifford Tryon's car. Chase Carter added that the medical examiner found a bottle of Xanax in Cliff Tryon's pocket after the FBI shot him dead, and the pills appeared to be from the same manufacturer as the half-pill found where Julia was shot.

"So now we've got three markers pointing to that shooting as an outlier," Lincoln said. He looked straight at Kit. "You think that's enough to say Tryon did it?"

"Yes. And I think it's enough to call that shooting an anomaly. The geo profiling confirms that. The death of Julia Rankin was unrelated to the other shootings," she responded.

Tom Packer sat lazily in his chair, lounging back and playing with his pen, his white shirtsleeves rolled up to his elbows. "You're not close to proving the mayor's connected."

"My suggestion," Kit said, "is that we cut that killing out from the pack, and let Virginia Beach take that on while the rest of us continue with the connected cases."

Lincoln nodded. His apparently endless wardrobe today featured a gray suit, lavender shirt, and a patterned lavender and white tie with fuchsia highlights.

Lincoln pointed to two Virginia Beach delegates. "You okay with that, boys?" They mumbled their assurance, and so he continued. "We are still getting calls on the tip line. But there's been a more personal contact. David, you want to update us on that?"

So he did. David told the group about the call to Piper Calhoun, and about the tap they now had on her phone. While he spoke, Kit watched Tom Packer. He seemed disinterested, inspecting at his fingernails with a bored expression on his face. What was the deal with Tom Packer? Why was he so antagonistic?

"And so," Lincoln said, "we've scheduled a news conference for today at five o'clock. In fact," he looked at his watch, "I've got to get going. Anything else?"

As the task force meeting broke up, Kit returned to her geo profiling, but not before signaling David to follow her. "I have an idea," she told him as he joined her in the small office where Candace had set up shop. "Look at this." She had printed the map produced by the geo profiling program on clear plastic. She laid it down on top of a street map of Norfolk. "We've pretty much narrowed down the UNSUB's prime locations to the city. By plotting the shooting sites, we're getting highlights here," she pointed to a residential area, "and here, with a smaller one over here near the Portsmouth shipyard."

"So you're thinking he lives in that area? And works one of those other places?"

"I can't be that specific," she said, "but what if we took a bunch of uniforms and flooded this area." She pointed to the residential zone.

"Why uniforms?"

"There's more of them, that's all."

"Wouldn't that run the risk of scaring him off? Pushing him somewhere else?"

"Maybe. But if geo profiling is applicable to this case, he wouldn't go far."

David rubbed his jaw. Kit could hear the sound of his hand on his beard. She loved that sound. Behind David, she saw Tom Packer walk by, hesitate in the doorway, then shake his head, and move on.

"So we go in there, and we start pulling people over for expired stickers and headlights out. And we pray for good law enforcement instincts."

"Right," Kit responded. "And if we get another shooting, we intensify that effort." She looked at him, her eyes bright. "If my hunch is correct, if he's not fleeing the area but hanging around to watch, then we want to see who comes back to the neighborhood."

"Yeah." David stood up. "I'll get going on that." But then his phone rang. "Right after this."

Kit listened as David spoke into his phone. "What's up?" she asked when he clicked it off.

David hesitated. His mouth tightened into a straight line. "I've got to go see my boss."

"Why?"

He sighed. "I got into a little trouble with Packer the other day. He's filed a complaint."

"Oh, David! What did you do?"

"Not half of what I wanted to."

✞ ✞ ✞

As David walked toward his boss's office at the Norfolk Police Academy, his mind raced forward. Would he be taken off the task force? Lose his job? Get charged with assault? Even misdemeanor assault would mean the end of his career. What would he do then?

He could teach PE. Coach. Maybe. Somewhere.

His heart was jumping in his chest. Walking down the hall, he was surprised to see another NPD officer, a member of the task force, walking out of the boss's office. Then he realized it was the guy Packer had been talking to the night David threw him up against the wall. Great. A witness.

The office door was partially open. David knocked.

"O'Connor? Come in," his boss, Darryl Minor, said.

The office was nothing fancy—just a gray metal desk and matching chairs, a flag, and a few pictures. As David walked in, he was surprised to see the chief of detectives occupying a chair.

"We've had a complaint," Minor began.

"Yes, sir." David's jaw felt wired shut.

"There's been an allegation about Detective Tom Packer."

"Sir?" David blinked.

"We understand you had a run-in with him a few days ago."

"Yes, sir. I was totally out of line. I let the tension get to me."

"We're not interested in that," the chief of detectives chimed in. "We want to know if Packer's drinking is impacting his work on the task force."

David's head started spinning. What? Packer was the target? This wasn't about him?

"So do you have direct knowledge of Detective Packer's drinking?"

David swallowed. "We don't socialize, sir. The only thing I can tell you is the day I," he hesitated, choosing his words carefully, "had a run-in with him, I could smell alcohol on him."

"And what time of day was that?"

"It was in the morning, sir, somewhere around ten o'clock."

And that was it. Five minutes later, David walked out of the office feeling fifty pounds lighter.

✴ ✴ ✴

Across the street from the liquor store stood an apartment building undergoing renovation. It was a simple matter for the man to park his white van behind the building, amongst all the other white vans. Then he slapped a hard hat on his head with an official-looking seal on the front that included the word "Inspector." He picked up a clipboard, and walked into the building.

It worked. It always worked. No one stopped him. No one cared. No one had the guts to ask to see his creds, not even the foreman. He was in control.

Just the way he liked it.

By the time he had climbed to the third floor, he had made up his mind. This would do. Nicely. Windows gave an easy view of the liquor store, below. A nearby freeway could provide quick egress. If the cops were as stupid as they had been, he could watch from a nearby parking lot, right across from the huge church, Saint Andrew's, the one with a clock in its towering spire.

He grinned. Fitting.

He'd spent nineteen years in the Navy, sworn to fight enemies, foreign and domestic. Now, he was the expunger of an even more personal evil.

He trotted down the stairway, whistling. Emerging onto the first floor, he smiled at a worker. "Looks good!" Then he climbed back in his van, threw the clipboard on the floor, and drove off. As he did, he looked for security cameras. None. Maybe one outside the liquor store, but then, it would simply catch the bloody victim falling to the ground.

The man glanced at his watch. The workers would be gone by six, he figured. Seven at the outside. That would give him time for a daylight shot. Or he could wait until nightfall.

He tried to figure out which would be more effective. Day or night?

Most of it had happened at night. After six, anyway.

He had to make this one count. He'd missed the 7-Eleven clerk. And the shot from the cheap hotel. So this one had to work. Had to work!

Because everyone knows, three strikes and you're out!

✞ ✞ ✞

"Everything okay?" Kit asked, as David rushed into the task

force office half an hour later. She stood huddled around a computer with Candace, Lincoln, and Chase.

"Yes. What's going on?"

"Another call. Listen." Kit pushed a key and the Sniper's voice emerged from the file.

"Tell them I am in control. Tell them I will decide who lives and who dies. Tell them to be ready. Because, when it's time, I will kill again, suddenly, like a hawk on a mouse, like an eagle striking a rabbit."

"Creepy," David said, "but there's that reference to a hawk."

"If this is the real sniper, we can say he is a male, middle-aged, probably white, a native speaker, high-school education or better," Candace said.

"He brings up time again."

"Right."

"And we couldn't trace the call."

"Also correct."

"So what do we do?" Lincoln asked.

Kit spoke. "We get ready. We flood the neighborhoods we're targeting. We look for anything that seems suspicious. And if there's another shooting, we watch to see who comes back in the targeted areas."

"I'll ask Chase to get overlays printed for all the teams," Candace said, "so everyone knows the areas we're targeting."

"Can we send them something digital, so it can go out to all the cruisers on their laptops?" Lincoln asked.

"Yes, I'll work on that."

David's phone vibrated. "Piper," he said, looking at the caller ID. He walked away from the group. When he returned a few minutes later, he simply said, "She's scared. And curious." He chuckled. "Probably more curious than scared."

Kit grimaced. "Reporters."

Lincoln and David left to get the red zone teams started.

☫ ☫ ☫

He paid particular attention to his ritual this time. Maybe he'd forgotten something. Maybe that's why he'd missed the convenience store clerk. Maybe that's why the maid had interrupted him. Maybe he'd missed a step.

At 4:50, he parked his van in the empty parking lot across from the church. He had his disassembled Bushmaster in a dark green canvas camp-chair carrying bag. In a matching backpack he carried the bullets and a bologna and cheese and mayonnaise sandwich, and a small carton of Yoo-hoo. His ritual meal. He waited in the van, watching, eyes half-closed, like a man resting after a hard day's work, until 6:45. Then he drove the van behind the apartment building being renovated, careful to leave it nose-out. As he had guessed, the workers were gone. At 6:55 he left the van. Carrying his bags, he walked up to the third floor.

The sun was down and night was falling. The man set up his shot, piling wood and bricks on a sheet of plywood set on two sawhorses, then placing his rifle tripod on top of that. He had positioned it about two feet in from the open window, to make it less likely someone would spot the muzzle flash.

He heard the clock strike seven. Multiple tremors ran through him, like successive waves hitting a breakwater. He closed his eyes and covered his ears. The image of that clock, that stupid clock in the hallway, flew in from nowhere. He cursed it away, cursed until the last tone from the church's clock tower down the street faded away. He shivered, then paced, paced away the fear by imagining the ax shattering the glass face of the clock in the hallway, splintered wood flying everywhere, his anger driving him to momentary victory.

Once he'd calmed down, once that stupid clock had stopped and he'd regained control, he looked around. He saw a five-gallon bucket and turned it over to make a seat. Now he had to wait, but that was okay. He had his routine.

He pulled a stack of old comic books from his backpack. Batman. Captain Marvel. The Green Lantern. The average becomes superior. The little becomes big and overcomes bad. Supernatural forces grant superpowers. But fighting evil, sometimes things got messy. Some people had to die so others might live. Might have a second chance at life.

How did he go from being his ship's Sailor of the Year to being dismissed from the Navy? It was in the Navy that he'd gotten his nickname, the Hawk. The Navy had embraced him, even when his wife divorced him and took his kids. When his world had fallen apart, the Navy had saved him.

Until that day.

Was it a delusion when the captain's face turned into his abuser's when he was giving him orders? Was it just his imagination that sparked the panic he felt when the captain opened his mouth? The panic that boiled over into anger that simmered and simmered until the Voice told him what to do?

All he knew was that to get rid of that man, the nightmares, and the fear, he had to follow the Voice. And so he had. He had attacked the Old Man. And then the Navy kicked him out.

In the declining light, the Hawk picked up his favorite comic books. He barely needed to see them; he had them memorized. So page by page he leafed through them, pulling himself back into his 12-year-old mind, reaching into the past, becoming little again so that then he could get big.

At exactly seven thirty, the man pulled the bologna sandwich and Yoo-hoo from his backpack. He slowly ate the sandwich, washing it down with the chocolaty drink. If he closed his eyes he could see his mother, nervously watching the clock while she made him his snack. If she fed him, and got him up in his room, she might be able to protect him. But if the Old Man got home …

At seven forty-five, with the world outside now dark, he carefully cleaned up. His stomach was tight. His mission was clear: Stop him before the top of the hour. Stop the Old Man.

He took the rifle in hand and looked through the scope. He was the hunter; the Old Man was the prey. How would he recognize him? He was tricky, now. He took different forms, but the Hawk would know him when he saw him.

A woman dressed in jeans and a leather jacket entered the liquor store. The man's finger twitched on the trigger as she walked into his crosshairs. But no, she was not the one.

The man relaxed. He glanced at his watch. Seven forty-seven. He had time. Two more people emerged through the garish red door. One, a man in a cowboy hat, the other, a short Hispanic woman. No, no, no. Not them.

The clock moved forward. Seven fifty. Every time he looked through the scope, he could feel his blood pressure drop. He grew calm and quiet inside, like a cat stretched out in the sun.

At seven fifty-eight, as the man peered through the scope, enjoying the relaxed feeling, *he* emerged from the store. This time, he was an older man, with gray hair, dressed in a gray suit and carrying a bottle in a bag. This was the one, the Voice said. This was the prey, and he was the hunter.

He sighted through the scope and as the gray-haired man walked into the crosshairs, the man squeezed the trigger. The gun roared.

But the sound of glass shattering made the sniper jerk up his head. Unbelievably, the gray-haired man stood. He stood! Unharmed!

How could he have missed? The Hawk cursed. His watched beeped. The church clock began to chime. The hour! The hour! Furious, the man turned, squinted through the scope, aimed his rifle toward the clock and pulled the trigger. He had to stop the clock. Stop the clock! He unloaded his rifle. The gun's retort echoed. People scattered on the streets below. And as the magazine emptied, the man realized he was in trouble. Too much noise. Too many shots. Too many people around.

Get away, get away! Panicked, he gathered his things. He shoved the rifle into the canvas bag. He jerked his backpack off of the floor. He raced toward the stairwell, sirens screaming in his ears.

Three strikes and you're out, little man! Three strikes …

No, no! The Hawk threw his gear in the van and started the engine. He eased out of the alley and onto a side street, moving casually, his mind racing. He had to get away, had to!

CHAPTER 21

"SHOTS FIRED, SHOTS FIRED!" SHOUTED Chase.

Kit's head jerked up. She jumped to her feet. "Where?"

"Hampton Road and 45th."

"Multiple shots?" David was sliding on his ballistic vest, racing toward the door.

"Let's go!" Lincoln shouted, gesturing. "Kit, you got this?"

"Absolutely," she said.

David jerked his car into gear and engaged his siren and lights. Multiple shots! That was different! Was the sniper falling apart?

Ten minutes later, he pulled up in front of the liquor store on Hampton Road. Shards of the shattered front window littered the sidewalk. Lights from multiple emergency vehicles danced on the buildings lining the street. David stepped out onto the scene. "What do we have?" he asked the uniforms.

"Guy was coming out of the store. He suddenly realized he'd forgotten something, and turned to go back in. That's what saved him."

"So no one got hit?"

The cop shook his head. "But the dude shot the heck out of the window," he gestured, "and that clock down the street."

David shielded his eyes from all the emergency vehicle lights. Two blocks down stood a large, cathedral-like church. Its spire held a clock, and even from a distance he could see the hands were stopped. "All right. Let's rope off the crime scene. Keep the reporters away. Where's the man who almost got shot?"

"Inside. He's pretty shaken up."

Lincoln arrived. "We're going to need access to that church," David told him. "We'll need to look for bullets. Can you get the ATF dog team here?"

"Yeah, sure, man. But let's go talk to this dude."

The "dude" was Frank S. Pearson, an accountant and avid golfer. "We're having company tomorrow and I was supposed to pick up bourbon and vermouth. I forgot the vermouth, and so I turned to go back in. That's when I heard the shot and the glass shattered."

They peppered him with questions. No, he didn't know anyone who would want to kill him. No, he wasn't aware of any enemies. His marriage was sound, his job intact.

Random. He was a random target. Just like the others.

"This is different, though," David told Lincoln afterwards. "Multiple shots. That means something."

"Like what?"

"The sniper could be escalating, or he could be falling apart." David looked across the street. "I want to go look in that building," he said.

"We have a team going through it."

"I want to see it for myself."

"Okay, I've got ATF on the way. We'll see about that church."

"I'll meet you down there in a bit."

✞ ✞ ✞

David entered the apartment building from the alley, climbing up the stairwell, flashlight sweeping the steps ahead of him. In all likelihood, the sniper would have shot from an upper floor, and so he climbed.

The third floor paid off. "I need the Evidence Response Team," David said, calling into his radio. In front of him were two sawhorses, some plywood, a brace of sorts, and an upturned mud bucket. The open window overlooked the liquor store.

He'd found the sniper's perch. He bent down, sweeping his flashlight over the floor, looking for shoe prints and found nothing. He peered out of the window, checking the angles. Then he began a broader sweep around the upturned mud bucket and across the room. "Make sure you check that for prints," he said, gesturing at the bucket when the ERT arrived, "as well as those sawhorses and the plywood."

"Everything's so dark, it'd be easy to miss something," the team leader agreed.

David took some pictures on his cell phone, and sent them to Kit.

His flashlight caught something near the stairwell: a hair, caught on an exposed nailhead. "Hey!" David called back to the ERT. "Come get this, will you?" He showed the tech the hair.

"It could be from anybody," the tech responded.

"Let's get it anyway."

✝ ✝ ✝

Back at the office, Kit monitored two teams of thirty officers each in the two hot zones she'd identified, and a smaller team at the Portsmouth red zone. "That's right, every expired plate or sticker, every taillight that's out. Get them pulled over. Then use your instincts. We're thinking it's a middle-aged white male, possibly military background. No accent. We're going to keep this up for at least two hours."

The minutes ticked by. Kit pressed the end of her pen on the table, flipped it, pressed the other end down, and flipped it again. Over and over, end over end, just killing time.

✝ ✝ ✝

Down the street at Saint Andrew's, the minister was ushering Lincoln and an ATF dog team through the building. They were about to climb the clock tower when David caught up to them. "I found the perch," he said, breathless from his run down the street. From the outside, he hadn't been able to see bullet holes, but the hands of the clock were definitely stopped at eight o'clock.

"Good job, man!" Lincoln said.

"In that apartment building under construction. How's it going here?"

"We'll know in a few minutes," Lincoln said, "once the dog starts putting her nose to work."

Sunny. A yellow Lab like Annie. David followed the others up the narrow steps. The walls of the stairway were stone, real stone, and he wondered how old the building was.

"Our congregation is declining in numbers," the minister complained. "So many gray hairs. I don't know how we're going to be able to afford the repairs."

The area at the top of the stairs was too small for all of them, so David remained on the stairwell. It was hot, and sweat soon dripped down his face. He didn't see how the dog was going to be able to work. The tower soared up a good thirty feet from the landing. Crossbeams braced the walls, but any slug that pierced the clock would be too high for the dog to reach.

The handler realized the same thing. "You all back down, and I'll let her go. But I don't see her finding anything here."

Lincoln, dressed in a suit, was dripping sweat. "I'll go down a few steps."

The minister followed him. The dog went to work. David watched as the yellow Lab's handler gave her a command. Within seconds, she jumped up on the side of the tower, and then sat down, her tail sweeping the floor. The handler looked up, shining his flashlight up on the wall. "She says it's up there," he said. "I see something that might be a slug, but we're going to need a ladder."

"Hold on," David said. He walked to the middle of the tower, and jumped. The first crossbeam was about seven feet up—within reach. He grabbed it, fixed his grip, took a deep breath, and pulled himself up.

"Holy smokes!" Lincoln said from the stairwell.

David's breath came hard. It had been a long time since he'd done that, and his body hurt. Struggling, he hoisted himself up on the crossbeam. "It's up here," he said. "The dog is right. I see one slug, anyway." He sat on the crossbeam, pulled his knife out of his pocket, and dug the slug out. He put both in his pocket, and stood on the crossbeam, looking for more. "You see anything else?"

"No, man. I don't," the ATF agent said. "You'd better come down before you fall."

David let himself down carefully, hanging on the beam, then dropping to the tower's landing. "Man, it's a hundred degrees up there." He wiped his brow on the bottom of his shirt. "You can get an ERT up here if you want, with a ladder. But at least we have one slug to start checking." He handed it to Lincoln, who had an evidence bag waiting.

"I just don't know how we're going to fix the clock," the minister said.

✟ ✟ ✟

David left the church and jogged back to his car, cataloging the evidence from this shooting in his mind. The shooter missed his target. Then he tried to take out the clock. That spoke to David about his mental disintegration. The sniper had never before taken more than one shot. He'd never shot an inanimate object. But clearly time, stopping the clock before it struck eight, was a crucial issue to him.

And it seemed obsessive. So in his mind, David began seeing an obsessive-compulsive white male with a history of abuse, good marksmanship skills, with access to weapons who was devolving and becoming more dangerous.

David reached his car and climbed in. He texted Kit that he was returning to the task force office, and pulled out of his parking place.

A block down the street, he decided instead to go to one of Kit's hot spots. Uniformed officers should be stopping cars, checking anything they could in hopes of spotting a suspicious man. He wanted to see the action for himself. Ten minutes and he'd be there.

He'd forgotten that Tom Packer had been assigned to the team covering the Lambert Point area. He started to move on, but then saw Packer had spotted him. He didn't want to appear to be avoiding the detective, so he parked and got out. "Detective," he said, greeting Packer. "How's it going?"

"This is a waste of time. Expired stickers don't float my boat, you know?" Packer put his hands on his hips.

"Mind if I drive through?"

"Suit yourself. You're not going to find anything."

Five minutes and three blocks later, David, saw something out of the corner of his eye that caught his attention. A battered white van pulled slowly out from behind a building, and then turned the wrong way down a narrow, one-way street.

Frowning, David turned quickly to follow him. What was this guy doing? It took two blocks to catch up to the van. David turned on his blue lights to pull him over. The van complied, but as David left his vehicle to walk up to the driver, the van took off, tires screaming.

David raced back to his car, jumped in, and began the pursuit. He radioed in his location and the description of the van and wondered why he didn't get a response.

The van was zig-zagging through the streets and it was all David could do to keep up with him. "Lambert's Point," he shouted into his microphone, "37th Street." But there was still no response and he threw the microphone down in frustration.

David dug in his pocket for his cell phone. As he did, he tried to think ahead. What was the van running toward? A big Norfolk Southern Railroad terminal and an industrial area. But it was essentially a dead end. Why would he go that way?

He found his phone and tried thumbing Kit's number. When nothing happened, he looked. Dead! He'd forgotten to charge it. Again.

He cursed and continued the pursuit. David lost the van, then spotted it again, then nearly had an accident, going through an intersection. His adrenaline pounding, he raced through the streets until he finally saw the van stopped up ahead—in a cul-de-sac. David pulled up behind him, drew his weapon, and carefully walked toward it. He used the mirrors to try to see the driver, began shouting commands, but he got no response. Finally, he walked up to the driver's side door, quickly opened it, and jumped back.

But no one got out. Using his flashlight, David peered into the vehicle. It was empty. Empty! Where'd the guy go? Then he saw something hanging from the rear view mirror that made his blood run cold. It was a dog collar. A green plaid dog collar, just like Annie's.

Fire raced through him.

Looking up, he saw a figure a good hundred yards ahead, running toward a long, weed-covered hill.

David took off. No way should he have given chase on his own, but all he could think about was the man disappearing over the brow of the hill. He put on speed. He wasn't going to let him get away.

He saw the man drop his backpack, but he still had a long

bag over his arm. David climbed a fence and entered a lot full of sea shipping containers. He grabbed his phone, tried dialing Kit again, stumbled, and dropped it.

The guy was getting away!

David began chasing him again. He saw he could gain ground by jumping off a ten-foot drop, onto the roof of a shed, then onto the ground. So he leaped and landed on the shed roof, but the shingles gave way, the roof caved in, and David felt himself falling, falling through the shed, crashing through metal and glass, until he landed with a thud on the floor. He started to get up, then everything went black.

⚜ ⚜ ⚜

What did the shooting of the clock mean? Was the UNSUB trying to stop time?

Kit looked at her watch—ten thirty. "Hey, Lincoln, where's David?" The new task force leader had come back looking hot and sweaty, his suit rumpled.

Lincoln frowned. "Last time I saw him he was playing Spiderman in a church clock tower. Did you call him?"

"He texted me. Said he was coming back here." Kit pulled out her phone. "I'll try him again."

But there was no answer, and that started a gnawing in Kit's gut. She told herself David was fine, that he'd just gotten distracted, and he'd be walking through the door soon. She asserted that he was impulsive and had probably just decided to go for a hamburger and had forgotten to tell her. And he had his cell phone muted. Again.

But as the minutes clicked by, her anxiety grew. She called him again. She texted him, adding 911 to the message to indicate its urgency. She used the radio. When all these means failed to produce contact, her adrenaline started pounding.

"I'll ask all the teams," Lincoln suggested.

But she was already sliding on a ballistic vest.

"Kit?" Lincoln stood between her and the front door.

"I know, I know! But if you think I'm going to hang back here while David is out there missing, you're crazy."

"You really think he's missing?"

"He's not answering calls. I don't know what's going on."

"Okay. But I'll drive."

They left Chase and Candace to manage the office. Lincoln asked Kit, "When do you think they can stand down the neighborhood teams?"

"At eleven," Kit responded.

"Okay, then. Eleven it is." Lincoln had stripped off his suit coat and tie, and had rolled up his sleeves. "Let's go find David."

The dark streets of Norfolk seemed ominously empty, like they were taunting Kit. "C'mon, David. Where are you?" she murmured.

Lincoln reached over and touched her shoulder. "He's a big boy. He can take care of himself. Did I tell you what he did at that church?"

"No. What?"

He told her, then, about David jumping up and pulling himself up on that crossbeam. "It was amazing, I mean, incredibly athletic for a guy…" he stopped himself.

"For a guy his age?" Kit laughed. "I'll tell him you said that."

They were retracing the route back to the last shooting site, but a call from Chase changed their direction. "Chase put a trace on his cell phone, but it's not pinging. But someone saw him talking to Packer," Kit said, clicking off her phone.

Lincoln turned the car. "Let's go then."

CHAPTER 22

WHEN HE SAW THE COP crash through the roof of the shed, he could scarcely believe his good fortune! He'd waited to see if the cop would emerge from the shed by some great miracle, but when he didn't, the Hawk couldn't resist—he crept over to it, and peered through the door.

The cop lay on his back in the midst of a pile of rubble. His eyes were closed. He looked dead.

But no—he moved. For a minute, the Hawk considered shooting him. One bullet to the head would end him. Sweet! But stupid. First, he'd have to take the time to reassemble his weapon, then what about the noise? The noise, the noise! And the area would be crawling with cops. Besides, he said, looking at his watch, it wasn't time. Not time!

Better to wait. Better to glide through the night and return to the nest like the predator he was. So he moved off, retracing his steps over the fence and up the hill. There were noises in the streets—car engines just a block or two over. He had to slip away, like a cop's bad dream.

And so he did.

☦ ☦ ☦

When David opened his eyes he saw stars through the hole in the ceiling above him. He tried to move, razor-sharp edges of metal debris pricked him. Assess your injuries first, he told himself. His head and back ached. His left leg (more specifically, his ankle) hurt like crazy, and he couldn't quite remember where he was or how he had gotten there.

Reflexively he pressed his elbow to his side, and felt the reassuring presence of his gun. He flexed his hands, and tried rotating his feet. The left ankle was no good—sprained maybe. And his right hand felt wet. Wet with what? Blood?

✞ ✞ ✞

"Well, where'd he go, Packer?" Kit had little patience for the man tonight.

"How should I know? He drove off that way, said he wanted to look around. That's all I know."

"All right, all right. I want everybody on this," Lincoln said. "Everybody on your team."

"I thought we were supposed to be looking for the sniper."

Lincoln dropped his voice. "Get real. This is a brother."

Packer grimaced in disgust. "What do you want me to tell them?"

Lincoln spread a map out on the hood of Packer's car. "I want a systematic search, a grid search, from here to here." He marked on the map, then glanced at Kit, who nodded her approval. "What's he driving?" he asked her.

She described his unmarked car. "I don't know the plate."

"Okay, we'll go with the description. Everybody gets the word on this, right? Everybody, Packer. Let's do it now."

✞ ✞ ✞

Light shone down through the hole in the roof. "The moon," David said out loud, as if acknowledging that would help orient him. He felt a lump on his left side and tightened his hand around it. His flashlight. Then he felt something on his legs, some movement. Alarmed, he jerked the light up and clicked it on.

A rat!

David cursed and scrambled to move. He felt metal slice his right arm and blood flow. But a rat! He staggered to his feet, adrenaline coursing through him. He heard a "squeak, squeak" and then rustling as the rat ran away.

His head swam, and he dropped to one knee. But he would not, he could not lie down again. "Stay up, stay up," he ordered himself. He shook his head and tried blinking away the blackness. "You have to go! Go!" Pushing hard on his good leg, he launched himself up. His ankle hurt like crazy and that focused his brain momentarily. His ankle was sprained. Maybe just twisted. Certainly not broken. He'd have to hobble. But he could do it. And he had to. Had to get out.

Rats!

His arm dripped blood. Jerking off his shirt, he wrapped it around the cut, making a tight wrap. He felt for his gun, and then his phone. One out of two wasn't bad. What had happened to his phone?

The door. Was there a door? His flashlight found it. David followed its beam, wincing as he moved. Outside, he took a deep breath.

Ah, yes. That guy. He was sure it was the sniper he'd been chasing. What had happened to him? Long gone, David suspected. But he'd seen him! At least he'd seen him. "4T238," he said out loud. Yes, the van's license plate was still in his brain. "Good cop," told himself. "Now, let's go."

But where? How? The fence and the hill before him looked insurmountable, considering his ankle. He had no phone with which to call for help. And the industrial area he had landed in looked deserted. *Walk the tracks,* he told himself. *They'll lead somewhere.* But as he started to walk forward, he got dizzy. He grabbed a pipe, and sat down quickly on an above-ground tank.

☥ ☥ ☥

Thirty minutes into the search, a Norfolk police officer found David's vehicle. "It's in a cul-de-sac fifteen minutes from here," Lincoln explained as Kit got in his car. "We'll be there in a flash."

The car, undamaged, sat parked in a residential neighborhood overlooking an industrial park next to the rail yards. "Dust it for prints," Kit said to some uniformed officers. "I want to know if anyone but David has been fooling with it." She shined her flashlight inside. No blood. Thankfully. She turned to Lincoln. "So where could he be?" The strain was evident in her voice.

"Does he have a girlfriend around here?" asked one unsuspecting cop.

Kit shot him a look. He closed his mouth.

"Let's look around," Lincoln said. "C'mon, Kit."

Flashlights in hand, they began looking through front yards and into backyards. A few dogs barked. A light switched on. Then Lincoln spotted the gap between houses.

"Look here." Beyond the gap was a weedy hill, and at the bottom, a fence and an industrial area. "Would he go down there?"

"If he was chasing somebody, he'd go anywhere," Kit responded.

"Why would he chase somebody without backup?" Lincoln asked.

"Because he's David."

Lincoln laughed. "Some people have heart attacks, others give them."

Two Norfolk police cars pulled up behind them. They turned to look at them. Tom Packer got out of one. The other was a K-9 unit. "I thought this might help." He motioned with his head at the other car.

Packer, being not only cooperative but helpful? "Thank you, Tom," Kit said, masking her surprise.

The officer's large black and tan German shepherd climbed out of the back. The officer brought him over. "You have anything of the suspect's?" he asked.

"It's not a suspect, it's a police officer," Kit responded.

"In that case, I'll keep Caesar on leash."

"Good idea," Lincoln said. "This is his car." He gestured toward the unmarked cruiser.

"Is it open?"

"Let's see." Lincoln opened the driver's door.

The handler, whose name was A. Jensen according to his name badge, walked the shepherd all the way around David's car, then directed him into the front, tapping on the driver's seat to get the dog's attention. "What's the officer's name?"

"David O'Connor." Kit's throat was tight.

Jensen stopped. "Coach? You're kidding!"

Kit's eyes widened. "You know him?"

"You bet." The handler gave the dog one more good sniff, then he commanded him to "sook," search.

✞ ✞ ✞

David sat on the above-ground tank, feeling oddly detached. The night air was chilly, and with his shirt off, he felt cold. He needed to move, but he didn't want to. He just wanted to sit and stare at the stars pricking the night sky with their silver light.

Kit. He had to get up for Kit. He shook his head to clear the cobwebs. Wow, that hurt. Then he lurched to his feet. Dizzy. Again. Kit. He had to find Kit. *Do it. Walk the tracks.* He pushed himself forward.

He only made it about twenty feet when he had to sit down again, this time on a concrete box. The shirt around his arm was soaked. He was losing blood. Maybe he should rest. He could sleep, maybe, just for a while.

No. *No! The tracks … follow the tracks.* He lurched to his feet, and stood there for a minute, trying to get his head cleared. Suddenly he saw a brilliant, white light right in front of him. He sat down fast and blinked, hard.

✝ ✝ ✝

Fifty yards down the hill, Caesar alerted on something. Jensen motioned Kit and Lincoln, who were struggling to keep up with the dog team. "This his?" Jensen pointed down to a cell phone on the ground.

Kit snapped on gloves before she picked it up, but she recognized it. "Yes, it's his." She thumbed the screen-on button. "It's either turned off or the battery is dead." No blood on it. That was good.

"So that's why tracking it didn't work!" Lincoln said.

Caesar had taken off again. Kit tucked the cell phone in her pocket and followed. Near the bottom of the hill stood a six-foot chain-link fence that stopped the dog. Jensen threw his flashlight back and forth, looking for an opening.

"You think O'Connor's over there?" Lincoln asked.

Caesar's barking answered that. "I've got wire cutters," Jensen responded, pulling something off of his belt. "They'll leave sharp edges, so be careful following me." He put the dog on a down-stay and began cutting through the fence. Then he bent back the wire. "It's old and rusty. Be careful."

"How did he get past it?" Lincoln asked.

"He went over it."

The chill of the October night cut through Kit as she passed through the fence. Overhead, the night sky was clear and dark. Thank goodness it wasn't raining. Could the dog follow a scent through rain? She followed Lincoln through a maze of massive shipping containers, some stacked two or three high. She heard the dog barking, and emerged from the containers in time to see him open a door to a shed and shine a flashlight in. She quickened her pace.

"Holy smokes," Lincoln said stepping into the shed. He moved aside to make room for her. Debris from old equipment and what looked like a tin roof created a metal jungle. "Things have been thrown in here for years!"

"Look!" Jensen shone his light up to the roof, then down to the metal below.

Kit didn't need an evidence tech to tell her what she was looking at—fresh red blood.

"Look here," Jensen was off again, following a trail of blood on the ground outside of the shed.

Kit hurried after him. Less than two minutes later, she saw the dog start to run. Then she spotted someone sitting on a box next to a pole. David? David!

✝ ✝ ✝

David looked up at the man standing in front of him. "Hey," he said.

Officer Jensen was radioing for an EMT when Kit and Lincoln caught up to him.

"David!" Kit said. "You're all bloody."

"There you are," he responded.

She snapped on fresh gloves. "Lincoln: handkerchief?"

He handed her one.

Carefully Kit began removing the shirt wrapped around David's arm.

"You sure you want to do that?" Lincoln asked.

"Not sure at all." She peered inside the makeshift bandage and quickly re-tied it. "Whoa. Handkerchief isn't going to help that." She looked at Lincoln. "You have a belt?"

"Sure." Lincoln removed it and Kit used it as a tourniquet on David's arm, up near the shoulder.

Kit checked her watch. She'd leave it on for fifteen minutes. Hopefully the rescue squad would be on the scene by then. "Where else are you hurt?" she asked David.

"My ankle." He extended his leg.

"It's swollen," Kit confirmed.

"Hey, I saw him," David blinked. "I saw him!"

"Who? The sniper?" Lincoln asked.

"I think so!" David took a breath. "I was chasing him. He

was driving that white van." He gestured up the hill.

"What van? There's no van now."

"It was there. Near my car." David closed his eyes. "'4T238' That's the license plate."

"Good job, good job. What else, man?"

David took a deep breath. "White guy, shorter than me, so maybe five-seven, wiry. But it wasn't Alex."

"Who?"

David dismissed his question with a wave. "Must not have had a handgun, or he would have shot me."

Lincoln pulled out his phone and called that in. "I want a BOLO issued. White van." Then he gave a description of the suspect.

David remembered something. "Hey, Jensen, he dropped something, like a backpack, up there on that hill. When he was running. Can he find it?" He gestured toward Caesar.

"Let me try him." Jensen jogged off with the dog.

David's head sagged forward. Kit sat down next to him and put her arm around him. She could hear sirens approaching. "You okay? Breathe, David. Keep breathing." He rested his head on her shoulder.

Lincoln stood about four feet away, jingling his keys in his pocket. "You did good, man. Help's coming."

CHAPTER 23

THE AIR SEEMED STIFLING IN his room, stifling! Worse than the engine room of the aircraft carrier. Sweat poured off the Hawk's face. How he wished he had a shower. But the small room he was renting in Mabel Grady's house came with a sink and a toilet only. A sink and a toilet and no questions.

He ran cold water in the sink, stripped off his shirt, and wet down a washcloth. Then he wiped his body off, beginning with his head and his face and continuing down across his chest and arms. The hair on his body stood up as the water chilled him. He flopped down on the bed.

It was only then, staring at the ceiling, that he realized the mistake he'd made. His backpack! He'd dropped his backpack running from that cop! If they found it, if they had his backpack, they'd have his prints.

A cold chill swept over him. He leaped to his feet. They could be coming! Now! He began throwing things into a duffel bag, cursing.

Maybe the cop died. Maybe it would take them a while to find him. Maybe nobody would find the backpack.

Maybe. Maybe. Maybe. But he couldn't be sure. And if they captured him before, well, before the killing was over, before the Voice freed him, he'd be cursed! Cursed forever! Never free of the Old Man. Never free.

He had to break away. He'd already switched the plates on the van. But now, he'd have to ditch it. Ditch the van, steal another car ... help, help!

He'd kill that cop if he could find him. Making him lose

his backpack. Making him lose!

Panic. Panic, panic, panic. He walked four paces across the room and four paces back. Four across, four back. Four and four, over and over, but his mind kept racing and his hands kept shaking and ... and ....

Stop. Stop! He forced himself to stop. Stop and think. This was his nest. This was his lair. He was safe here, right? Safe?

But not with the backpack lying on that hillside. He trembled all over. Maybe he could sneak back and ... no, that was stupid. A stupid thought.

Look, he still had his rifle. His rifle and two pistols. He needed to pack those in ... in what? He'd lost his backpack! Stupid, stupid, stupid! His legs jerked. He wanted to pace again, pace again, but he closed his eyes and counted instead. His chin trembled. He got to forty-seven, his favorite number, and opened his eyes. Pillowcase. His pillowcase would do.

So he grabbed it and ripped the pillow out and began stuffing his handguns in, protecting them with T-shirts. Ammo. How much did he have? He checked his drawer, pulled out the boxes that were there, and put them in the pillowcase, too.

What else did he need? Clothes. His passport. What money he had. The bottle of whiskey at the head of his bed. His pills, precious pills. And his box. His memory box. That was it.

When everything was packed, the Hawk slipped out of his room. He checked his watch. Eleven fifteen. The old lady had better be sleeping! He left the house, slid open the door of his van, and stuffed his rifle, his duffle bag, and the pillowcase inside, along with a reusable grocery bag holding his clothes, the whiskey, and the box. The old lady never stirred.

Okay, okay. How to do this? He started the van and drove off slowly.

But what if? His mind raced. What if they were already looking for him, looking for the van? What if, what if? Flash, flash—different scenarios flashed through his head.

He had to ditch the van. He had to get another vehicle.

He had to be … elusive.

At night, with fewer cars on the road, he'd be more conspicuous. But in the daytime! Wow, the traffic. He could blend in. So, brilliant! He'd ditch the van. Steal an inconspicuous nothing little car, and hit the road. Not Route 13. They'd pick him off on that twenty-mile stretch of openness across the Chesapeake Bay Bridge-Tunnel. No. He'd go 64 or maybe 664, up through Portsmouth. Depending on …

Wait!

If he ran, he couldn't complete the job. He couldn't end the terror.

But what if …

What if he could draw them to him. How could he do that?

Another shooting?

He had a better idea. Maybe he could use Miss Fedora herself.

He needed her. He could use her. It was only right.

First, he had to sleep. He knew a place off the Lafayette River, a place he could hide the van in the bushes, sleep some, then push it in the water. They'd never find it. Never! He'd steal a car from the neighborhood, and then escape, hidden in plain sight in mid-morning traffic. Then, he'd get Miss Fedora.

Perfect. Perfect. He reached in his pocket and pulled out a bottle. Prescription sleep aids. And roofies. Yes, he had them. Perfect.

ⴕ ⴕ ⴕ

Fourteen stitches, a tetanus shot, a couple of X-rays, and an ankle brace later, David was patched up. "Now, let's go get my car," he said to Kit.

"You won't need your car. Not for a while. Come on, I'll take you home."

"No way. Kit, this is hot now!"

She rolled her eyes. "Somebody once told me that there were three hundred other officers that could work that case. You need to take care of yourself. Your body needs to remake all that blood you lost."

He pressed his lips together.

But she was right. He fell asleep in the car on the way home. Kit helped him into the house and he collapsed again once Kit got him into his own bed.

That's when Kit noticed the box in his bedroom, addressed to her, care of David. Her heart took a double beat when she read the return address. Her mother's.

What had her mother sent her?

It was three in the morning. Kit wanted to go back to the office, but now she was curious. All those years she'd never opened a single letter, a single card her mother had sent her. She'd kept them all in a box, a memorial to her abandonment, an altar for her anger. But now, for some reason she felt drawn to this package.

She carried the box out to David's kitchen. Finding a knife, she cut through the packing tape and pulled the box open. Inside was tissue paper, then something else ...

A quilt. She pulled it out. She spread it over David's couch so she could see it better.

It was not just any quilt, it was an art quilt, a beautifully designed picture wrought in fabric.

The background fabric was off-white dotted with tiny blue stars. On it was appliquéd a rough map of the United States in blue. The profile of a woman's face, peach colored, formed the coastline of the State of Washington. Her eyes were closed. Her long blonde hair flowed down over the Rockies, the Mississippi, the Midwest, the Appalachians, and curled around Hampton Roads. Other national icons were represented: the cacti of the desert southwest, the St. Louis Arch, New York skyscrapers, and so on. And the woman's eyes shed red, heart-shaped tears that followed the trail of her hair, swirling across the journey her mother had taken, and clustering around the coast of Virginia, Kit's home.

The backing, in the same blue as the map, held a signature block with her mother's name, the date, and a Scripture reference: Isaiah 49:15-16. The design, the construction, the handwork spoke of someone who was, indeed, an artist.

Kit grabbed her phone, opened the Bible app, and found the verses: *Can a woman forget her nursing child, that she should have no compassion on the son of her womb? Even these may forget, yet I will not forget you.*

Stunned, Kit began to weep. Gathering the quilt in her arms, she collapsed on the couch and held it close.

David must have heard her. He appeared in the doorway, his eyes scanning the scene. Kit grabbed a tissue and blew her nose. "I'm all right," she said, sniffing.

He hobbled to her and she moved the quilt so he could sit down. He took her in his arms. "What's going on?"

"I'm sorry I woke you up," she said.

"No, no, it's fine. This was in the box?"

She nodded. She stood and stretched her arms wide, holding the quilt so he could see it.

"It's beautiful!"

"Yes." She sat back down and nestled up against him.

"Something's changed," he said softly.

"In that pond, I was so close to death, and so close to God at the same time. I see, now, that ..." Her voice trailed off into tears.

"That's okay," he said, "we'll talk later."

✞ ✞ ✞

David woke up at five-thirty. He sat propped up on the couch. Kit was asleep in his arms, wrapped in her mother's quilt. Perfect, he thought. Thank you, God.

Trying to move as little as possible, he checked his phone.

Good old Lincoln. He'd kept him updated with texts throughout the night.

Retrieved backpack.

Checking for prints on pack and items inside.

Prints found and identified.

2 a.m. BOLO issued for a "person of interest," Henry Raymond Hardison, 42.

So, they had a suspect. Great!

✞ ✞ ✞

Half an hour later, Kit stirred. She opened her eyes, realized she was leaning on David, and sat up. "Oh, David! I didn't mean to fall asleep. Was I hurting you, lying on you like that?"

He grinned. "Not hardly."

"What time is it? I need to get to work."

"Lincoln's handling it." He showed her the text messages on his phone. "How about I scramble us up some eggs?"

"No, I'll do that. You need to stay off your feet. You can call Lincoln while I get breakfast."

Over eggs, David updated her. Hardison wasn't at his last known address, which was logical, because his ex-wife lived there. She confirmed he was an obsessive compulsive control freak whose life had recently begun falling apart. They divorced four years ago. Then two years ago, Hardison had received a general discharge from the Navy for insubordination. Recently, she'd had a protective order issued against him. And he was forbidden to see their children.

Precipitating incidents? Yeah, you bet.

"Give me fifteen minutes to get dressed," David said, "and we can go in."

"We? No, you're supposed to rest," she replied.

He argued, but when he bent over to tie his shoes, he got dizzy.

"Please, stay here and take care of yourself. We'll keep you in the loop."

Reluctantly, David agreed.

✝ ✝ ✝

He had to sleep; he had to sleep! Why couldn't he sleep? He'd pulled the van behind some bushes next to the Lafayette River. No one could see him from the road. The day had turned out cool and cloudy. Few people would be out on the water. If they saw the van, they'd assume he was fishing.

He had it all planned. But now, he couldn't sleep.

Frustrated, he left the van, walked to a fast food place, picked up a burger and fries, and then walked back. He consumed the food, sitting on a rock, staring out over the river. Stupid people. Stupid people and their stupid ways.

All of his phones were in his backpack. So stupid! So he'd bought three more at a convenience store, his baseball cap pulled low to elude the security cameras. Now, with his belly full, he could make his phone call. That would relieve some tension. He could almost hear his mother saying, "That's one of your crazy ideas." Yeah, but look where his crazy ideas had gotten him! Front page news all over the country. Hampton Roads in his control. Crazy? Ha!

✝ ✝ ✝

Kit stood in front of her white board, staring at the map she'd posted on it, and the trail that had led to suspect Henry Raymond Hardison. He'd been found in a geo profile red zone. Where would he go next? That was the big question.

She heard a noise and looked up as Lincoln walked in with a fifty-something guy dressed in a gray suit, white shirt, and red tie. Then she realized it was FBI Director Joseph D. Prather and his entourage.

Lincoln looked almost casual, in his khaki cargo pants and golf shirt, standing next to the director. How strange.

Kit stepped back as the director stopped in front of the board. "Impressive," he said. "Show me the investigative flow."

"Sir, Special Agent McGovern here would be the best one to do that," Lincoln said.

The director turned to her and smiled. "McGovern? Ah, yes. I've heard about you."

Kit cocked her head. Prather's piercing gray eyes were edged with amusement. "Sir?"

"That human trafficking case. My friend Steve Gould said you were right on top of that."

Friend Steve Gould? Kit had a sudden feeling Special Agent in Charge Samuel L. Jones was in deep trouble. "Yes, sir, thank you."

"Explain this to me." He gestured toward the white board.

She spent the next ten minutes summarizing three weeks of investigation.

"Geo profiling. I like that," Prather said. "So what's next?"

"Sir, that's up to Agent Sheffield, but if it were me, I'd have extra security at the tunnels and major freeways. I think that's how this guy is traveling. I'd flood the media with pictures of him and send uniforms in to question anyone they can find."

"Makes sense."

"And one more thing, sir: I'd have every report of a stolen car in Norfolk sent straight over here, because I think he's going to dump that van."

Lincoln raised his eyebrows.

Prather looked at him. "You agree?"

He cleared his throat. "Yes, sir. It's a plan."

† † †

David stretched out on his bed, listening to the police scanner, trying to rest. He kept going over the events of the night before. The chase especially. What else could he remember about this guy?

Frankly, a lot of it from after he fell through the roof was foggy. But that wasn't the important part.

He could see the van in his mind's eye. He could see that dog collar hanging on the rear view mirror and something else—food wrappers?—on the front passenger seat. The rear seats had been pulled. That's right. The rest of the van was empty, like maybe the guy could sleep in there.

Or shoot from there.

He called Kit.

"Okay, David," she responded. "I'll pass that along."

"Anything new?"

"Not really," Kit said. "Are you resting?"

"Absolutely."

"Try to sleep."

No way could he sleep. "Yeah, I will."

He hung up with Kit. He didn't have his city car and his own car had been wrecked. That left him isolated. Kit probably wanted it that way—she'd made no offers to get his city car back to him.

Then, he had a thought. Packer. Kit would never suspect he'd ask Packer for a favor.

He called Packer's cell. "Hey, man, thanks for coming up with that K9 idea. It might have been bad if he hadn't found me so quickly."

Packer muttered something. David wondered if he knew he was being investigated for alcohol use. Had he thought how David's testimony might impact that? "I need another favor," David said.

Three minutes later, Packer had agreed to get David's police car delivered to his house.

† † †

All day long, Kit and the task force chased leads. Then, at eight p.m., Steve Gould walked back into the office. Kit wanted to hug him. He looked good—tan even, like he'd gotten a day or two at the beach. She approached him. "I met your *friend,* Director Prather, a couple of hours ago." She smiled at him.

He lifted his chin. "Same new-agent class." He looked down at a piece of paper and continued. "He's not much for SACs playing politics. Especially with crooked politicians."

Kit wanted to laugh. Sing maybe. Dance. But she stayed professional.

"So update me," Steve said, and so she did. "And where's David now?" he asked.

"At home. In bed. Or at least, sitting with his foot propped up."

Steve got a funny look on his face, but Kit didn't ask what that was all about.

✝ ✝ ✝

When the officer brought David his car later that day, he knocked on the door. "Hey, thanks a lot," David said, taking the keys.

"Sure." The officer started to leave, then turned back. "This your dog?"

Dog? David stepped out onto the front porch. "Annie!" A very dirty yellow Lab wagged leaped toward David. "Thanks, man! Did you find her?" he asked, rubbing Annie's ears.

"She was just lying there on your porch when I came up," he said.

"She's been missing," David said. "Hey, thanks for bringing the car!"

"You bet, man."

Thankfully, the cop turned to go before he could see the tears in David's eyes. "Where have you been?" he asked the dog as he ran his hands over her, checking for injuries. Thank God, Annie was home!

She appeared to be unhurt. So he put the dog in the shower and cleaned her up, then he found some food for her —some hamburger mixed with leftover vegetables.

With his ankle aching, he sat down on his couch and propped his leg on the coffee table. Annie jumped up on the couch and curled up next to him, resting her head on his leg. He texted Kit the good news, then leaned his head back. For a moment, life felt almost normal.

✞ ✞ ✞

Piper Calhoun sat in her fancy motel room imagining what it would be like to live like this all the time. To be on the road. She'd always wanted to be an investigative reporter, traveling across the nation, reporting on the big stories. She could imagine herself living out of a suitcase, dining in ethnic restaurants, sitting at a bar late at night with a cop she was interviewing.

The ringing of her cell phone jarred her out of her daydreams. She checked the call ID and froze: it was him.

The man's voice, though distorted, still was littered with expletives: "Report this: They think they know. They don't know! They'll never know! I have stopped the clock, and I can start it again. I am the Hawk. I killed time and I will kill again. I am the predator. You are the prey. No one can stop me except the Voice. Now I'm gone. I will be back. Someday."

"Okay," Piper said cautiously. "I should be able to get that in. Not for tomorrow…"

"Yes! Tomorrow! Tomorrow! Or more will die."

Piper checked her watch. Eight forty-five. She could make the deadline if she tried. "Okay, I'll try. Don't get your shorts in a wad!" That probably wasn't smart. It just came to mind.

The guy laughed. Maniacally. And hung up.

Piper rose. Cara was in the bathroom. Getting ready to take a shower. Probably she should tell her.

Certainly she wouldn't.

✞ ✞ ✞

"How odd!" Kit said. Several members of the team were clustered around the recorder at the task force office, listening to the call Piper had received.

"Sounds delusional," Candace said.

"Yeah, what's this stuff about 'the Voice,'" Lincoln asked.

"He may be hearing voices. He seems to think he is, anyway."

"Do you think he's really gone?" Kit asked. "Out of the area?"

"I doubt it."

"Would you call that demonic?" Lincoln asked. "That stuff about the Voice?"

Candace didn't respond, and Kit hesitated. Spiritual warfare was not her area of expertise. An awkward silence followed. "I don't know," Kit said finally.

Candace spoke. "I think it's time to update our profile. I want to consult with someone else on this, but I think it's safe to say that our suspect is panicking and experiencing psychotic breaks. He's never been more dangerous than he is right now."

CHAPTER 24

PIPER TRIED TO THINK: HOW could she get this story in? This exclusive, exciting, over-the-top story? Who was on duty as night editor? Was it someone she could trust? Jared. Jared Thomas. Oh, no way. If she was ever going to blow this town, her work had to be great. Awesome-sauce. And Jared's idea of awesome was limited to getting "only" in the right place.

That wasn't going to cut it. She had to get into the office herself. Had to make the story soar. Maybe, just maybe, her collection of stories would be Pulitzer material!

Up until now, she'd been emailing her articles in. But this one? Not this one! No. She wanted her fingerprints all over this. She had to be sure what she wrote got in exactly the way she'd written it. She had to guarantee it.

Cara was in the shower, and up until now, Piper had avoided making an appearance with her at the office. Police protection was embarrassing and unnecessary. She'd never hear the end of it from the other reporters. Worse, they might question her "collusion with authorities."

Piper's mind raced. The shower cut off. She sat down on the couch, and when Cara emerged ten minutes later, dressed in sweats and a T-shirt, drying her hair with a towel, Piper made sure her groans were audible.

"Hey, what's wrong?" Cara asked.

"Oh, nothing," Piper said, curling into a ball.

"Are you in pain?"

"It's just … just an ovarian cyst. It happens now and then."

"Oh, no! Can you take something for it?"

"Meds. But they're back at my apartment." Piper put on her best sad puppy face.

"Well, let me call and find out who's watching your place." She turned to go to her room.

She's getting her phone! Piper thought. "Wait," she said. "There's a CVS two doors down from here. Any chance you could just go get some Midol?" Piper had to come up with something Cara may not have herself. She groaned again. "Midol and … and a Coke. That will help so much—and it would be a lot quicker!" She smiled weakly.

"Sure. I can do that. Let me grab my purse."

Three minutes later, Cara, her hair still wet, was out the door. Piper scribbled a note: *Sorry to ditch you. Had to meet a police-shy source. Back in a bit.* She laid it on the coffee table and waited to hear the elevator motor grind on its trip downstairs. Two minutes later, she grabbed her purse and her tote bag and took off.

Why had she brought her tote bag? Her notes were in her purse. Duh!

Too late to go back. But she didn't want to leave it visible in the car. Too many busted windows lately in that area. Junkies looking for anything they could sell. She sure didn't want to have to deal with that. Not right now!

She got to the office in record time. Tossing her tote bag in the trunk, she hurried inside.

✟ ✟ ✟

At ten that night, David's phone rang.

"O'Connor, this woman you asked me to babysit? She's gone!"

"What?" David sat up. Cara was steamed.

Cara, lacing the story with swear words, told him what had happened.

"No sign of forced entry?"

"No! And she left a note." She read it to him.

"So, did you check outside the building?"

"Of course I did. She's not there."

"How long has she been gone?"

"An hour."

And you're just now calling me, David thought. His mind

started cataloguing the possibilities. "Did you try the newspaper?"

"No one answered. Plus, she's already filed her story for tomorrow. We talked about it. So why would she go there?"

"Okay, okay, look. You wait there. I'll be there shortly. With any luck, she'll have come back."

A little voice told David he should just tell Kit and let her or Lincoln handle it. But no. He was so restless. No way could he just stay home. Piper was his problem.

He changed into tactical pants and a golf shirt. His ankle was still too swollen for boots, so he rewrapped the Ace bandage, reapplied the brace, and slid into his most supportive athletic shoes. He checked his gun and ammunition. His department-issued shotgun would be in his car. He was going to be ready for whatever happened.

He found a mixing bowl and filled it with water for Annie. "I'll be back," he said to her. Hopefully, wrangling that crazy reporter wouldn't take all that.

☥ ☥ ☥

Mission accomplished. Piper shifted her story to "editing" then stood over Jared's desk, watching to make sure he didn't destroy it. When he sent it to on to pagination, she dawdled at her desk. When the page went to press, she finally relaxed. Yes.

Shutting down her computer, she waved goodnight to Jared and walked out of the newsroom. A chill in the dark October night made her question her decision not to bring a jacket. She walked hurriedly to her old Chevy. Didn't the Pulitzer come with some money? Maybe she could afford a new car!

Cara was going to kill her. Oh, well. She'd told David she didn't want anyone staying with her. She put the key in the car door. Then her eyes widened as a hand came over her mouth, and some hard object jammed into her ribs.

☥ ☥ ☥

At 11 p.m., a night-duty agent learned that SAC Samuel L. Jones had been "promoted" to a special assistant position at FBI Headquarters in Washington, which he would begin immediately. One of Director Prather's deputy directors would temporarily lead the Norfolk office. That juicy bit of gossip had just reached the task force when they also got word that a uniformed officer canvassing a neighborhood in the red zone area happened to knock on the door of one Mabel Grady. Indeed, she did know the man in the picture the officer showed her.

The buzz at the office would have pegged the meter had there been one. "You want to go see this guy's room?" Lincoln said, bursting into the geo profiling room.

Jones was gone. "Yes!" Kit slid into her tactical vest.

The room was dirty and dank. Built as an addition onto a 1940s-era house, it looked more like a shed than human habitation. A mattress on the floor, a sink and toilet in the corner, and an old dresser comprised the decor.

"Wow," Kit said, stepping in behind Lincoln.

"You called it, though. It's right in the middle of one of your red zones."

The evidence response team was already dusting for prints. "Let's get out of their way," Kit said. "I'd like to talk to the landlady."

Mabel Grady wasn't too happy having her late-night TV infomercial interrupted. "You tell him he owes me rent when you catch him," she said.

"How much has he been paying you?" Kit asked.

"Fifty a week. Been late every time."

"What's he like?"

"Charles?"

"Is that his name?" Kit asked.

"Yeah. Charles Bettcoe. You should'a known that."

Kit glanced at Lincoln, who was writing the alias down. "So what is Charles like?"

"Quiet. That's all I care about. I don't want no loud parties or nothing going on."

In that room? Kit blinked.

"When's the last time you saw him?" Lincoln asked.

The woman looked up at the ceiling. "Let's see. Maybe Sunday. He seemed mad about something. I got out of his way."

"Was he ever violent?"

"With me, no. I've got no complaints. 'Cept about being late with rent. A day late, every time." She glanced toward the people moving in and out of the back room. "I'm guessing he's gone for good. Lemme know when I can get the rest of his stuff outta there. Clean, maybe. I got to put an ad up at the grocery store."

Kit shifted her weight. "Mrs. Grady, when he rented the room, did he give you references?"

"He gave me fifty bucks a week. Cash. That was the beginning and the end of it."

"Conversation over," Kit said as she and Lincoln walked away. Overhead, clouds shrouded the stars and the moon. Kit rubbed her arms in the chill. "Our problem is, where has he gone?"

"I've got people on the bridges and the interstates. Every white van is getting stopped."

"But he'd know that, right? So how's he avoiding it?"

"That's one place all the water around here helps. It's hard to leave Norfolk without using an interstate or a bridge."

"Exactly. So I think he's laying low. We need to check relatives, friends, anybody who might put him up."

"He may steal a car, like you said."

"Right. That, too." Kit tapped her lip. "Trouble is, he could steal a car in the middle of the night and get out of Norfolk before the owner even knew it was gone." She looked at Lincoln. "This is still going to be hard."

"We'll have to coordinate closely with jurisdictions outside Norfolk, and the Virginia State Police. We can do this, Kit! We can do it," he said. Then he smiled at her. "If you'll just tell me how."

☦ ☦ ☦

"Who are you and what do you want with me?" Piper yelled as the man secured her hands with plastic strip ties.

"You know who I am."

The man shoved her into the back seat of her own car. It was littered with old newspapers, a magazine or two, fast-food wrappers, and water bottles. The thought occurred to Piper that she might want to clean out her car sometime.

Still, her reporter's eye started cataloguing some details. He was short, five-six or seven, wiry, with dark hair that hung over his ears and collar. He smelled funny and she wondered what mixture of alcohol, drugs, and sweat would produce that odor.

"I need you," he said, his breath foul in her face, "to write my story. That's what you do, right? You write. Nothing more."

"Yes," Piper said. "I'm a reporter."

He started to stuff her mouth with a bandanna. Piper panicked. "Stop! I'll be quiet. I promise!"

He looked at her skeptically.

"It'll make me throw up. You don't want to ride in a car smelling of vomit, do you?" She smiled weakly at him.

His eyes narrowed. "You lie there and be quiet, and nothing will happen. You move, you try to get attention, I'll kill you with my own hands." He wrapped his hands around her throat to emphasize the point.

Fear pulsed through her. He was surprisingly strong. "Okay, okay!" she said. "I'll … I'll just lie here."

She wiggled to get as comfortable as she could, dislodging a half-empty water bottle. Outside the car, she saw the man going through her purse. He found her cell phone and she saw him toss it. Then he slid into the driver's seat. Oh man, she thought, what a story this is going to be!

✟ ✟ ✟

David sped over to the extended-stay hotel where he'd set Piper up. Cara was fit to be tied. Pacing. Angry. David got her to calm down enough to tell the story from beginning to end.

"Did you hear the call she got from this alleged source?"

"No, I was in the shower."

"Okay," he said when she finished. "You stay here. I'll go to the newspaper."

Crazy Piper. What would she do next? He drove to the *Norfolk Times* building. The thought crossed his mind again that he should call Kit. Or Lincoln, maybe.

No. He felt fine. No reason to distract them.

Most of the newspaper building was dark. David checked his watch: 11:15. There had to be someone in the building. David hobbled over to the only window showing any light. He tapped on the glass. He tapped harder. Finally someone peered out. A young man. David held up his badge. The guy motioned toward a door.

"Yeah, she was here," Jared Thomas told David, after explaining he was just wrapping up for the evening.

"When did she leave?"

"About half an hour ago," Jared replied.

"Was she meeting with someone?"

Jared frowned. "Not that I know of."

"She filed a story for tomorrow, right?"

"Yeah, she did." Jared yawned. He neglected to mention it was her second story of the day. "Look, if there's nothing else …"

David took a deep breath. "Can I have your number? In case I think of something?"

Jared gave it to him, and David turned to leave. "One more thing," he said, turning back. "What does she drive?"

David called Cara after leaving the newspaper office. Of course, she had no good news for him. Piper hadn't come back. And she was still steamed. "Listen, do me a favor, will you? She drives a Chevy Spark. Red. See if you can find out her license plate number. And get someone to ping her phone."

Not knowing what else to do, he drove back home. Piper was going to get an earful from him when she finally showed up.

✞ ✞ ✞

The Norfolk Police Department reported an average of five vehicles stolen every day. Kit stood in the task force office, trying to figure out how to process that information and turn it into something usable. "We've got to put BOLOs out on every vehicle stolen until we find this guy," she murmured out loud.

Candace stood nearby. "Would he try to use public transportation?"

"He couldn't get on an airplane, hopefully. So that would leave buses." She turned to Chase Carter. "We've alerted TSA, right? He's on the no-fly list?"

"Yes. We did that as soon as we had a name."

"All right. Contact the bus companies as well. He'd have to go to Newport News to get on a train, but it wouldn't hurt to alert Amtrak."

"Got it."

"He's been great," Kit said to Candace as she watched Chase walk away.

"Kit, you get some rest. Chase and I will track the information coming in."

Kit eyed her. Rest sounded good, but she didn't want to miss anything. "Especially the stolen cars?"

"Yes, especially the cars."

✞ ✞ ✞

"Look, I'll write your story," Piper said, "but I want some coffee first."

The guy looked at her like she was crazy.

She was sitting in the back seat of her car, her back propped up against the passenger side door, her reporter's notebook in her hand. At gunpoint, she'd managed to find several half-filled ones under the seat, after insisting he free her hands. "I want coffee. It's late!" she pointed out when he hesitated. "There's a drive-thru two blocks ahead, on the right. Vente, black."

He cursed, but he did what she asked.

"While you're at it, see if they have a chocolate croissant. I'm hungry, too."

After getting the coffee and the croissant, he drove her to a place near some water. Piper didn't quite recognize it, but she had the feeling she wasn't far from ODU. In fact, she realized, she was close to David O'Connor's house. Maybe she'd see him!

Oh, he'd be so mad.

The man pulled up behind a white van. Piper made note of the license plate and make. No way could she guess the van's year. "Okay, let's get started," she said as cheerfully as she could. She had to write his story before he'd let her go. Already she was trying to decide if it would be serialized or one big spread. "First of all, what's your name?"

The man reclined the driver's seat a little, like he was tired. "I am the Hawk," he began, and Piper started scribbling notes.

✞ ✞ ✞

At 1 a.m., with no sign of Piper, David decided he really had to alert the task force that she had gone MIA. Should he call Kit?

No, he decided. He'd just go in. Better to deal with this in person.

"You stay here," he told Annie, after letting her out briefly. Frankly, she seemed exhausted. Before he was out the door, she was curled up on his couch.

☩ ☩ ☩

Oddly, the coffee she was drinking seemed to be making her sleepier, not more awake. Piper yawned and scratched her head. "Okay, where were we?" She squinted at her notebook.

The Hawk turned and looked at her.

"What? I'm tired!" she said. "Why don't we finish this tomorrow?" Her words seemed to slur. Weird.

"Yeah," the man said.

Piper nestled down on the seat and drifted into sleep.

CHAPTER 25

KIT SLEPT FOR A FEW hours, then got up. When she walked into the task force conference room she was surprised to see David bent over some maps with Lincoln. What was David doing here? She thought he was at home. "David?"

He looked up when he heard her voice. She saw him wince as he put weight on his ankle. She frowned at him.

"Guess what? Piper's missing." Lincoln said.

"What?"

David told her the story. "At first, I thought she'd actually gone to meet a source," he said. "I could see her doing that. Now," he checked his watch, "it's 3:15 and I'm not so sure."

"Why didn't you call and let us know?"

"I'm the one who brought her into this. I thought I should deal with her."

Kit sat down. "What are we doing to find her?"

He filled her in. "Her cell phone pinged near the newspaper office, but the unis couldn't find it. I'm wondering if she just accidentally left it at her desk."

"Well, that would be stupid, since we've tapped that phone," Kit said. "Did she get her story in? About the phone call?"

"Paper won't be here 'til about four-thirty," Lincoln said.

David leaned forward. "Wait, what?"

Kit realized they hadn't told him what they'd heard via the tap. "She got this weird phone call around 8:45." She filled him in.

"Wow. I wish I'd known that. It puts a different spin on it."

"What?" Lincoln asked.

"Well, look. She gets a call from the guy demanding a story. Her deadline is probably, what, 11? Ten-thirty, maybe? So she's in a time crunch, so she runs over to the newspaper …"

"Wait—why not just write the story and email it in? Hasn't she been doing that?" Kit said.

David hesitated. "She has, but who knows? In fact, Cara told me she'd already emailed one in yesterday, by dinnertime."

"So?"

"So this is color-outside-the-lines Piper we're talking about." He tapped his finger on the table. "The sniper didn't know where she was or that she could email stories in. By demanding space in the next day's paper, he might have been trying to lure her out." He looked at Kit. "And maybe, just maybe, she went into work to do it and he grabbed her."

"Why would the sniper want her?" Kit asked.

"To take her? Use her as a hostage?" Lincoln suggested.

Kit checked something on her phone. "It's here! The online version of the paper has her story. Wait! David, you're right—it has two stories!" She looked at the men. "I think we'd better get a BOLO out on her car."

✝ ✝ ✝

When the reporter snorted in her sleep, Hank "the Hawk" Hardison jerked awake. Good. She didn't rouse. He peered carefully out of the car. No cops. Nearly thirty-two hours and still they hadn't found him.

He knew how to hide! Stupid cops.

What now?

The reporter stirred. The amount of Z he'd given her should make her sleep until eleven at least. Then they'd move. That was the plan.

He rubbed his arms. It was cold now, and he wondered if he dared start the engine so he could get some heat.

He started to reach for the key in the ignition, then heard a noise and froze. A dog stuck its nose out of the woods, sniffed at the tire of the van parked in front of him, and wandered off again. How long could he stay here and not be found? He trembled a little. Was he pressing his luck?

Sudden terror overtook him. What if…? What if …?

Could he give her another Z? He had to! He got out of the car and moved around to the back passenger-side door. Cradling the reporter—what was her name? Piper something?—half upright, he forced the pill down her throat and followed it with a little water. She coughed and sputtered but the pill stayed down.

Now, what to do, what to do? He laid her back down and got back out of the car.

He needed his stuff. His guns. His memory box. His whiskey. They were in the van, and it might be hot.

But this car was a mess. And how would he get away with her in the back seat? The minute she woke up, she was a danger to him.

But he needed her. They weren't finished with the story. His story.

She wasn't very big. And he was strong.

He moved to the rear of the car and opened the trunk. Lots of junk. Nothing hazardous. Nothing she could use as a weapon. No tire iron even. If he put her back here, he could put his stuff, his guns, near him in the back seat. And she would be contained until he needed her again.

The Hawk opened the back passenger side door, lifted her up, and laid her in the trunk. "I hope you can breathe," he said before closing the lid. He sure didn't want a dead body decomposing in the back of the car!

He transferred all his things from the van to her car. He took license plates he'd stolen and replaced the ones on her car. Then he drove the van to a place where there was a short, cleared slope down to the water. He opened the door, slipped the van into Drive, and jumped out.

The van rolled slowly down the slope. It splashed into the water, settled, sputtered, and stalled. But would it sink? Why wouldn't it sink? It sat there, like some giant bobber, taunting him! Hank cursed. But he couldn't wait any longer. He turned and walked away.

♱ ♱ ♱

Early the next morning, Lincoln walked into the task force conference room where Kit and Candace were quietly talking. He plopped a copy of the *Norfolk Times* down on the table. "Are police getting closer?" the headline screamed.

"Are we?" Lincoln asked.

"Something's going to pop," Kit said. "Let's go get breakfast." Someone had supplied the coffee room with bagels and yogurt. "David?"

"Bring me back something," he called. He checked his watch. At 8:30 he was going to call his elderly neighbors and ask them to let Annie out.

✝ ✝ ✝

Piper knew she was uncomfortable and she knew it was dark and she felt like she was moving but where was she? And why?

She felt groggy. Nauseated. She couldn't see a thing, so she reached around to see what she could feel. Fabric. Paper. A fast-food cup with a straw. A tire. What?

A trunk! She was in the trunk of a car! Panicked, she tried to sit up, hit her head on the top of the trunk lid, and laid back down.

Oh my gosh, she could hear him! Hear the sniper. What did he call himself? The Hawk. She searched her memory. Why was she in the trunk? He must have drugged her! That coffee! The more she drank, the sleepier she felt. Oh, man!

Whose car was she in? Had to be hers. In the dark, she found a long, slim reporter's notebook. Oh, and some clothes —her jeans and a bra she'd grown tired of wearing one day.

Then she felt something that triggered a memory—a tote bag. Wait! Her tote bag. The one she was using the day ...

She rustled through it and yes! Her hands found it. The burner phone Detective O'Connor had given her! The one she'd refused to carry in case they were tracking it. It was in the tote bag she'd tossed in the trunk. Yes!

✝ ✝ ✝

David had spread a map of Norfolk and vicinity out in front of him on the table. He'd marked from memory Kit's red zones, highlighting the area in which he'd spotted the sniper. Then he tried to imagine how he would get out of there if he wanted to elude police, using a highlighter to mark his ideas.

He paused.

It was fairly useless, not knowing where he was starting from. Would he hide in a red zone? Had he already left Hampton Roads?

David didn't want to think about that. So, he concentrated on studying the interstates and connecting roads leading out of the Norfolk area. His phone rang at eight-thirty. He didn't recognize the number. "O'Connor."

"David! Detective O'Connor!" a voice whispered.

He stood up, his adrenaline pumping. "Who is this?"

"Piper!"

"Where are you? What's all that noise?" A roar in the background made it difficult to hear. He pressed his right ear closed.

"I'm in the trunk!"

"The trunk? What trunk?"

"I'm in *my* trunk."

"Why? Who's driving?"

"*He's* driving! The sniper!"

David started moving toward where Kit and the others had gone. "Are you sure?"

"I can hear him cursing. And singing. Ow!"

"What's wrong?"

"Bump."

"Where's he headed?"

"I don't know!"

"Okay, okay. Stay calm. They're monitoring your calls, remember?"

"Not on this phone!"

David looked at his caller ID again. "What phone is this?"

"That burner you gave me."

"Okay, okay. Look. I've got the number. I'll get them on it. Don't panic. Stay calm. We'll find you. Is it your car, for sure?"

"Yes, my car. And Detective? I don't feel so good."

ቿ ቿ ቿ

"Call me back in a few minutes, Piper." David clicked off his phone, wrote down her number, and hobbled as fast as he could to where Kit, Lincoln, and Candace stood drinking coffee. "Kit! Piper's in her trunk!"

"She's what?" Kit said, trying to process his words.

"She just called me." He held up his phone. "The sniper has her in her trunk. He's driving somewhere."

"What do we do?" Lincoln said.

Kit thought she could hear panic in his voice.

"I told her to call me back in a few minutes," David said. "She's on a burner."

That made tracking it harder. "Okay," Kit said, getting into gear, "we need a tap on your phone and we need to triangulate on hers."

"Got it!" David hobbled off.

"Chase," Kit said, "go with him!"

Candace had the Hampton Roads map projected on the SmartBoard. Kit looked at Lincoln. "We need an alert to go out to all task force members and participating agencies. State Police as well. We need eyes open for Piper's car. You have the details on that?"

Lincoln nodded.

"You get that going and then come back. When we start to get a signal on the phone she's using, we can narrow down the search area."

Lincoln started to move. She stopped him. "Every officer needs to be told not to shoot at the car. Piper's in the trunk. We want to protect her. No shooting. It doesn't work anyway in most cases."

He nodded and left.

"How would you leave Hampton Roads if you were trying to elude police?" Candace mused, staring at the map.

"By helicopter," Kit said, her voice dripping with sarcasm. "Traffic's a mess. Always."

✞ ✞ ✞

Curses on Norfolk traffic! An accident in the Midtown Tunnel had the Hawk sitting in stopped traffic on 337. Stopped traffic. Anyone could recognize him.

That stupid reporter. His face was on the front page of the *Norfolk Times*! The front page! His *face*! Who gave her the right to do that?

He shielded his now-public face from the guy in the car next to him, propping his elbow on the window frame and resting his head in his hand. C'mon, c'mon! His knee bounced uncontrollably. He glanced over. The man was on his cell phone! Was he calling the cops?

The Hawk saw an opportunity to exit. He turned right, then swiftly moved through neighborhood streets, working his way back to 26th Street, which he took to Lafayette, then Chesapeake, then Norview.

So far so good. Now, onto 64 … Oh, no! No! Two police cars sat at the entrance ramp. Swiftly he cut right, into a residential neighborhood and wound his way through those unsuspecting streets.

✞ ✞ ✞

David and Lincoln returned minutes later. David had on his ballistic vest. "Really?" Kit said, giving him the eye.

"I got her into this."

"She got herself into this. Has she called you back?"

"No."

"Lincoln, you're in charge. How do you want to proceed?"

"Honestly? I want to be out there. I want to see this guy go down."

"Somebody's got to stay here."

The door opened. Steve and three other task force members hurried in. "What's up?"

Kit deferred to Lincoln. He updated the newcomers.

Steve stroked his chin and walked toward the projected map. "He'd be an easy target on 13," he said, pointing to the twenty-mile long Chesapeake Bay Bridge-Tunnel. "If he knows this area, he won't go that way."

An officer from Suffolk chimed in. "To get to the Monitor-Merrimac Bridge Tunnel, I-664, he'd have to head west first. That's a long way."

"I-460 is a possibility," Steve said, "but there's a lot of cross streets on that route and a lot of deputies in between Norfolk and Richmond."

That left the infamous and perpetually jammed Hampton Roads Bridge Tunnel.

Lincoln took a deep breath. "I want to go out there. Steve, you know these roads better than most of us. Would you be willing to coordinate from here?"

"Yes."

Kit felt resentment begin to stir. Was she being relegated to desk duty? A support role?

Lincoln turned to her. "Would you come with me? I'll drive. I'm the least familiar with this area, but if you'll navigate and help me figure out how to take this guy down, I think we can do this thing. And I think I'll learn a lot."

"All right!"

David stared at his phone. "Right now," he said, "the HRBT is green. No delays. If he takes that tunnel, he could run up I-64, or even follow Route 17 up toward Gloucester. I'll get on the other side and coordinate a chase team if he comes that way."

The other two nodded.

Steve took over. "Okay, Lincoln, you and Kit stay loose, over here, near the intersection of I-64 and I-264. That'll give you some options and let you get behind him if he heads to the HRBT. We'll have a third team over here, where I-464 comes in," he pointed to an intersection near the Downtown Tunnel, "and a fourth up here in Chesapeake."

Everyone nodded. The Suffolk officer said he'd head up the team in Chesapeake and someone else took the I-464 job.

Meanwhile, Chase, on headphones, was monitoring the scanner. "Patrol officer radioed he was four cars behind a red Chevy, stuck in traffic on 58," Chase reported. "Before he could get close enough to pull him over, the Chevy exited onto 403, but then he saw him on I-264 westbound."

"Has the dispatcher alerted cars in that area?" Kit asked.

"Yes, ma'am, he did. But then the guy ducked down onto some surface streets. They've lost him somewhere around Virginia Wesleyan."

"He'll resurface."

"All right let's go!" David said.

✟ ✟ ✟

The October sun cast soft edges on the day. Sixty degrees going up to seventy. Kit and Lincoln climbed into his SUV and headed for their quadrant. She looked over at him. He was wearing tactical pants and a golf shirt with his ballistic vest and raid jacket overtop. Nothing fancy. He looked ... normal.

Lincoln glanced at her. "Thanks for coming with me." He wore humility well, she thought.

Kit adjusted her seatbelt. Running without lights and siren, it would take them about twenty minutes to get to their assigned location. Steve had assigned someone at the task force office who would support each field coordinator. Chase was her contact. She radioed him with their status.

Meanwhile, the dispatcher was reporting an officer had spotted a red Chevy on Indian River Road. He tried to catch up to him, but the driver turned left and zig-zagged through neighborhood streets.

Another cop saw a red Chevy racing through the parking lot behind strip-mall stores; another spotted him entering an unpaved access road. "I think that's him. He knows this area," the cop said.

But so did the cops, and soon they were in hot pursuit. "Block off the entrance to 64!" Kit radioed.

That was smart, but it didn't stop the Chevy.

✞ ✞ ✞

Fortunately, Hank the Hawk had saved some road dope— amphetamines—for the trip. He was already smarter than the cops; now he'd be smarter and faster, right?

The streets screamed by in a blur. He drove like a man possessed, darting in and out of traffic, his eyes flicking from his rearview mirror to the road ahead and back again. Once he'd lost those last cops in a maze of houses, he decided to ditch the Chevy. But wait—what about the reporter? What if she was waking up? She could be a problem. Nuts. He'd stick with the Chevy.

"I got this," he said out loud. "I got this!"

✞ ✞ ✞

"Suspect is in a dark red Chevy in the vicinity of ... Newtown Road, Newtown Road! Traveling west, no eastbound!"

"Which is it?" Kit muttered.

"C'mon, guys," Lincoln said.

"Regardless, he's east of us. Let's go!"

Lincoln checked his side mirror, ready to pull out into traffic. "Give me directions."

"Take the exit. Then head right!"

David radioed he was in position on the Hampton side of the HRBT. Part of Kit hoped the sniper wouldn't run that way. Part of her knew he would. All this jockeying through surface streets was a feint. He was just trying to throw them off.

"It's going to take more than good police work to stop this

guy," Lincoln said.

"You're right."

"Jericho Road, westbound, red Chevy," an officer reported.

What? That was opposite the way Kit had directed Lincoln.

"Double-check that 28," the dispatcher said. "We had him on Newtown Road."

"I'm seeing a red Chevy, driven by a white male. Now he's northbound, Witchduck Road."

"10-4. Got that."

"We're okay," she said to Lincoln. "He doubled back."

The dispatcher said, "He appears to be headed for 13, the Bridge-Tunnel."

"Take a right up here?" Lincoln said, gesturing toward a sign.

"No way," Kit said to Lincoln. "He's not going that way. He's faking them out. Let's wait ... he'll either double back and take 13 back to I-64, or he'll try taking 60 to the HRBT."

"Okay, what do I do?"

"Pull over. Then we'll be in a position to go either way."

CHAPTER 26

THE HAWK WAS SOARING. HE'D swallowed another bennie and was racing, racing! He felt like he could see cars faster than they could move, and he zig-zagged in and out of traffic on the four-lane road. He saw a cop car ahead at an intersection, took a quick right turn, ran a pattern through a neighborhood, and came out ahead of the cop. Yeah! This was flying! "Route 13, here I come! You can't get me. You'll never get me!" His language devolved and he bounced in his seat, his head spinning as violence spewed from his mouth.

Oh, that felt good! Stupid girl, stupid cops! "In-de-pen-dance Boulevard," he said, laughing at the street sign. Yeah, independence! He was going for the Bay Bridge-Tunnel. Sure he was! Sure!

Traffic ahead! He ran up a right-turn lane then swerved left at the light. He heard brakes squeal behind him. "Don't follow me so close!" he laughed. "Get outta the way!"

They'd be expecting him to turn onto 13. So he did.

But only for a quarter mile. "Let's do this!" he shouted and jerked off 13 onto Pleasure House Road. "Yeah, yeah, yeah!" As he drove under 13 he could hear sirens.

Ha! Not one cop in his rear-view mirror. Not one!

Left on 60, left on 60. Go, go!

☦ ☦ ☦

"We've lost him," an officer reported.

"What? What?" Lincoln hit the steering wheel in frustration.

"Attention all units. 10-29 Dark red Chevy. Suspect last seen on Independence Boulevard. Be advised suspect is armed and dangerous. Hostage may be in the trunk. All units respond."

"He's going for the HRBT," Kit said.

"How do you know?"

"Too many cops between him and freedom. If he makes a dash for the HRBT, he just might make it." She tapped the dashboard. "Let's head that way. I think we can intercept him."

"Red Chevy northbound, on 60, intersection First View Street," an officer radioed.

"He's ahead of us!" Kit said. "Light 'em up!" How did he get ahead? "Let's go, let's go!"

Lincoln raced through town, lights flashing. He was a pretty good driver, Kit thought. They joined up with Route 60 at Little Creek.

Kit peered through her windshield, searching the traffic ahead, as she negotiated the road. Right before the tunnel, she saw him. "I've got him, I've got him! HRBT, westbound!" She gave her location and the description of the car to the dispatcher. "We are a quarter-mile behind. Can we get a spike strip out somewhere?"

That would be difficult, though. The heavy traffic entering the two-lane, one-way tunnel under the James River was dangerous enough without trying to spike a fugitive's tires. What to do? "Who's in the tunnel?" Kit asked.

The dispatcher responded, "No one, yet."

She switched radios. "David? Coming your way!"

"West end is covered!" he responded.

Looking ahead, Kit saw the Chevy swerve into the left lane. The driver of a pickup truck he cut off apparently took offense and began tailgaiting the Chevy. "Look at that!" Kit said. "The black truck is tailgating him," Kit said.

"Oh, good," Lincoln responded. "Road rage with a psychopath."

"He'll get ticked off and do something. Just watch."

Sure enough, seconds later, the Chevy's brake lights lit up. To avoid a collision, the pickup braked and veered left. It hit the Jersey barrier, which became a ramp and launched the pickup over the low guardrail. The truck hit the water with a huge splash.

"One in the water," Kit told the dispatcher.

"Mile marker?"

There was never one when you needed it. "Just off Willoughby Spit," Kit said. "Left side." That would have to do.

☦ ☦ ☦

"Wow, wow!" Hank the Hawk watched in his rearview mirror as the pickup truck went airborne. "I wish I could watch you drown," he said, laughing. "Yeah, yeah! You go, guy! Ride my tail again!"

This was fun, so much fun. The cars in front of him scattered like chickens when they saw him coming. Sometimes he changed lanes just to see if he could fit in a space. He caught nervous looks from passengers and fearful reactions from drivers as he careened down the long causeway to the tunnel. He was flying, flying fifteen feet from the water which stretched out on both sides—the James River, Chesapeake Bay, and Atlantic Ocean all converging into an endless expanse.

Oh, how he hated the Navy. He'd loved it at first, loved the structure, the orders, the uniforms, the commands. And he was good at it, very good. Smarter than his captain. Able to see things the captain couldn't imagine. And that's what got him in trouble. Being too smart.

An eighteen-wheeler lumbered in front of him. He skirted around it, then dodged in front to see what the trucker would do. Blaaaaah! The trucker protested with his horn and Hank the Hawk laughed and swung left again.

Then in his rearview mirror he saw a light. A blue light. Cops. They were catching up to him? Ha! He could handle them.

And then he had an idea, really it was the Voice's idea, that would be fun, so much fun. The timing would have to be just right, the circumstances perfect. But the Voice told him that he could do it, that he should do it, and then it would be over. And he'd be free!

Ahead, Hank saw the open maw of the tunnel. Cars and trucks streamed inside the fifty-year-old tube.

Where was the cop? Hank checked his side mirror. The blue light was maybe a dozen cars behind him, coming up fast. His ears popped as he descended down into the tube. Fluorescent lights gave everything a stark, cold look.

It would drive the cops crazy to be stopped. Blocked. He could see it now—himself driving into the distance and the frustrated cops piled into a bloody mass. Yes!

He slowed to approximate the speed of the rest of the traffic. Fifty-five. Fifty-five and stay alive. Or not.

Wait for it. Wait for it. At the exact bottom of the tunnel grade, Hank swerved right, straight in front of the eighteen wheeler, and then hit the brakes. Blaaaaah! The truck's horn screamed and its brakes locked, screeching against the pavement. Hank sped up to keep out of its way. In his rear-view mirror he saw it swerve as the driver lost control. The cab swung to the left. The truck jackknifed. The huge trailer swung forward.

But it swung a little farther than Hank had anticipated, and it clipped the rear of his car, pushing the rear wheels to the left. The Chevy spun and slammed against the left wall of the tunnel and stopped about forty feet ahead of the truck, which lay crosswise across the tunnel.

Hank cursed, then screamed with fury, then laughed as *bam! bam! bam!* one car after the other plowed into the truck and tunnel traffic came to a complete halt.

ᛏ ᛏ ᛏ

Kit saw the Chevy cut the truck off and saw the truck jackknife. "Watch out!" she yelled.

But Lincoln had it covered. He slammed his brakes. Thank goodness the guy behind them did, too. But she and Lincoln looked on in shock as one vehicle after another plowed into the crosswise tractor-trailer. Another car hit theirs, and their airbags deployed, choking them with white dust. The SUV came to rest in a mass of wrecked cars.

ᛏ ᛏ ᛏ

David sat nose out at the west end of the HRBT, listening and praying, adrenaline coursing through his body in waves, praying for protection for Piper, praying for guidance, praying for Kit. His window was down and the soft October air was a sweet contrast with the noise of the traffic.

Then he heard Kit's voice on the radio, heard she was following the sniper, heard they were headed for the HRBT, so he sat up, alert. He would be ready to intervene in the chase, and cut the guy off. He had five cruisers with him, ready to chase this guy.

His plan was working, until he heard a horrendous noise, almost like an explosion, and Kit's voice reporting the crash came on the radio.

The tunnel was blocked, but where was the suspect? More cars emerged—presumably they were ahead of the crash. But was the sniper? And where was Kit? His heart pounded. His hands twitched on the steering wheel. What should he do?

✝ ✝ ✝

Lincoln's door was jammed. "You okay?" he asked.

"Yeah, you?"

"Yes. Let's go!"

"Grab the shotgun if you can!"

Lincoln crawled over to the passenger side, shoving the air bag out of the way, choking and coughing on the dust. A car was smashed against theirs. There was just enough room to squeeze out. "Can't get the shotgun out!" Lincoln said.

"Come on!"

Kit had her pistol, her backup weapon, and several magazines. She looked around. People were beginning to climb out of their cars. Others were screaming and crying, trapped. She could smell gasoline. What an inferno a fire in the tunnel would create! Fear raced through her. "Go! Run!" she yelled to the people, pointing back up the ramp. "Run!"

What about the sniper? Where was he? She motioned to Lincoln and they moved forward, toward the semi truck, climbing over bumpers and stepping on hoods of cars. As far as she could tell, they were the closest officers to the front of the crashed cars.

Had the sniper gone on through?

David! Had he intercepted him?

She neared the tractor-trailer. She heard yelling. She peered underneath it and saw the red Chevy, smashed up against the side of the tunnel. She motioned Lincoln forward.

Then Kit heard shouting and cursing and then gunfire! *Boom! Boom! Boom!* Three shots! It sounded like cannon fire as it echoed against the tile walls. Kit plastered herself behind a truck wheel and motioned for Lincoln to do the same. She peeked around, and saw a man on the ground. The truck driver? Someone climbed into the Chevy, then she heard the engine trying to turn over. How could she get to a place where she could see?

✝ ✝ ✝

The roar of multiple crashes in the tunnel had David's mind racing. A Virginia Department of Transportation worker jogged over to his car. David had told him who he was and why he was here.

"We've got multiple accidents in the tunnel."

David handed him a clipboard. "Show me."

The man drew the tunnel, drew a truck crosswise at the very bottom, with cars piled up behind it, and then another crash on the up ramp. "People must have panicked, when the saw the accident in their rear-view mirrors. We've got multiple cars involved in that second crash after the tractor trailer. Pedestrians are running up the ramp!"

"I'm looking for a red Chevy."

"Cameras are black and white, but this here vehicle," the man said pointing to a rectangle in front of the wrecked truck, "may be what you want. It's a Chevy, for sure."

No red Chevy had emerged from the tunnel. David had been watching for that. So the sniper was either in the mess behind the truck. Or he had caused it.

The man straightened up. "We're holding up emergency response until we have clearance."

"Any chance of fire?"

"Always a chance of fire, sir, with crashes in the tunnel."

Another VDOT worker came running out of the building. He shoved a bunch of papers through David's window. "Screen shots," he said breathlessly, "so you can see what's going on."

"Thank you both." David started leafing through the grainy black-and-white shots. Then he saw what he was looking for: a dark Chevy crunched up against the left wall of the tunnel. He looked back at the workers as he laid the printouts on the front seat. "I'm going in."

✝ ✝ ✝

Kit climbed up the big rig's tractor, pulled open the driver's side door, and crawled inside the cab. If she could just see! So far, the shooter didn't know she was there. If she could get the drop on him…

"FBI, FBI, put down your weapon!"

Lincoln! His challenge was answered with a hail of bullets, one of which penetrated the cab.

Kit slid back out. "Hey! What are you doing?" she said.

"Sorry, sorry."

Kit could see Lincoln was wired—his eyes were wide and he was almost twitching with adrenaline. "Okay, look," she said, "you stay here, behind the tire. I'm going to see if I can sneak around the back of the truck."

"There's gas leaking. I can smell it."

"I know."

"The others," Lincoln motioned backwards with his head, "are getting the people out. The whole tunnel's blocked, Kit."

Would David come from the other direction? She wondered. Would that be smart? What would he do? "Let's see if we can hold this guy off until we get reinforcements."

"Or we die in a fire. One spark and this place'll be an inferno!"

"Talk to him while I move back." Then she said, "Remember, pop and drop, Lincoln. Don't be a target."

Lincoln nodded. Then he called out, "FBI, Hardison. You're surrounded. Drop your weapons." His voice echoed through the tunnel.

Kit crawled over the cars smashed up against the truck. Inside one, an unconscious woman lay crumpled against the window. She couldn't help her. Not now. Not with Hardison shooting. Kit crawled around crashed cars to the back of the truck and crouched behind the tire. Then she peeked around the wheel.

✞ ✞ ✞

David told the officers waiting with him at the west end to stay put. He put on his flashers and began driving slowly down the up-ramp of the HRBT. No blue lights. No siren. He wanted to look like a confused civilian.

People were streaming out of the tunnel on foot. One old

guy was using a walker. A mom had two children with her. A young man ran.

Halfway down the ramp, multiple wrecked cars blocked him.

Boom! Boom! Gunfire! David jumped out of his car and peered down the ramp. The Chevy and the semi were still out of sight. His mind raced. He'd have no cover if he kept going on foot. None. One side of the tube was just a wall. The other side had a small catwalk but nothing to hide behind.

Then his phone rang. "Piper?"

"He's shooting!"

"I hear it. Stay put. Don't panic. We're here and we're going to get you out."

"David, he's crazy!"

"Are you still in the trunk?"

"Yes."

"Stay put!" He clicked off his phone. He didn't have time to relay Piper's message. He'd have to trust the guys at the office to do that.

David looked around at the wrecked cars blocking the tunnel. One, an old Toyota truck at the back of the heap, looked like it might be drivable. He jogged over to it. There was furniture in the bed. A dresser, a table, chairs, a sofa, and a grandfather clock. That stuff might block bullets aimed at the back window.

He tried the door. Unlocked. He slid in. No keys.

More gunfire. And shouting.

Kit?

Could he hotwire it? Maybe. Then he had a better idea.

✞ ✞ ✞

Kit crouched behind the double tires at the rear of the tractor-trailer. Bullets flew all around her, pinging off the walls and thudding into rubber. She made herself as small as she could. Then she heard Lincoln shouting again, drawing the sniper's attention to himself. *Thank you,* she thought as she peeked around the tire. Hardison was trying to move the Chevy, trying to start it, but he might have been panicking—the engine wasn't turning over.

Good! Lincoln must have thought he had a shot. He fired

his weapon, boom, boom, boom, boom, six shots in a staccato burst. Did he hit him? Kit peeked around the tire. No. The gunman came back full force, firing over and over until Kit thought her eardrums would burst. Then she heard Lincoln cry out.

Was he hit?

The gunman stopped. Maybe to reload? Kit looked around the back of the truck toward Lincoln, and saw him huddled next to the front tire, holding his hand. He anticipated her coming to his aid, and waved her off. Steve's voice registered in her ear bud. "Kit, Lincoln, evacuate the tunnel. Leave, now!"

How could they? With the sniper right there? And Piper in the trunk?

Lincoln looked at her, shrugging a silent question with his palms up.

No, she indicated. She wasn't leaving. She'd beg for forgiveness later. Lincoln frowned, but he stayed put.

Kit peeked back at the Chevy. She jumped as gunfire came her way again. Seven shots and then a maniacal laugh. This guy is crazy, she thought. Crazy!

Then she saw some movement further ahead in the tunnel. A driverless truck, a small pickup, was drifting down the ramp backwards. How odd! Had its owner left it in neutral?

Right near her, on the back of the semi, a ladder provided access to the top of the trailer. If she could get up there, it might give her an angle to pick off the sniper. Kit looked toward Lincoln and motioned to him. If he could just keep the sniper's attention …

He nodded. "Hey, Hardison!" he yelled, drawing the sniper away from Kit.

Kit reached for the ladder and began pulling herself up. "Evacuate, McGovern! Now!" Steve's voice exploded in her ear.

So close? Are you kidding?

She reached the top of the trailer and began belly crawling into position.

And then she smelled it. Fire. She turned. A spark from one of the bullets had ignited gas under one of the wrecked cars about fifty feet behind her. Soon, a wall of flame was cutting them off from the agents and the cops on the east end of the tunnel. Black smoke began curling toward the ceiling of the tube.

"Time to quit, Hardison! You don't want to die in here." Lincoln kept talking.

Kit's heart was pounding. She had to calm down and make this shot. Because once Hardison knew she was up there, she'd be an easy target.

"You're surrounded, Hardison, by hundreds of cops. There's no getting out of this."

She could hear the fire behind her, flames licking at the wrecked cars. She could smell the smoke, acrid and hot. A drip of sweat ran down the side of her face. She crawled forward. Her pistol hand shook. Should she leave? Run, while she could? But what about Piper?

"Kit, get out now!" Steve's voice again. "Fire! The sprinklers aren't working! Get out!"

She jerked the ear bud out of her ear.

And then she saw something. She blinked. The driverless truck was swinging slowly in an arc toward the left wall of the tunnel. Her eyes widened. From her perch, she could see someone in the cab. And she knew in an instant who it was: David.

David!

God, please, please keep the sniper looking at Lincoln!

She stretched her arm forward. She took aim. She pulled the trigger back part way. She would wait until she had a clean shot. Because she might get only one. How fast could she scramble down if she missed and Hardison shot toward her? Fear gripped her but also determination.

Suddenly, the small truck began to move faster. Had it gotten away from David? It slid down the tunnel and slammed into the left wall. When it did, the grandfather clock swayed, then toppled off the truck. Pendulum, weights, and chimes clanged as it hit the pavement.

When Hardison heard the sound of the clock, he jumped up and turned around, clearly alarmed. And Kit saw she had a head shot, and she squeezed the trigger, *BOOM, BOOM, BOOM!*

She saw him fall. She saw David emerge from the truck and hobble toward Hardison, his gun drawn. She kept her gun trained on him as well. Then David turned, gave her a thumbs up, and yelled something she couldn't understand.

Boom! Somewhere behind her something exploded. A car?

Kit clambered down from her perch. Lincoln met her at the back of the truck. She was shaking and so was he. "Gutsy move!" he said, but her ears were ringing and she couldn't understand his words.

David stood over Hardison, gun still drawn. Kit moved quickly to him. "I think he's dead," David said.

His words were muffled. She pointed to her ear.

David nodded and motioned for her to take Hardison. She cuffed him. "Dead," she said, and gave him a thumbs up.

Smoke filled the upper third of the tunnel. Kit started coughing. She saw Lincoln on the radio. "We've got to go!" he said. "Now! Leave him!"

"I'll get Piper," David yelled. He popped the trunk on the Chevy. Empty! He looked again, saw the back seat was down, and jerked open the back door. Piper Calhoun looked up at him and grinned. "I couldn't see what was going on from the trunk!"

"Come on!" he said. He grabbed her hand and started to move.

She pulled away from him. "My notebook!"

"Go, go, go!" David yelled as she finally started up the tunnel.

Halfway up the ramp, the fire suppression system initiated. Water poured down, soaking them all.

"Wow, what a story!" Piper said. "Wow!"

EPILOGUE

SPECIAL AGENT KIT MCGOVERN STOOD on the steps of the Federal Courthouse, along with David, Lincoln, and Steve. A gaggle of reporters stood below, waiting for the Acting Special Agent in Charge to begin the press conference.

"IT'S OVER!" the headline on *The Norfolk Times* had screamed that morning. And indeed, twenty-three days of terror in Hampton Roads had ended. People had poured out on the streets in celebration, shaking the hand of the nearest cop, and honking horns like it was the end of a war. The fear had lifted. Relief felt sweet. Piper's stories, which would be serialized over the next five days, were making single copy newspaper sales skyrocket. Everyone was happy.

The sun was beginning to make its descent as the SAC began. Kit's hearing was still impacted from the tunnel shooting, and she had to work to understand what he was saying. She felt David's arm touch hers, and she knew it was intentional. She bit her lip to keep her tears back. He'd made it, and she had, too.

Henry Raymond Hardison's life was falling apart, the SAC said, and he had decided to take it out on Hampton Roads, where his ex-wife lived and where he was discharged from the Navy. He continued outlining what they knew, much of it from debriefing Piper.

The news conference lasted twenty minutes, and after that, they were off to David's house. He told her he had some steaks he wanted to grill for dinner.

While he puttered in the kitchen, Kit looked at his house

with fresh eyes. It felt comfortable, homey. She picked up a conch shell, and recognized it as one they'd found on Assateague Island, where they'd first met. More and more memories followed as she touched one artifact after another. The last was a small oil painting of her grandmother's house on South Main Street on Chincoteague Island. David was renting that house when she met him. She picked the painting up, remembering her grandmother, thinking of David.

"Hey," he said, entering the living room, "let's go out on the dock. I want to watch the sunset."

"Aren't you hungry?" She put the painting down.

"It can wait."

He took her hand and they left the house. It somehow seemed natural to have a dog padding along behind them. Kit was looking down, watching her step as they walked. When she lifted her gaze, she saw flowers in a vase at the end of the dock. Her stomach tensed.

David put his arm around her. He kissed her head. "Look at that," he said, pointing toward the west. Then, just as the setting sun touched the waters of the Lafayette River, he pulled something out of his pocket, and dropped to one knee.

What? Her heart beat fast.

"Katherine Anne McGovern," he said, looking up at her and opening the small box in his hand, "will you marry me?"

"Yes!" she said, tears filling her eyes. "Yes!"

He stood and slipped the ring on her finger, and she threw herself into his arms. He kissed her, a deep, long, passionate kiss. "Let's make it soon!" she whispered.

✝ ✝ ✝

Kit stood on the beach at Assateague Island, right near the place she'd first met David. The midday sun, high in the sky, made the sixty-degree November day seem warmer. She was wearing a long-sleeved, white lace dress, and sandals. Her highlighted hair was swept up. From her ears dangled two diamond earrings.

David stood facing her in a tux, holding both of her hands and smiling. She'd never seen him in a tux. He was so handsome. The sun cast a warm glow on the side of his face.

To his right, her left, the breakers rolled in, one after the other in an eternal parade.

"This is forever," he said quietly, "like the ocean."

"I know."

Overhead, they heard loud honking as a flock of snow geese made their way to the pond on Assateague. The white birds put on a show, whirling down from the sky like skeins of silvery yarn, honking and calling.

Kit laughed. "They're early this year."

"I invited them to our wedding," David said, squeezing her hands.

Behind David stood his best man, her friend Ben Heitzler, along with her father and brother. And Steve. And Lincoln and Candace and Chase and about a zillion other people who had wanted to come, including Piper Calhoun, who looked like she was taking notes, and who definitely had a camera. Kit's matron of honor, Connie Jester, stood behind her, holding her bouquet. Next to her was David's sister, Maggie, with tears in her eyes, and a special guest, courtesy of David—Kit's mother, Renee Boudreau.

She was, as David had said, artistic. Frail. Gentle and kind. Timid, even. Kit's height, thin, with long, blonde hair. The minute she met her, Kit felt years of bitterness falling away. When she saw her father and stepmother welcome Renee, Kit finally understood. People are human. Whatever had happened over twenty-five years ago was history. It was time to move on.

As the pastor led them through their vows, Kit looked into David's eyes, those golden brown eyes she had first fallen in love with.

Because of him, walls had come down. Because of him, healing had begun. Because of him, she had finally begun to understand forgiveness and love.

But she knew that's not what he'd say. He'd say it was all because of God.

Later, after a party at Rita's, their favorite restaurant, Kit and David said goodbye to their guests and drove to South Main Street. They walked out onto the dock across from her grandmother's old house. The Chincoteague Channel flowed steadily toward the sea. A pair of ducks paddled in the marshes. Headlights from a few automobiles glittered on the causeway.

David put his arm around her. He nuzzled her ear. "I can't believe you're finally my wife," he said.

The bright orange sun touched the horizon. The water in the channel and the sky turned purple, blue, red, orange, and yellow in a vibrant display, water and sky reflecting off each other in a symphony of color that changed with each passing moment.

"It's beautiful," David whispered.

"Golden," she replied, and she leaned her head against the man she loved and let the glory fill her soul.

The End

Acknowledgements

This book, like all my books, is the product of many minds. Dru Wells, retired FBI agent, generously shares her expertise with me. Michelle Buckman provided expert editing—I am responsible for any mistakes that remain. Chris Cepulis gave me valuable feedback. June Padgett, of Bright Eye Designs, patiently worked with me to create the cover. (Her husband, Charlie, actually shot a map to create the image. Thank you, Charlie!)

I'm fortunate to have sisters, biological and spiritual, who cheer me on, pray for me, and patiently listen when "writer insecurity" surfaces. And my intrepid agent, Janet Grant, of Books & Such Literary Agency, always provides the wisdom and business acumen I need.

Jane and Jon Richstein, owners of Sundial Books on Chincoteague Island in Virginia, are wonderful supporters of the arts, hosting me and many other writers, artists, and musicians in their store and creating an enriching cultural hub in my favorite place on earth. I appreciate their support!

Finally, my husband, Larry: He was the first to believe I could write a novel and the first to insist that I not give up when obstacles arose (as they have, multiple times). Years ago, he dragged me over to the FBI Academy so I could learn how the Bureau works; more recently he taught himself the publishing process when we decided to go Indie. Together we've managed forty-seven years of marriage, three kids, four grandkids, seven dogs, and six books. Throw in a pony and my life is complete. Thank you, Larry!

About the Author

Linda J. White writes FBI thrillers and is a national award-winning journalist. Her husband, Larry, worked at the FBI Academy for over 27 years. They live in rural Virginia and have three grown children, four grandchildren, a cat, and a Sheltie who loves to herd them all. Linda is available to speak to library groups, book clubs, and other organizations.

> Web site: lindajwhite.net
> Email: rytn4hm@verizon.net
> Facebook: Linda J. White Books
> Twitter: https://twitter.com/rytn4hm
> Visit Linda J. White's Amazon page

Now that you've read Sniper!

Enjoy more novels from Linda J. White, available at amazon.com, christianbook.com, barnesandnoble.com, and wherever books are sold:

Bloody Point

Young FBI agent Cassie McKenna searches for serenity by retreating to her sailboat on the Chesapeake Bay after her agent-husband is killed in a car wreck. But serenity proves elusive. A series of violent events around the Bay seem far from coincidental, and when her former FBI partner, Jake Tucker, is assaulted and left for dead, Cass knows it's time to get back in the game.

> "[A] powerful combination of page-turning plot and real-life characters who struggle with the 'Why, God?' questions we all sometimes ask."
> Marlene Bagnull, author and director, Greater Philadelphia Christian Writers Conference and Colorado Christian Writers Conference

Battered Justice

FBI Special Agent Jake Tucker works hard to be an excellent investigator and a great dad to his two kids, even if he is divorced. Having Cass McKenna as his partner helps with both goals. When a shot in the dark takes out a colleague, Jake and Cass set out to find the shooter. They discover a shadowy trail of drugs and criminal conduct connected with a casino—and the battered, bloody body of Jake's ex-wife, Tam. Jake is sure Tam's new husband, a powerful state senator, killed her. But Lady Justice can be battered, too, and soon Jake finds himself in a new fight—a fight of faith, the fight of his life.

"Linda White is a masterful storyteller who continues to impress. Her novel, 'Battered Justice,' grabs your attention from the first page. This edge-of-your-seat thriller weaves murder, romance, deceit, and faith together into a suspense-packed story with characters that have you hooked through the last page."

Dr. Sharon S. Smith, SA, FBI Ret.

Seeds of Evidence

FBI agent Kit McGovern's vacation to her grandmother's Virginia island home is interrupted when the body of a young boy washes up on the beach. Who is he? How did he die? And why has no one reported him missing? Kit's only clues are the acorns in the boy's pockets and the tomato seeds in his gut. Teaming up with D.C. homicide detective David O'Connor, Kit follows plant DNA evidence to track the killer, clues that lead them into the dark world of human trafficking.

"[A] suspenseful story sown with fascinating investigative details, planted on a picturesque island, and cultivated by characters you care about."

Sarah Sundin, author of "With Every Letter"

Words of Conviction

Terror grips Senator Bruce Grable and his estranged wife when their five-year-old daughter is kidnapped from her bedroom. The perpetrator provides the clues to solving the crime: his words. FBI agent MacKenzie Graham, a forensic psycholinguist, analyzes the kidnapper's notes. But will her analysis solve the case in time? And could Grable's guilt have contributed to the crime?

> "I have just two words to say about this book: READ IT!"
>
> Ann Tatlock, author of the Christy Award-winning
> "Promises to Keep"

The Tiger's Cage

Northern Virginia, 1993: FBI Special Agent Tom Donovan has two great passions: his family and locking up bad guys. He's about to nail his current nemesis, Angel Ramos, when the drug kingpin does the unthinkable—he kidnaps Tom's eighteen-year-old son, Kenny. Tom is furious, his wife is terrified, and Kenny must cling to his newly forged faith to survive.

> "The Tiger's Cage" is a compelling read, a crime story rich in details about FBI procedure. At the same time, it's a winning story of family and faith."
>
> Howard Owen, author, winner of The Hammett Prize